"Stunning suspense tale." —*BookRak*

"Gericke's smart and suspenseful book will keep you turning the pages . . . then get you up in the morning hiding your board games away." —Deborah Blum

"A very ambitious project, with lots of layers in both the killer's psyche and the life of Emily . . . Gericke has created a complex, suspenseful thriller." —*BookBitch*

"Shane Gericke's thriller actually did blow me away. When a killer forces a 911 operator to listen as he kills a cop . . . the reader knows it will be nonstop action." —*Lesa Holstein Reviews*

"*Blown Away* is exceptional. The characters, the pacing, and the thriller aspects are all top-notch and indicate a very talented writer." —*Reviewing the Evidence*

"High marks for action . . . the tautly written prologue is especially chilling . . . dynamic cast of characters." —*Hidden Staircase Mystery Reviews*

"*Blown Away* tightens the plot around Emily Thompson like a terrifying noose." —Thomas Frisbie

"With insightful grace, Shane Gericke weaves vivid characters and nonstop action into a compelling page-turner. He emerges as a rising star of the police-thriller genre." —Peter Haugen

CUT
TO THE
BONE

Shane Gericke

SHANE
GERICKE

PINNACLE BOOKS
Kensington Publishing Corp.
www.kensingtonbooks.com

PINNACLE BOOKS are published by

Kensington Publishing Corp.
850 Third Avenue
New York, NY 10022

All Kensington titles, imprints, and distributed lines are available at special quantity discounts for bulk purchases for sales promotions, premiums, fund-raising, educational, or institutional use. Special book excerpts or customized printings can also be created to fit specific needs. For details, write or phone the office of the Kensington special sales manager: Kensington Publishing Corp., 850 Third Avenue, New York, NY 10022, attn: Special Sales Department; phone 1-800-221-2647.

This book is a work of fiction. Names, characters, businesses, organizations, places, events, and incidents either are the product of the author's imagination or are used fictitiously. Any resemblance to actual persons, living or dead, events, or locales is entirely coincidental.

PINNACLE BOOKS and the Pinnacle logo are Reg. U.S. Pat. & TM Off.

ISBN-13: 978-0-7860-1814-7
ISBN-10: 0-7860-1814-3

First printing: June 2007

10 9 8 7 6 5 4 3 2 1

Printed in the United States of America

To Jerrle,
who turns thunderstorms into blue skies

ACKNOWLEDGMENTS

My very first thank-you goes to Michaela Hamilton, my remarkable editor at Kensington Publishing Corp. She saw the story I wanted to tell, and cleared the trees to get me to the forest. If you enjoy this tale of derring-do—and of course you will!—it's in no small part from her skill and patience.

Next I want to thank my tireless agent, Bill Contardi of Brandt & Hochman Literary Agents, and my showstopping publicist, P.J. Nunn of Breakthrough Promotions. Your long hours and large enthusiasms on my behalf are noticed, and a joy.

Then come the many folks who help me understand the world Emily Thompson inhabits, from police operations to criminal intent to firearms to medicine to psychology to newborn children to underground gasoline tanks and the trucks that fill them. They are Chief David Dial and Sergeant Elizabeth Brantner Smith of the Naperville Police; Chief Raymond McGury of the Bolingbrook Police; Roy Huntington, editorial director of *American Cop* magazine; Dr. Barbara Emery-Stolzer, MD; Sharon Rymzsa, RN; Lisa Gray, LCSW; Susan Siy, LCPC; Joseph Altier, general manager with BP Products North America; manuscript whisperers Bill and Jan Page; my fellow authors at International Thriller Writers Inc., particularly the extraordinary Gayle Lynds, who continues to offer such selfless support; and Victoria Lynch, Pat Ghent, Doris Blechman, David Robinson, Kendra Panek, and Julie Hyzy.

I must not forget Dave Smith, Raimondo "Ray" DeCunto, and Jim Glennon, the pros from Calibre Press. They invited me to participate in their two-day "Street Survival" seminar, which teaches cops around the nation how to win against the most murderous criminals society can offer. Their hospitality is greatly appreciated, and their theories infuse Emily's approach to her work.

And finally, to novelist Scott Turow, whose crucial early advice gave me the direction I needed to transition from newspaper journalist to fiction writer. I wish you good cheer and many thanks.

Prologue

The blue velvet curtains drew back like it was movie night, allowing Johnny Sanders to stare through the bullet-proof window.

Twelve sets of eyes stared back.

The eyes of the people who'd come to watch him die.

Sanders half-smiled in acknowledgment.

Some returned it. Others looked away. One skinny guy flinched, like Sanders had snaked through the glass and tickled him.

Sanders thought that hilarious. He was strapped to a quarter-ton chair, which was bolted to the floor, which was anchored to reinforced concrete.

He wasn't tickling anyone.

He was waiting. For the end.

Which would come in, oh, a minute and a half.

He tried to relax by taking deep breaths. No good—the air stank of quicklime and paste wax. The former from the fresh-cured concrete that formed the execution center's floors, ceilings, walls, and corridors. The latter from the chair itself.

He traced his fingers along its wide oak arms.

Slippery as drool.

The paste wax, he figured. Humidity. Restless fingers of the condemned, rubbing the wood like a rosary. . . .

Sanders shivered, suddenly chilled. He wondered why. The execution center's furnace was pumping heat like the devil opened a hole in the earth.

Maybe I'm getting sick, he thought. *Hope I don't catch my death of a cold.*

The little joke made him smile.

He glanced at the official clock over the curtains.

The smile faded.

He wasn't sick, he knew.

He was scared.

He shouldn't be. But he was.

Go figure.

"Gonna work this time?" the official executioner asked the electrician.

"Damn well better," the electrician said.

"I hear ya. Did you replace the power cable?"

The electrician slapped the control panel. "New, just like this. I triple-checked every connection. Polished the electrodes. Replaced the switches. Rebuilt the buzzer box." He shook his head. "This time she sings like the fat lady."

"She doesn't," the executioner warned, "Covington sticks us both in the thing."

Sanders worked his teeth into the heavy mouth guard. Like the doctor said, it'd be stupid to crack his molars if clemency came through during the burn.

He chomped till rubber suckled his gums.

Praying the phone would ring.

"Fifteen seconds," the executioner said. "Get on those push-buttons."

Black silk touched red plastic.

It was part of the dress code, the silk. Like the rest of the staff, the executioner and his two assistants dressed business casual—tan Dockers and navy sport coats. But in addition they wore black silk hoods and gloves, to shield their identities from the condemned.

A couple of months ago, he'd asked his California counterpart why that mattered. "Dead men tell no tales," he'd quipped over single-malts at a corrections conference. He received only a shrug and a muttered, "Who the hell knows why we do anything?"

Sanders's mouth was so dry he couldn't swallow. Yet sweat poured like a broken hydrant.

Weird.

The chaplain walked in. Told him to stay strong, he was going to a better place, Jesus forgave, and he wanted to pray now, yes?

Sanders didn't answer.

The chaplain asked more insistently. Sanders kept mum. Let Rev. Michaels sweat a little himself, wondering if he'd done something wrong.

"Five seconds," the executioner said, eyes on the stuttering clock. "Four. Three . . ."

* * *

When the red hand joined the blacks at twelve, the executioners would take a deep breath and push. One of the buttons—and only one, so each could secretly believe he wasn't the real executioner—would send several thousand volts of Illinois electricity into the condemned prisoner. Killing him.

Or so everyone hoped.

Last time, the multimillion-dollar death system didn't kill anything but the lights. Prompting an apoplectic Illinois Governor Wayne Covington to boot the Justice Center's director. If it didn't work exactly as promised from here on, the governor warned, "I'll fire every single damn last one of you."

Nobody wanted that.

"Two. One. Now," the executioner said, breathing fast and shallow as the second hand completed its march to the sea.

Their thumbs kicked so symmetrically they could have been Rockettes.

Sanders cringed at a warmth he hadn't felt since third grade. "Oh, man," he whispered, flushing with shame.

The Justice Center director swaggered in, grinning so hard his eyes vanished. "You're one hell of an actor, Johnny!" he boomed. "You looked so scared when that buzzer went off I thought you'd wet your pants."

Yeah, well, Sanders thought.

He decided not to mention that.

"I'll tell you what's really scary," he said, slurring from the mouth guard. "Those twelve official witnesses."

"Them?" the director said, pointing to the state employees milling about the other side of the viewing window. In the back, arms folded, was the man playing Martin Benedetti, the detective commander who'd arrested the killer and would view the burn for real. "Why?"

"They just sat there, staring. At me. Like vultures and I was roadkill."

"They were supposed to, Johnny. That's their job."

"I know," Sanders sighed, wriggling against the slats to murder an itch. "I get that they were playacting. But right at the end, when the buzzer went off? I swear they wanted me dead."

"For real?"

"Yeah. Creeped the bejeezus out of me."

"That's great!" the director barked, clapping his hands in glee. "Means they did a hell of an acting job, too. Covington will be pleased."

"Good," Sanders said. "That's good."

"You got *that* right, brother," the director said.

Today was the third in a series of dress rehearsals for the execution of Corrigan "Corey" Trent, whose monstrous crimes rivaled those of John Wayne Gacy and Richard Speck. Covington built the electric chair especially for Trent, and ordered these endless rehearsals to "make sure the bastard roasts to perfection."

Which is why Sanders found himself in a six-by-twelve cell at Stateville Prison, the maximum-security fortress near Joliet that housed Death Row. Sanders, a state historian, was organizing more than two centuries of official execution documents. He'd volunteered to play Trent in the dress rehearsals to get a better feel for the people he was reading about. "Wow, a Method historian," his boss kidded when Covington gave his blessing.

He was tossed in the one-man cage at noon yesterday, to the jeers, threats, and hurled feces of the real condemned, led by Corey Trent. Correctional officers—"COs" in prison parlance—restored order. Sanders sat in his bunk the rest of the day, heart thumping, chin in hands, wondering what exactly he'd gotten himself into.

At sundown, a flying squad of COs shoved him in an armored car and sped north. A half hour later he was flung into the condemned cell at the State of Illinois Justice Center in Naperville. The staff let him call his "lawyer" for updates on his "clemency petition," then served his last meal—Coke, cheddar fries, and a rare T-bone. Prompting the center's director to joke as he swallowed the last bite, "Don't worry, Johnny, we'll make sure *you're* well done."

The doctor arrived at nine to make sure Sanders was healthy. "If you weren't, we'd postpone. We don't execute sick people," he'd said, without a hint of sarcasm.

Then it was lights-out. Sanders lay wide awake in the concrete gloom, wondering how even monsters like Trent survived the Row without biting out their wrist veins. Best not to think about it, he supposed. He fell asleep.

At sunrise, the chaplain asked if he wanted to pray. Sanders said no, not now, but he'd sure appreciate a visit just before the sentence was carried out.

"That's when I'll really need your help, Reverend," he explained. "You know, in getting square with the Lord."

The young chaplain agreed eagerly, and Sanders grinned to himself. Messing with the clergy was fun. They were so earnest.

Then he was shaved, diapered, dressed, manacled, marched down the hall, strapped into the electric chair, ministered, witnessed, and "executed."

To ensure Sanders wasn't accidentally injured, the live power cables weren't attached to the chair. They plugged instead into a test box in the rear of the chamber, which, unlike the remainder of the cement complex, was tiled for easy cleanup. The box was chockablock with resistors and capacitors that mimicked the human body. If the power spurted out of the generator and ran the circuits properly, the box would buzz, signaling death.

Which it did.

Which is why everyone was smiling.

"What happens now?" Sanders asked as the guards unbuckled the last of the leather straps that pinned him to the oak.

"You take a break," the director said. "Have a smoke, hit the john if you need. Then we run through it again." He pinched his chin divot, thinking. "This time, fight the guards all the way to the chair. Hard as you can. Give us a good show."

"Cool," Sanders said.

"Yeah, everyone likes that part," a guard said.

As Sanders headed to the bathroom, the director dictated notes. Then he strode to the telephone—"safety yellow," per OSHA regulations—bolted to the wall.

The hotline to the governor's office in Springfield.

It was there if Covington changed his mind. Or some court somewhere changed it for him.

The latter was always possible, the director knew. The former wasn't. Covington wouldn't cancel an execution if his life depended on it. That kind of thinking hadn't been in the man's makeup since 1966. But having a hotline was part of the execution protocol, and as such, it needed to connect loud and clear.

He put receiver to ear and waited through the clicks.

"It went perfectly, Mr. Governor," he said when Covington picked up downstate. "No more circuit problems. The Justice Center is up and running." He listened a few more seconds, then grinned. "That's right, sir. We're ready to burn the trash."

FRIDAY

1

"Ready for next Friday?" Emily Thompson said.

"Let's talk about that later," Martin Benedetti said. "I'm enjoying myself too much."

Emily smiled. "So you're glad you changed your mind."

"Oh, yeah, this is great," he groaned as the attendant shoveled on more steaming mud. "I feel like the marshmallow in the hot chocolate. Why didn't you make me do this years ago?"

Her face pats left stripes on both cheeks.

They were at a "mud spa" on Ogden Avenue, on Naperville's Far North Side. She'd been asking Marty for months to try the tub for two. He'd kept declining, saying he wanted nothing to do with "exfoliants and lite FM." Then, on her forty-second birthday, he'd bowed, handed her a gift certificate for two, and said, "Slap my chaps and call me Mary . . ."

She squished deeper.

Their cheerful attendant described the 104-degree mud as a "mystic Zen formula" that "detoxified and cleansed" body and spirit. Emily knew better. It was the same peat moss, volcanic ash, and tap water she dumped in her flower beds. She didn't care. Its clinging heat whacked her stress like a hit man. Having Marty cheek to cheek was a bonus—they could make fun of it later as they snuggled up in her bed, all Zenned.

The attendant filled two Waterford flutes with Soy-Carrot Infusion Juice. The lead crystal glowed tangerine in the soft mood lighting. She offered to swaddle their eyes with cucumbers dipped in chilled lemon water. "So your inner child stays cool," she murmured.

Emily tilted her face to accept them. Marty declined, muttering about needing a testosterone patch. The attendant giggled, shoveled on the final steamy layer. "I'll step out now, let the Zen work its magic. Call if you need me."

Marty thanked her, waited for the door to latch, cleared his throat.

"You're not going to tell anyone about this, right?" he said.

"About what, darling?" Emily asked, hearing the *skritch-skritch* of his fingers worrying the side of the redwood tub. She smiled into the lemon-scented darkness.

"About my parking my hamhocks in a tub of goo."

"And liking it," she said.

"Don't rub it in."

Emily threaded her fingers into Marty's. "Don't worry, tough guy," she said, squeezing tight. "I won't tell anyone your precious secret—"

A chorus of screams echoed through the spa room.

The cucumber slices flew as Emily's eyes popped open.

Marty was already fighting out of the tub. Emily struggled against the black quicksand. Marty pulled her slender wrists till her top sucked free.

Their attendant raced into the room, slamming the door

so hard the glass shattered. "A man just killed Zabrina!" she screeched with plate-size eyes. "Hide or he'll kill us all!"

"Get our clothes!" Marty roared, mud flying as he fought to stay upright on the pebbled glass.

"No time!" Emily shouted, shoving her heels against the bottom of the tub. Her hamstrings twanged, and the rest of her popped free.

She swung her rubbery legs over the ledge. Lunged for her black leather purse. Slipped on the glass and fell sideways, banging her head off the cornflower wall tiles as she hit the floor.

"Ow!" she yelped.

"Emily! You all right?"

"Go! Go! I'll catch up!" Emily gasped through the bells clanging in her head.

Marty knotted a bath towel around his waist. Emily reached up, ripped her purse off the peg, and pulled out two Glocks—hers 9-millimeter, his .45.

The attendant shrank into a corner. "Don't hurt me," she begged. "Please, miss, I'll do whatever you say."

"We're police!" Emily said, holding up Marty's gun like the Statue of Liberty. He snatched it and bolted. A moment later he reappeared, threw Emily a thick white robe, and rushed off.

Emily grabbed the pitcher of Infusion Juice and poured it over her head. She gasped as the icy slush melted on her steam-ironed body. The bells fell silent. She scrabbled to her feet, punched her arms through the sleeves of too-large terry-cloth robe, wrapped her hands around the butt of her gun, and sprinted to the lobby.

"Good Lord," she breathed at the explosion of tomato soup.

Marty was on his knees, blowing air into a young, pretty woman. Her face was white as spun sugar. Blood fizzed from her chest and neck when Marty exhaled. Emily knew instantly the CPR was form, not substance.

"I'm a Naperville Police detective!" she announced, ready to fire if the shooter popped out of the crowd. "Which way did he go?"

No answer, just a frantic fear-buzz.

"Did he leave?" she demanded. "Come on, somebody talk!"

"He didn't say a word," a manicurist blubbered. "Just shoved a knife in Zabrina and took off."

Emily looked around, didn't see a weapon. Maybe still on him. "Which way?"

The manicurist pointed at the main door.

"Parking lot," Marty said, looking up. "Watch yourself, Detective. I'll be there soon as someone takes over." He surveyed the crowd. "All right, who knows CPR?"

Emily charged across the striped asphalt, robe flapping, eyes everywhere. Nobody fleeing. Nobody sauntering too nonchalant. Nobody jumping in a Dumpster or darting behind a store.

She ran her emerald eyes over the closest group of cars. Nobody hiding. No doors slamming. Ditto the next, the next, the next—

"Look out!" Marty yelled.

Emily whirled to see an Audi streak from a slot and charge her. Shooting was useless—it'd be on her in a heartbeat. She jumped straight up, desperately clawing air to clear the metallic blue bumper that would mash her to roadkill—

"Aaaah!" she screamed as her body shoveled up and over the hood. She crashed into the windshield, heard a sickening crunch. Glass or shoulder, she didn't know which.

The driver jammed the gas pedal. The sucker punch of acceleration flipped her up on the roof. She windsurfed a moment, scrabbling for a hold on the hot, slick metal.

A sharp swerve bucked her off.

She slammed into the rear gate of an ancient pickup truck. She and rust rained to the pavement. She rolled the moment her body touched, to avoid breaking her neck. The Glock skittered out of her hands. She quick-crawled after it, vision jangled, skin on fire.

Marty triggered a pair of hollowpoint bullets. She saw the flames but didn't hear the blasts. The rear passenger window shattered.

She reached her gun and fired at the driver's head. Three sheet-metal craters opened in the door. Too low. She adjusted, reaimed.

The Audi careened onto Ogden. She couldn't shoot. Too much traffic.

She grunted to her feet and broke into a sprint, triangulating the lot, gulping and blowing, trying to cut the gap with the fleeing—

She toppled, clutching her leg.

"Officer down!" Marty bellowed. "Someone tell nine-one-one!"

"I'm not hit!" Emily yelped.

"What is it, then?" he said, flopping down next to her.

"Scar!"

She'd taken a bullet in her left calf two years ago during a nightmare encounter with a serial killer. The knotty wound healed enough to pass the department's medical exam, but when pushed to extreme physical limits—like now—it could squeal like a ripped pig.

"Dig into it, Marty," she begged. "Make it stop. Oh God, it hurts." She prayed the sirens were paramedics bearing needles of painkiller.

"I've got you, Em," Marty reassured, his big knuckles drilling for oil. "I've got you . . ."

The first Naperville Police cruiser skidded into the lot.

She clutched Marty's waist and pulled herself sitting,

fighting the sudden blizzard of panic. Her killer was back, choking her life away. She made herself breathe deep and slow, four seconds in, four seconds out. In. Out. In. Out.

Better.

"Woman's . . . dead?" she wheezed, massaging both sides of her neck.

Marty nodded.

"Who knifes . . . receptionist . . . at a spa?"

"Dunno," Marty said, hugging Emily close. "But we're sure as hell gonna find out."

2

The Executioner whipped into an empty slot, his blue eyes pulsing radar.

No cops. Not even a curious civilian.

He turned off the engine. As he'd learned from his numerous practice runs, this medical-office parking lot on Sherman Avenue—thirty seconds from the spa, nicely screened by trees and buildings—made an ideal place to switch cars.

Though the advantage wouldn't last if he dawdled.

Leaving on his gloves and Chicago Bears cap, he peeled the fake red beard from his jaw. He wiped the rubber-cement boogers into a white supermarket bag, and added the beard and bloody knife. He crumpled it tight, looked around once more, ready to escape.

An olive-green minivan was pulling next to the curb.

Dammit.

He had to wait now. He couldn't risk the woman behind the wheel telling a cop about the maroon Subaru wagon that peeled rubber when the sirens got close. *Get out of here,* he warned silently, each tick of the cooling engine loud as artillery. *Thirty more seconds and you die, too.* Not that he minded, but the kill would take time he didn't have. *Leave. Now.*

She didn't.

He gripped the .40-caliber Sig snugged in his waistband.

Five seconds . . .

His left hand squeezed the chromed door handle.

Three seconds . . .

Exit, walk, shoot till dead, walk back, drive away. Easy.

Two seconds . . . one second . . .

A skinny girl in pigtails hopped out of the van and dashed through a door with a sign shaped like a molar. The woman made a three-point turn and exited the lot.

Lucky you.

The Executioner slid out, tossed the keys down the storm drain. Hopped into the Subaru with the bag, started the engine with a gasoline-heavy *vroom*. Nosed out on Sherman then onto Ogden Avenue. Quickly scooted to the middle divider to let a police cruiser scream past. The cop hunched over the wheel made a little wave, "Thanks."

He waved back, amused.

He drove the speed limit to Wisconsin Avenue, cranked the wheel in a quick hard right, and began his side-street escape from the city.

3

Governor Wayne Covington tipped back in his buffalo-hide chair, allowing him to rest his crisp, white-blond hair against the paneling. He steepled his fingers, blew a thin river of smoke.

"What about riots?" he asked.

"Won't be any," Naperville Police Chief Kendall Cross said.

Covington snorted. "The antiexecution sissies agree with you, do they?"

"Yes."

Covington's tapered eyebrows flicked in surprise.

"Publicly, the protest groups will 'take it to the streets,'" Cross said, tapping a tail of ash into the governor's Baccarat ashtray. "But their leaders assure me privately it's marching and singing only. They've forbidden any forms of violence."

"Joe Citizen's tolerance for that garbage ended September 11," Covington said.

"Right. So I believe them when they say no rioting. But if it happens, we're prepared." He mimicked the swing of a riot baton. "We'll talk softly but carry a big stick."

Covington smiled, spun the brightly lacquered humidor.

Cross surveyed the fat Cohibas with the oily, dark-chocolate wrappers. Governorship hath its privileges. He took one and accepted the wooden match. He sat back, flamed the end bright, took a deep mouthful of smoke. He savored its mineral sharpness a moment, then released a perfect blue ring. It fluttered toward the window, where an air blower broke it into wisps.

He turned his attention to Covington, who suddenly seemed lost in thought.

"Your brother?" Cross asked gently.

"Ah. Yes. You've known me way too long," Covington said, puffing furiously to cover the crack in his news-anchor voice.

"Since you were our county's state's attorney. And now you're smoking Cubans in the Governor's Mansion." Cross tipped his head. "Helluva run you've had, Wayne."

"I'd give up every bit to have Andy back."

"I know," Cross said, flexing his mutilated backside. Damn that shotgun blast. "I'm sorry I never had the pleasure of knowing your brother."

Covington blinked. "You two never met? I'd have sworn— oh, that's right. We buried him well before Naperville hired you as chief. Time flies."

They smoked in silence.

"Earl Monroe murdered my brother in 1966," Covington said after a while. "But it feels like yesterday. I still catch myself driving by our old house sometimes, seeing if he's in the yard." His eyes got bright. Cross stared out the window to allow him the moment . . .

"Sorry," Cross said, reaching for his warbling pager. He

checked the display, frowned. "Use your phone, Wayne? My cell doesn't work in here."

Covington pushed it across the coffee table. "NPD?"

"Nine-one-one from Hercules Branch," Cross said, speed-dialing his chief of detectives. "He knows I'm here and wouldn't interrupt unless—hey, it's Ken. What's happening?"

His expression darkened.

"How many dead?" he grunted.

Covington jerked straight up. He stabbed a button, and a wall of plasma TVs sprang to life. Each sported a news anchor with practiced motions and perfect hair. Each crawl spat "Naperville" and "dead" and "kill" and "slay."

"All right," Cross said. "I'll be back as soon as I can." Stiff with anger, he disconnected.

"You remember my detective Emily Thompson?" he asked.

"Sure," Covington said. "From two years . . . oh Lord, *she's* not dead, is she?"

"No. But she came this close," Cross said, pressing thumb to forefinger. "Someone walked into a spa she was at and stabbed the receptionist."

"And Emily?"

"She ran outside and tried to capture the killer. He hit her with a car."

"Goddamn murdering scumbags!" Covington bellowed, flushing so dark his eyes glowed like high beams. "How bad was she injured?"

"She bounced off instead of going under the wheels. Nothing serious."

"Thank God. Was she able to—"

Cross shook his head. "Car absorbed the bullets. Manhunt's under way." He stubbed the cigar. "If we're done . . ."

"Yes, yes, by all means get going," Covington said. "You want my jet? It'll get you home in thirty minutes."

"No, that's all right," Cross said. "Branch is acting chief when I'm out of town. Nothing I can do that he won't do better." He smiled, but it held no humor. "Just tell your troopers I'm driving a Naperville black-and-white, and I'm not stopping for any speeding tickets."

4

"You want tickets, lady?" County Sheriff's Sergeant Rayford Luerchen mumbled as the maroon Subaru wagon wove over the yellow line. "I'll give you tickets."

He'd gotten lippy in a roomful of brass the other day, airily correcting one of the lieutenants without dicks about some point of law she'd been droning about. Payback came this morning in the form of a new assignment—traffic citations, and nothing but, for two months. Him! A senior sergeant. A leader of men. Pulling over jerk drivers like some carrot-brained newbie.

He tried groveling. "I was wrong, ma'am, and I'm very extremely sorry," he'd said. No good. She'd insisted on her pound of flesh.

So he'd write up every two-bit violation he could muster. In Naperville.

The people in this snooty burg would raise hell for getting ticketed one mph over the limit. Or putting a toy in their back window—"dangerously obstructed view"—or sporting an unwashed license plate. Enough flame-throwing to the sheriff from the gentry, Luerchen reasoned, and lady lou would get the message.

Don't cross Ray Luerchen.

He accelerated.

The Executioner stiffened. He was well away from the spa, in a quiet residential area. Five miles under the limit. Signaling every turn. There's no way he should be pulled over.

So then why was this cop swooping down in his rearview?

He caressed the Sig's walnut grips as he sorted his options.

Luerchen shook his head, wondering what to do. His computer wasn't connecting because Plank Road was a cellular "dead zone" with its steep hills and valleys. He couldn't ask the dispatchers to run the plate—they were swamped from the spa murder. *Like I should be.* He dare not wait for either problem to clear because lady lou would rip him for loafing.

"Awright, awright," he decided. "I'll write it up now and call it in later."

He flipped on his roof lights and burped the siren.

The Executioner spotted the colorful wooden sign for Seager Park. Nodded. He knew Seager. Lots of trees for concealment. With no playground equipment to attract children, usually deserted this time of day. It should work.

He put on his signal and crunched up the gravel driveway.

* * *

"Park it while we're young, pal," Luerchen muttered, scratching his sunburned scalp.

As if hearing him, the Subaru pulled underneath a towering maple. Brake lights flashed, window went down, engine shut off. The driver shrugged dramatically—"What did I do, Officer? I didn't do anything! Why are you pulling me over?"— but kept his hands in plain view, as the Rules of the Road encouraged.

We have a winner! Luerchen thought, smirking. The guy's panties were already in a bundle from being pulled over. When he found out he'd pay triple-digits for bumping the yellow line during his oh-so-careful turn from a side street . . . well, he'd be just the type to phone the sheriff. Even better, send one of those snippy "I pay your salary" letters to the local paper. Those always made cops hoot with laughter.

He grabbed his ticket book, already thinking about the next jerk.

"Focus," the Executioner murmured as the cop widened in the side mirror. "Do what you have to do, then get out." He hung his left elbow out the window like he was preparing to defend his driving skills, and let his right hand slip casually into his lap.

"Good morning, sir," Luerchen said, dipping his head to the driver's level. "Do you know why I pulled you over—"
Blam!
Luerchen fell back screaming as the .40-caliber hollow-point tore away his jaw. Blood and teeth spattered into his eyes, blinding him. His left hand clawed for the Mayday button on his radio. His right fumbled with his safety holster, trying desperately to free his gun.

The Executioner jumped out of the Subaru, leveled the shiny barrel.

Blam! Blam! Blam!

Luerchen collapsed with a single, strangled huff.

The Executioner waited till blood quit flowing, then kicked the cop in the right temple, making sure he wasn't faking.

The snapped neck said no.

He ran to the cruiser, slid into the hard, grimy seat. Found the switch that controlled the roof lights. Toggled it.

Siren whooped.

Untoggled, tried another.

The flashing stopped.

He put the cruiser in gear and backed it next to the splayed feet. Plucked handcuffs from the stretched-out gunbelt around the cop's belly. Snapped one cuff around the left ankle, the other to the cruiser's tow ball.

Taking care to not drip sweat on anything, he climbed back inside and stomped the gas, dragging the cop into the trees. In the rearview, he saw the head bounce-bounce-bounce off rocks and roots. It reminded him of those World's Funniest Videos. He smiled.

Then he braked, threw it in Park, and ran to his Subaru, finger on the trigger just in case.

Not necessary.

He returned the Sig to his waistband and drove out of Seager Park. Made sure he used his turn signal. Got back on Plank Road and continued his escape.

5

"Enough already," Emily groaned, shooing the para-medics who'd been poking, prodding, and painting her scrapes antiseptic-purple. "I gotta get dressed."

"Before CSI bags our clothes as evidence," Marty agreed. He grasped his waist towel with one hand, offered Emily the other.

She grabbed his fingers and pulled herself to her feet. The movement shook up her vision like a snow globe. She blinked a dozen times to clear it, then began walking toward the spa, planting one foot firmly before lifting the next. She'd feel silly tripping in front of the Fire Department.

"Wait up!"

Emily turned to see a blonde in a black-and-white. It was Lieutenant Annabelle Bates, commander of the Naperville Police SWAT team and Emily's closest girlfriend.

They stopped to let her catch up.

"We were serving a warrant when we heard the officer

down," Annie said, eyes dusting Emily for injuries. "We just got back. Are you all right?"

"A little banged up," Emily said. "But nothing broken."

Annie whistled her relief. "I understand we found the car."

"Patrol spotted it a few minutes ago," Emily said. "In that medical mall on Sherman. We know it's the killer's because Marty and I shot it."

"For what little good that did," Marty grumbled. "Canine units are searching, but I'm betting he stashed an escape vehicle and took off." A dirt fog erupted as he scratched his mud-crusted forearm. "Unfortunately, nobody at the mall saw anything."

"Security cameras?" Annie asked.

"Only inside," Emily said. "Guarding the drugs and equipment. None point at the lot."

"We're never that lucky," Annie said. She squeezed Emily's arm, her petite features tight with concern. "Are you sure you're all right, hon? Branch said you got run over."

"Well, sort of," Emily said. She explained.

"She jumped right up and chased the bastard," Marty added. "Might have caught him, too, except for the charley horse."

Annie's eyes dropped to Emily's calf. "Again?"

Emily nodded, disgusted the two-year-old injury was still getting the best of her.

"Well, you're standing now," Annie said. "Took half the day to do that last time your calf went nuts. Progress."

"Enough that I can be useful here," Emily agreed.

Annie's face twisted. "You don't think you're working this case, do you?"

"Of course I am," Emily said. "I'm a detective."

"You're a witness," Annie pointed out. "A participant. You're involved."

"I tried to apprehend a murder suspect. That's the extent

of my so-called participation," Emily argued. "I'm not a witness. I didn't see the killing. I only heard the screams."

"It's true," Marty said. "We're only ear-witnesses."

Annie still looked dubious.

"It's like back at the station," Emily said, grasping for another straw. "First detective to answer the phone gets the case. I was first detective here."

"Totally by accident," Annie said, kicking at the ragged hem of Emily's robe.

"Still counts."

"And your leg?" Annie pressed. "You can walk and kneel and perform crime-scene tasks?"

Probably not, Emily thought, feeling the lobster pinch when she put weight on it. But she wasn't going to miss a homicide because of a stupid cramp.

"I'm fine," she said, massaging her scalp with her hands. Mud flakes rained. Talk about a bad hair day. "Besides, I already talked to Branch. He's inside with the victim."

Annie's faint smirk said she knew Emily was tap dancing—talking to Branch wasn't the same as getting approval from Branch—but would ignore it because she'd do the same thing. "Well, hell, why didn't you say so?" she said, aiming Emily at the spa. "Let's find your clothes so you can get right to work."

She looked over her shoulder at Marty, cranked the smirk to full wattage. "You go finish your bubble bath, dear. You missed some dirt behind your ears."

His reply was blacker than the mud.

6

The Executioner slapped the turn signal so hard he bent the stick.

Cursing his adrenaline-fueled ham-handedness, he turned onto Royce Road on the Far South Side. Headed for the secluded split-level he'd purchased when Covington announced he was building the electric chair in Naperville. The radio squawked bare bones about the spa. Nothing about Seager Park.

Excellent.

He studied the rearview. Narrow, winding blacktop shaded by oaks and maples. Drainage gullies left and right, here and there. Kids running free in long, sloped yards. Cars going both ways. None ugly or plain enough to be unmarked police.

The DuPage River Park to his right was dotted with worn structures from century-old farmsteads. The land skidded hard to the water below, which twinkled blue-green in the merciless August sun. The cloudless sky held no helicopters or low-flying planes.

He drove slow and wide around the trucks idling on the shoulder. Checked peripherally to make sure no SWATs were hiding in the cab, waiting to attack. Nope. Just City of Naperville water crews, backs bent, elbows flying, digging up a main.

Bowie, waiting for him at the house, would chuckle at this excess of caution.

But he'd understand.

7

Emily sniffed cautiously as she entered the lobby, wondering if she'd need the nose soap.

She sneezed, shuddered, sneezed again.

Yup.

Death had short-circuited the woman's bowels and bladder. The smell mingled with the congealed blood, whirlpool chlorine, and jasmine from the mood candles. Fear-stink pulsed from employees and clients, who couldn't leave till detectives took their statements.

Which Emily couldn't do till she learned some basics.

"What's her name, Captain?" she asked the big man over the little corpse.

Hercules Branch raised an index finger that said, "With you in a minute."

"OK." She turned to a uniformed patrol officer, whose fiercely jutting jaw reminded her of a sweet potato. "*Please* tell me you brought Vicks VapoRub."

"Don't leave home without it," he said, pulling a tin from his pocket.

Emily thanked him and smeared a gob under each nostril. The stinging menthol fumes helped mask the stench of death. A cheap cigar was even more effective, but a year ago Chief Cross banned smoking at crime scenes. Too much risk of contaminating evidence.

The building was an old Chinese buffet reincarnated as an elegant day spa. This was its lobby—what the foot-high calligraphy over the reception desk called the "client welcome center." The thirty-foot ceiling came to a series of peaks, reminding Emily of the circus tents she'd adored as a little girl on Chicago's Southwest Side. Fringed Oriental rugs softened the pearl granite floor. The walls were rag-rolled, navy blue with robin's-egg highlights, and held a series of art prints that were as indefinite as jazz.

She took notes.

Champagne-colored curtains covered the tall, narrow windows. A dozen chairs, the same lacquer black as the frames of the art, surrounded a glass table filled with women's magazines. The manicurist occupied the chair farthest from the main door. Next to her sat the woman who'd attended her and Marty. Her mud-streaked head rested on the manicurist's bony shoulder. A cappuccino maker steamed in one corner. A water dispenser gurgled in another.

"Zabrina Reynolds," Branch said. "With a Z."

He flipped to the middle of his notebook.

"She was twenty-three, according to the manager," he said. "She's worked here a couple years. Lives with her boyfriend in a condo on Route 59."

"Should I notify him?"

"I already did," Officer VapoRub said. "These ladies had his cell phone number. He's in Taiwan on a business trip. His boss confirmed his presence."

"Ruling him out."

"For the time being," Branch agreed.

The manicurist began wailing.

"We loved Zee," she sobbed. "So happy all the time, so much fun." Her lower lip pooched out. "She wasn't supposed to be here today."

"Why not?" Emily asked.

"Zee had a cold. I told her to go home, I'd cover the desk. You know what she did?"

Emily shook her head.

"She patted my cheek. Like my grandma does? Then she said, 'It's more fun here with you guys.'" Her face crumpled, and the floodgates opened anew.

"Why don't you take her outside for some fresh air?" Emily told the attendant. "I'll find you when I'm ready to take your statement."

The attendant nodded, trundled her out the door. Emily glanced at Officer VapoRub.

"I'll keep them company," he said.

"Thanks."

She started to join Branch at the body, then felt a presence against her back.

"You found your clothes," she said, reaching back to pat his leg.

"Along with a hot shower," Marty said. "Branch, I'm gonna head to the office and write my statement. I'll e-mail you copies when I'm done."

Branch gave him a thumbs-up, and Marty swung his attention back to Emily. "Want to work on the house when you're done?" he murmured.

She bumped her head "yes" against his chest. Easy to do because he was a foot taller than her five-six. "I'll call you," she said. "Be awfully late, though."

"Doesn't matter." He rubbed her shoulders, then gently pushed away.

"Aw, Marty, tell her you wuv her," Branch said.

"I'd better not," Marty said. "She'd insist on smooching me, then you'd have to fire her for sexual harassment and we'd all be embarrassed . . ."

Cop humor, Emily thought as they chuckled. Like these two homicide veterans, someday she'd be an expert at whistling past the graveyard.

But not today.

Not with Zabrina Reynolds staring at her.

Marty headed out.

Emily finished scouting, then turned her attention to the corpse.

8

The Executioner drove into his attached garage, heart singing at his success. When the door merged with the concrete floor, he eased his grip on the Sig and hopped out.

Plunked the bloody knife in a pail of Clorox. Donned coveralls and fresh gloves. Scrubbed the getaway Subaru top to bottom, then stem to stern. Vacuumed the interior. Removed the dust bag and stuffed it in a can of paint. Washed windows and mirrors and wiped down the interior.

Then did it again.

Satisfied the car was as clean as he could make it, he threw a nylon cover over the roof and secured it with bungee cords, snapping them with a satisfying *thwack*.

He added both sets of gloves to the can, along with the beard, hat, and bleached knife. He hated to lose the stabber—he'd sculpted it from a single bar of steel—but he had plenty of others. He watched it disappear in a bubble of barn-red latex.

The bulk squished the paint to just below the brim. He

added a capful of drying catalyst. In twenty-four hours, the evidence would be sealed like a bug in amber. He hammered on the lid, put the can in his Land Rover, and went into the house.

"Hi, Bowie," he greeted with a salute. "You won't believe the day I had . . ."

He detailed the kill while eating his favorite lunch from childhood—bologna and cheese on white bread, with lettuce, Miracle Whip, and a dash of pepper. Then he showered, changed, confirmed his morning departure with the airline, and reviewed the plan again.

Airtight.

He told Bowie his schedule from now till Monday—"I probably won't call, I don't want anyone tracing my calls back to you"—then hugged him good-bye. He grabbed his carry-on and headed for the garage. Wished again he had eyes on top of his head so he wouldn't strain his neck looking for police aircraft.

As he backed the Land Rover out of the garage, he debated whether to swing by the mud spa. It wasn't smart, he knew. He should stick to the plan—drive south, pick up the interstate, get to St. Louis to start the next phase.

But the woman from the windshield beckoned. He'd realized who it was as soon as he reached Ogden Avenue, and was enormously thankful he hadn't killed her.

Yet.

He turned north.

9

Emily judged Zabrina Reynolds five-five and 120 pounds. She had a tiny waist, flared hips, and medium bust. She lay faceup, arms at her sides. She hadn't fallen that way, Emily remembered. Marty repositioned her for the CPR.

Her delicate hands were cupped, like she was holding water. Her waist-length hair was blond with lime-green streaks, an affectation that somehow worked for her. The hair was so askew the overheads sparkled off her scalp. Zee had enormous green eyes with perfectly tweezed brows. Her full lips were painted coral. Her skin was taut. No blemishes or scars. One tattoo, a kitten, above her left ankle.

More notes.

An alligator belt cinched her pale yellow sundress. Her sandals had medium-high, but wide, heels. Stylish, but still practical for spending time on her feet. "A sensible girl," Emily's mom would have said approvingly.

Befitting August, Zee's legs were bare. Befitting an employee discount, her nails were perfectly manicured, and painted the same coral as her lips. They appeared natural, not glued on.

Branch grunted.

Emily turned to see him trying to exit the chair he'd taken to ease the strain on his bad hip. His face was mottled from exertion, his expression stained with frustration.

"Need a hand?" Emily asked.

"Not unless you can go potty for me, Detective," he replied.

"Gosh, no, Captain," she said, batting her eyelids. "But I'm certainly willing to learn. Is there a school for that?"

Branch snorted as he pried himself loose. He straightened his trousers, then limped toward the men's room, leaning on the black thornwood cane. His big hand squeezed the top knob, which was carved into a bug-eyed man bellowing at the top of his lungs.

Emily smiled. It was a sly joke from Marty, Branch's best friend besides his wife, Lydia.

Two years ago, Branch was raked by submachine-gun fire. His myriad injuries healed over the course of four hundred physical therapy sessions, but walking sans limp was still maddeningly elusive. Marty talked to a woodcarver pal. A month later, he had what he wanted. He wrapped it in Dick Tracy comics and gave it to Branch last December, at the NPD party.

"You are such a dick," Branch murmured, shaking his head. Everyone knew it was cop-speak for, "Love you, too." Applause erupted even as heads turned to hide damp eyes.

The bathroom door closed, and she went back to her examination.

"Sheriff's dispatch to Commander Benedetti."

Encrypted band, Marty noted. Unusual. Not surprising,

though, given the patrol frequencies were so clogged from the manhunt.

He picked up the mike. "This is Benedetti. Go ahead."

"It's Marge. Are you still in Naperville?"

"Yep. Just left the spa, heading back to the shop." As chief of detectives, his office was next to the sheriff's in the county building. "Why?"

"I can't raise Patrol Nineteen. I tried everything but smoke signals."

"Who is it? And what's he or she doing?"

"Luerchen. Smiting evildoers on Plank Road."

Marty grinned, having heard how badly Ray stepped on his weenie at the lieutenants' meeting. Apparently, so had Marge. "Bunch of dead zones along Plank. Probably can't hear you."

"I know. But the lieutenant needs him back ASAP."

"Probably wants her wastebasket emptied."

He heard Marge giggle. "Probably," she agreed.

"So what do you need from me?"

"Your body."

"So many women tell me that."

"They don't mean it like I do, dear," Marge said. "Listen, I'd send a patrol unit, but they're all tied up on jobs. I hate to bother Naperville. They've got their hands full."

"Say no more." He U-turned in front of the McDonald's and headed back toward Plank Road. "I'll find the miscreant and send him your way."

"Thanks, Marty. You're a doll."

"Yeah, but don't tell anyone. I'd never hear the end of it."

"Your secret's safe with me."

The fun, flirty banter reminded him of how sensational Emily looked popping out of that mud. Not as good as being slathered in whipped cream, one of the many fantasies he'd cooked up about the first woman he'd loved since his wife died of cancer. But close.

"Appreciate that, Margie," he said, making a mental note to stop at the supermarket after finding Ray. "Benedetti out."

Emily studied Zabrina's cuts. Each was an inch long and very thin, with smooth edges. Deep, to have killed her so fast. One was on her chest, where her barely there bra crossed her heart. Another was on the left side of her neck, into the jugular vein. Air-blackened blood crusted around each, freshened by the occasional flush of scarlet.

"A long, narrow, unserrated blade," she said. "Like a fillet knife."

"Agreed," Branch said.

"Crime of passion?"

"You tell me," he said.

Emily stuck her hands in her jeans. She wouldn't lose her breakfast—her stomach was far stronger than two years ago—but those three cups of French roast were bubbling more than she liked. "Part of me says yes. Knives are intimate. You have to get close to kill someone."

"Arm's length," Branch said. "At the most."

"Meaning Zee's killer was near enough to look into her eyes," she said. "Hear her gasp. Watch her bleed. Meaning he hated her."

"Or loved her, or was jealous."

"Passion's a powerful trigger for murder."

"Suggesting the boyfriend?"

"We already cleared him," Emily said. "But maybe he hired a hit man."

"Or woman," Branch said.

She ceded him the point and looked at the waist-high reception desk. The reddish-black stickum near the back edge was enough to account for her broken nose.

But not the rest.

"Where'd all the blood go?" she asked.

Branch's smile said, *Attagirl.* "Inside the body," he said. He removed his sheath knife and laid the tip on his own chest. "He pushes straight up, under the rib cage," he said, miming it. "The tip punctures the heart. Because of the shallow angle and thinness of the cut, the blood doesn't drain back through the hole. It stays inside her body."

"In the chest cavity?"

"Nature's own Tupperware."

"I get it," she said, examining Zee's swan neck. "Same with her jugular?"

"Uh-huh. But there, he angles down." Another mime. "He sliced her esophagus, too, so the jugular blood had a place to drain."

"Her stomach," she said, patting hers.

"Yes. Some sprayed out of the wound, as you can see. But most stayed inside. That's why the room's not awash."

Emily shook her head. "How could he possibly accomplish all that?"

"Either he's so lucky he should be in Vegas," Branch said, "or he's an expert with a blade."

"Suggesting the hit man."

"Or an extraordinarily angry friend. Dealer, lover, rival, doctor, lawyer, Indian chief—"

"You're giving me a headache," she complained.

"Great cure for that," Branch said. "Find him and ask."

"Or her," she shot back.

He chuckled, and waved for her to get to work.

"Come on, Ray, show yourself," Marty said, eyeballing each side street as he worked his way west on Plank Road. "I've got a report to write."

He slowed at Seager Park. Prettier place than most to fill out paperwork, he knew from his own years in patrol. Or, considering the sergeant's abject laziness, steal forty winks.

He crunched his way up the gravel, hoping it was the latter. He'd sneak as close as he could and crank the siren. With any luck, give Ray a heart attack . . .

He skidded to a halt.

A five-foot circle of parking area wasn't the dusty beige of the rest.

His senses sharpening in a way that warned, "Here Be Dragons," he bailed out and hustled to the discoloration.

It was blood, all right. He couldn't detect the telltale scent of old pennies—battery-acid fumes had long ago burned away his sense of smell—but he knew by the color, sheen, and crust.

And the hundreds of circling flies.

He glanced around. Saw four brass cylinders just outside the circle. Small, empty, and resting on their sides.

Handgun cartridges.

He pulled a handkerchief from his pocket, turned over the closest.

".40," the bottom read, under the deep indent of the firing pin.

Not Luerchen's caliber, Marty knew. The sergeant carried .45s.

Meaning there'd been a shooter.

He bent his head to the gravel to examine the blood from a flat angle. He noticed very faint drag marks pulled out of the northwest side. They pointed toward what looked like an opening mashed into the treeline.

Roughly the width of a police cruiser.

He hustled back to his car.

"Marge," he radioed, breathing slow to control his fast-pumping heart.

"Go ahead, Marty."

"I'm at Seager Park on Plank Road. Send backups, Code Three."

"What's happening?" she asked. "Did you find Luerchen?"

"No. But there's blood and shell casings. A car-sized opening in the treeline."

"Oh, no."

"Round up detectives, forensics, and canines. Put SWAT on standby. Find the sheriff, tell him what's up." He scratched his head, trying to anticipate all possibilities. "Call Branch. His cavalry can get here faster."

"You going to wait for them before you check out the opening?" Marge asked.

"No. If Luerchen's there he'll need help. Tell everyone I'm in the trees so don't shoot me."

"Understood, Marty. Please be careful."

"Will do. I'll call when I know more."

No sense assuming a jacked-up cop wouldn't take a shot at a heavily armed man prowling the woods, so he popped his trunk and slipped on his body armor. SHERIFF glowed atomic yellow from both sides. He cinched the straps tight, then pulled out the M-4 combat assault rifle he kept for emergency firepower.

He jacked in a round of .223, tucked the butt into his shoulder, and walked into the woods, feeling a little bad about the heart-attack joke.

Emily divided the lobby into three-foot squares. She tucked her gloved hands behind her back and searched each square in order.

She stopped, cocking her head.

"What?" Branch asked.

"There's two burnt matches. Behind the door."

"*¿Que?*"

Emily squatted, wincing at the ripple in her calf. They were wood. Eighth-inch square, two inches long. Kitchen matches—Ohio Blue Tip or a clone. Available anywhere in the world.

She closed her eyes and visualized scraping one against the sandpapery strip glued to the cardboard box. The bulb head flared bright orange, then steadied. The flame crawled down the stick. When it ran out of wood—or hit a finger—it died.

She opened her eyes, compared visualization to reality.

Pretty close. The bulb heads were charcoaled. But the burns ended right away—the sticks were untouched. Suggesting the matches were lit and immediately extinguished.

She relayed the information, and Branch pointed to the mood candles.

"I've visited this spa enough," Emily said, shaking her head, "to know they light their candles with butane torches."

"That's not it, then. Do they allow smoking?"

She pointed to the large slash-in-a-circle over the water cooler. "They called nine-one-one once when a guy wouldn't put out his cigarette. And he was out on the sidewalk."

"Smoke Nazis," Branch grumped, shifting his grip on the cane. "Interesting where you found those matches."

"Behind a door, and nowhere close to a desk or chair," she said. "I think it's a clue."

"Almost certainly."

"But what on earth could it mean?"

"Hey, you're the detective," Branch said. "Find out."

Marty hissed when he saw what hung from the bumper. He took a close look, hissed again.

Backed slowly out of the crime scene.

10

The kid at the window snatched the Executioner's twenty. Mumbled into the headset. Played the register like a Steinway. Made change. A few minutes later, he handed over a bag with an oil stain so translucent the burger wrappers showed.

The Executioner drove to the parking area.

He unwrapped his food, ate quickly. He loved that first hot spurt of beef juice. How it so nicely coated his tongue and ran down his throat. Marvelous. Good thing he ordered three. Even with the bologna sandwiches at home, he was starving.

Killing did that.

He finished the second burger, bit into the last—

Froze.

A Naperville black-and-white was nosing into the lot. The burly cop behind the wheel wasn't heading for the drive-through.

The Executioner's thighs went numb.

Thirty minutes earlier he'd crept past the mud spa, gawking at the circus like a hundred other drivers. He looked for Windshield Emily. She wasn't there. He looked harder, becoming so distracted he drifted into oncoming traffic.

He was saved by the screech of the oncoming car.

The Executioner waved, then ducked his head in what would look like shame but was really to hide his unbearded face. The other driver kept going, apparently accepting his "apology."

Now this.

The cop crept up one aisle of parked vehicles, down the next. Stopped to bring a radio mike to his lips. Hopped out of the cruiser to peer into a car.

The burgers congealed in his belly. His extremity numbness spread. His thin lips parted to suck extra oxygen, and his field of vision narrowed. He recognized the feeling—adrenaline dump. Telling his body to fight or flee.

He untucked his shirt, wrapped his fingers around the Sig. The checkered grips bit into his gloved, finely scarred palm.

The cop crept closer.

He gripped tighter.

Closer.

Tighter.

He flicked the window button. The electric purr sounded like a chain saw, so acute were his senses. August humidity swirled though the Land Rover. It mixed with the frigid AC and shot dew all over his windshield.

The cop pulled even.

Looked up at him.

The Executioner prepared to fire . . .

The cop finished the last aisle and bumped out the exit.

Safe.

He wiped the gloves on his pants, drained.

* * *

A few minutes later he steered to the garbage can topped with a plastic clown. He threw napkins, cup, and oily bag into its yawning mouth.

Followed by the evidence-laden paint can, which he'd tucked inside a beat-up cardboard box. By tomorrow it'd be in a landfill, crushed by a thousand tons of Naperville castoffs.

He kicked up the AC till the jungle air turned polar, then headed south.

Noting with approval the line of drivers dumping trash on top of his, and the absence of anyone who cared.

11

"I hate rubbernecks," Emily grumbled, passing out sandwiches behind the mud spa. Her stomach had started growling, so she volunteered to drive to Grandma Sally's, the family restaurant a few blocks west on Ogden. "There I was, minding my own business, and some idiot in a Land Rover nearly hits me head-on."

"Gawking at the pretty flashing lights, huh?" Officer Vapo-Rub said.

"He was so not paying attention he drifted into my lane," Emily said. "I had to slam on my brakes. Fortunately for him, he straightened up and waved his apologies."

"Should have pulled him over anyway," VapoRub said, biting into a drippy gyro. "Teach the dope a lesson."

"And let the food get cold?" Branch said. "What kind of cop *are* you?"

Everyone laughed.

Branch's phone burbled. Still chuckling, he plucked it off his belt.

The long scar on his cheek began twitching. Emily knew what that meant. Her tuna on whole wheat began tasting like cardboard.

"What?" she said when he disconnected.

"It's Marty at Seager Park—no, no, he's fine," Branch said, hastily adding the last when Emily blanched. "A sheriff's dispatcher couldn't raise one of her deputies. She thought it might be radio trouble, asked Marty to find him."

"And?"

"He did, just now. Dead. His name's Rayford Luerchen—"

"Ray?" she gasped.

"Uh-huh. Do you know him?"

The brutality of the submachine-gun attack had erased parts of Branch's long-term memory, she knew. Traumatic amnesia, the doctors called it. Branch simply didn't remember her ugly history with Ray Luerchen.

"Uh, yes, I do," she said. "Go on."

"Marty found Ray deep in the woods, handcuffed to the tow ball of his cruiser. He'd been shot four times—jaw, chest, forehead."

"Jesus," Emily groaned as the other cops shuffled and spat. While she despised the misogynist creep, she didn't wish him murdered. "Did he get any shots off?"

Branch shook his head. "Gun's still in his holster. Let's just hope Ray scratched his assailant. Maybe CSI will find some skin under his nails."

"Or jammed in his boot treads," VapoRub said. "If he managed to kick the scrote."

"Even better."

Another thought occurred to Emily. "Maybe we're looking at the same killer."

"As Zabrina Reynolds?"

"Yes."

"Unlikely," Branch said. "Ray was shot, Zabrina stabbed.

Most doers stick with one or the other. Too hard to be good at both." He stroked his blue chin. "Then again . . ."

"The timing," she said.

"Yeah. What are the odds of two killers roaming Naperville at the same time?"

Emily tossed her sandwich in the garbage. "Maybe he was driving the side streets, trying to escape. Ray pulled him over. Not because he suspected anything, but just to write a ticket."

"Makes sense," VapoRub said. "Ray would've had his gun out if the stop was anything other than routine. He ain't the bravest chicken in the coop."

"Shooter pulls into the park," Branch said, nodding. "Blasts Ray when he walks up. Cuffs him to the tow ball, dumps him in the trees."

"And escapes," Emily said, the word fizzing bitter on her tongue. "Again."

"Looks like. I need to call Ken."

She leaned against the faded brick wall, wondering why she was suddenly so cold.

12

"Grab whatever bodies you need," Cross said, straining to hear his speakerphone over the whine of tires on interstate. "I'll shuffle the paperwork when I'm back."

"Will do. Is the sheriff OK with me leading the task force?"

"As long as Marty handles the Seager Park side."

"Fine by me," Branch said. "Our people will concentrate on the spa."

Cross confirmed. "We'll run the combined operation out of our station. It's closer to both crime scenes than the county building."

"Already heard that, so I put more phones and laptops in the auditorium," Branch said. "Our tech guys are setting up the database. Their media sergeant volunteered to be our official spokesman, and I accepted. Both canine units are sniffing the park."

"They find anything?"

"Picked up a scent in the woods. Lost it in the parking lot."

"Shooter escaped in a vehicle, then. Not on foot."

"Uh-huh. I put up roadblocks, but they won't do any good. Too much time elapsed before Marty found the body. Shooter could be in Iowa by now."

"Goddamn Ray," Cross grumbled. "Why didn't he tell his dispatcher what he was doing? At least we'd know what the shooter was driving."

"He might have tried," Branch said. "I'm no fan of Ray's"—Marty had refreshed his memory of the self-important blowhard—"but the dead zone might have kept him from connecting. His lieutenant was on him to pump tickets, so he said screw the radio, I'll call it in later."

"You're probably right. We've all been there," Cross said. "Moving on, what evidence did—"

"Hang on, Chief, can't hear you."

Cross waited for the static to ease.

"What evidence did you find in the park?" he continued.

"Blood, bullets, footprints, cruiser, and Ray," Branch recited. "Along with the usual park trash—beer cans, take-out, condoms, whatnot."

"Lots for the crime lab to process."

"With more coming. CSIs are just starting the detail sweep."

"I'll ask the state lab for help. What did you find at the spa?"

"Nothing useful. Emily did spot something unusual, though." He explained.

"Interesting," Cross said.

"I thought so," Branch said. "I'll make sure she follows up."

"Good. Sounds like you've got everything under control."

"Till the next shoe drops. Where are you?"

"Northbound I-55, passing Bloomington," Cross said. "I'll be in Naperville in an hour."

"It's 110 miles!"

"Your point?"

"I'll call with news," Branch chuckled. "Assuming you live through the fireball to hear it."

Cross smiled, then disconnected.

He called the mayor and city manager with updates. The sheriff to coordinate assignments and offer condolences. The state lab for help. And finally, the governor. Covington had offered to take over execution security so Cross could concentrate on the double homicide. Cross considered it, but decided to say no. Matter of pride. He'd meant what he said in Springfield—nobody was better than his cops.

"Are you positive you can handle both?" Covington said after Cross explained.

"Yes," Cross said. "But if that changes, I'll call."

"Make sure you do," Covington warned. "I don't care if Martians land on that Riverwalk of yours, Trent is going to die at noon Friday. It's your job to make sure that happens."

Cross looked at the cell phone. "I told you I can do both, Wayne, and I will. But the homicides take priority if push comes to shove."

"Goddammit, Ken, that's not what I want to hear—"

"If they're not solved ASAP, chances are they won't be," Cross said. "Since one's a police officer and the other a young woman, failure is not an option." He shook his head. "Your execution, on the other hand, can easily be rescheduled."

"*Rescheduled?*" Covington roared, his voice greased with anger. "Have you lost your mind? That monster cut a baby from a mother's living womb!"

Cross turned down the volume.

"Trent's so inhuman his parents moved out of state when

he was convicted. One sister changed her name, the other hangs up on reporters when they mention his name. His brother told *Newsweek*, 'Our heart goes out to those poor victims. Our family neither fathoms, nor forgives, this monstrous act. Corey is no longer our blood, and we won't be there for him. Ever.'"

"Gee, I didn't know that," Cross said. "It's only led every newscast this week. Whatever you pay your press secretary, it's not enough—"

"He's going to burn!" Covington raged, a full octave higher. "In my electric chair! Till smoke comes out his ears! You screw this up, Ken, I'll fire your ass and—"

"Don't you threaten me, Wayne," Cross shot back. "I don't work for you. As for Trent, he *is* a jackal, and I'll light him up Friday as requested. But a guarantee? You don't get one. There are no guarantees in this business, and you know it. What the hell's wrong with you?"

A long, hollow silence.

"Just make sure it gets done, Chief. If you know what's good for you."

"Threaten me again, Governor, I'll turn this car around and kick your—"

Click.

Cross ended the call, shaking his head. Covington had always been overbearing on the topic because of brother Andy, but this was ridiculous.

Passing the state prison in Pontiac, where Death Row was housed before Covington transferred it to Stateville for its proximity to the new Naperville Justice Center, he visualized Emily bouncing off the hood of the getaway car. Imagined Miss Reynolds drowning in her own blood. Saw Ray Luerchen drain into the wormholes of a hot, lonely parking lot.

He pushed the cruiser to 140.

He flipped on the siren when other cars appeared but otherwise kept it silent—too hard on the ears. Twigs and gravel banged off the glass, disappeared in the slipstream. The steering wheel shook. He wondered how long he could hold this speed without breaking something.

As long as I have to.

13

The family in the next lane stared at the highly agitated driver talking to no one.

The Executioner glared back, peeling his lips off his long white teeth.

Dad tromped on the brakes. The trucker behind rode the air horn.

You've got to relax, the Executioner told himself. *You escaped Naperville just fine. Don't blow it now by attracting attention.*

"I'm on Interstate 55," he told Bowie over the hands-free throwaway cell. Billboards flew by at 65 mph. Each promised Big Laffs in the upcoming TV season. He doubted that. "Nobody saw me. Nobody's following."

The rearview was smudgy from all the times he'd made sure.

"I'll get a couple of stiff drinks in St. Louis, then a nice supper. Fly out in the morning."

His muscles began leaking tension.

A million-to-one shot, Emily Thompson smearing his windshield. But truth *was* stranger than fiction. No way she could identify him, of course. Not from the half-second she spent before blowing away, and not with how well he'd altered his appearance.

He'd left no fingerprints thanks to his skintight, flesh-colored gloves. Deposited no hair thanks to body shave, hairnet, and orange-and-blue Bears cap, which were hardening with the paint. He'd rented the Audi with a fake driver's license and prepaid credit card. Ditto Subaru and Land Rover. It was so easy to forge credentials with Photoshop, Internet, and card burner.

"Time to sign off, sport," he told Bowie. "See you when I'm back." Several moments' pause. "Yeah, me, too."

He disconnected, then punched the radio preset. Drummed his fingers through weather, sports, and nausea/bloat/hygiene commercials.

Finally the news.

The announcer said a woman was shot this morning in Naperville. Said the upper-middle-class city of 150,000 was thirty miles west of Chicago and the nation's best place to raise kids. Said the woman died instantly. Said cops found the getaway car, launched a dragnet. Said a female police detective was inside the spa and heard screaming.

So that's how Emily got there.

Said the detective chased the killer but got run over. Said the detective wasn't seriously injured. Said her name was Emily Marie Thompson. Said two years ago, she was a hero.

The Executioner whistled "Zippity-Do-Dah" as he disengaged cruise control. What the announcer *didn't* say was a description. If Emily had seen him, that would have led the story. Ditto the fat cop in the park. He was utterly, completely safe.

He put on his turn signal and pulled to the shoulder. Slow, deliberate, a total Calvin Careful. Traffic whizzed past inches from his door, the wind shear rocking him like a hobbyhorse. He saw a black-and-white police car running full-boogie in the northbound lanes. He didn't care. His hands were steady as iron plates.

He pulled a spiral notebook from his poplin sport coat. It had a canary cover and light-blue page rules. He clicked a Fisher Space Pen—the one the astronauts used, which was cool—and ran a line through Zabrina Reynolds. His all-caps lettering was precise, and touched neither rule. He unclicked and counted the ink lines.

One, two, three, four, five, six, seven, eight, nine, ten.

Followed by three still un-inked. Two were out west.

The last was back in Naperville.

He smiled.

Emily Thompson was already dead.

She just didn't know it yet.

14

4:18 P.M.

"Who could have done this to my Zabrina?" Cassie Reynolds wailed. She curled sideways on her daughter's bed, knees clutched to her chest. "Who? Why?"

"We don't know, ma'am," Branch said. "Not yet."

"You're the police! You're supposed to know! What's taking you so long?"

"We've put on every available resource," Branch assured. "Chief Cross and the county sheriff assembled a joint task force. Our best detectives, CSIs, and canine units are in the field looking for clues. The state crime lab's on board. And we've issued an all-points bulletin on the killer."

He didn't mention that nobody knew what he looked like—all the manicurist remembered was the gleaming blade—where he was headed, what he was driving, or if he *was* a he.

Cassie had stumbled into the police station at 2:16 P.M., drained white from her frantic drive from Milwaukee. Her husband, she said, was in Amsterdam on business. She'd caught him between meetings, and he was taking the next flight home. The task force debriefed her face-to-face, then him via cell.

Nothing useful.

The coroner wasn't ready for the formal identification, so Branch offered to drive Cassie to her daughter and boyfriend's condo. Perhaps she'd see something to spark a helpful memory.

That wasn't working, either.

"Think hard, Mrs. Reynolds," Branch urged. Zabrina's lime-green streaks hinted at a wild side, so he steered the conversation that way. "Did she have enemies? Owe someone money? Any arguments with her boyfriend? Or other friends? Did she use drugs—"

"No!" Cassie screamed, pummeling the bedspread till dust flew. "No, no, no! Zee was a good girl! She didn't do anything like that!"

Branch waited out the cloudburst.

Finally, Cassie rubbed her glistening cheeks, turning the mascara into fingerpaint. "Our daughter was a dream come true, Captain," she said. "It was hard for us to conceive. My mother had the same problem with me. But finally, it happened, and Zabrina was born."

Her smile became wistful, Branch noted. Happier times.

"She was a kind, wonderful girl," Cassie said. "I never had a lick of trouble with her, not even the mother-daughter fights you expect. We were very close."

"Yet Zabrina lived here," Branch pointed out. "Not in Milwaukee."

"Her boyfriend landed a job in Naperville, so she decided to move," Cassie said, with a little head bounce that said she hadn't been exactly thrilled. "We offered to buy her a place near us so we could see her more. But she wanted her independence. You know, cut the apron strings." Her eyes refilled, and she lifted Zabrina's pillow to her face.

Branch saw that a lot with survivors—scent was a such powerful reminder of their loved ones. He let Cassie breathe awhile, then asked the next question.

"She took the spa job right after she moved in with Barry," she said, lowering the pillow. "Only temporary, while she looked for something that paid better. But she grew to love it. She took a night job for extra money."

"Doing what?"

"Waitressing. One of your downtown steakhouses." She pursed her lips. "Or maybe it's seafood? I forget."

Branch made a note to track that down.

"I heard something you might like to know," he said. "The ladies at the mud spa genuinely looked forward to seeing Zabrina walk in every morning."

"Really?"

"That's what they told me."

Cassie glowed, straightened a little. "That's wonderful to hear, Captain. You always like to believe people adore your children. And it proves what I'm saying—she wasn't on some mobster's hit list. She didn't gamble, take drugs, cheat on Barry, or do those other horrible things you said. She was killed by some random nut."

The precision of the knifework suggested otherwise, but he let Mrs. Reynolds hang onto that particular pillow as long as she could. She'd need it. "Why do you think that?" he encouraged. Half of what detectives found useful came from the informal rambles at the end.

"You see it all the time," Cassie said. "The Amish school. Columbine. Post offices. The Middle East. Someone goes nuts and innocent people die! In this case, my only child! My baby!" Her eyes leaked grief. "You see it all the time . . ."

"The poor dear," Donna Chen said, delicate fingers fluttering against her linen blouse. "I pray she didn't suffer."

"No," Emily said. "Zabrina died instantly. I know she didn't feel a thing."

"Oh, I'm so happy," Donna said. She immediately flushed.

"It's OK, Mrs. Chen. I know how you meant it."

"Please, Detective, have a seat."

Emily eased into the striped wingback. She declined the proffered lemonade—she was pounding down too much sugar today as it was. While Branch questioned Zabrina's mom next door, a dozen task force members canvassed the condo complex, knocking on doors in search of leads. Emily drew the neighbor.

"So you've lived here a while?" she asked.

"Oh, gracious, many years. Nine at least," Donna said.

Emily smiled to herself. That *was* a lifetime in Naperville. Unlike her old Chicago neighborhood, where your neighbors were your neighbors till you joined the great bowling league in the sky, the population here turned over every couple years from corporate upsizing, downsizing, re-orgs, and transfers. Moving vans were as every bit a symbol of this white-collar city as the Riverwalk.

"Zabrina moved in two years ago," Donna continued. "She and Barry were ideal neighbors. Thoughtful and hard-working, always ready to lend a hand. My husband admired Barry's ambition to succeed, and we girls got along famously." She put her hand to her mouth. "Oh, listen to me! I'm no girl any more."

"It doesn't show," Emily said.

"Thank you," Donna said, touching Emily's hand. "That's sweet of you to say. It's all because of this marvelous facial moisturizer I found . . ."

They chatted about that for a minute, then Donna started reminiscing about fun times with "Bee and Zee." Emily took notes.

"So Zabrina had no enemies," she said, wrapping up. "No one you can imagine killing her."

"Not in a million years," Donna declared. "Not that darling young woman."

"How about her family? Did she ever mention any enemies they might have?"

"No," Donna said, crossing one leg over the other. Emily envied their shapely slimness. "Zabrina invited us to dinner once when her parents and grandmother came to visit from Milwaukee."

"Her dad's mother?"

"Maternal grandmother," Donna said.

Emily tried recalling the name from the rushed background reading she'd done before beginning the canvass. "Was that Myla?"

"Leila," Donna corrected. "Leila Reynolds. She died just last year. Very classy, with perfect manners and an engaging spirit. Cassie and Zabrina clearly inherited those genes. The father was just as nice. He was senior vice president of a Chicago bank, but didn't put on a single air. Believe me, Detective Thompson, those people have no enemies."

Emily kept writing, not surprised at the response. Every single person they'd interviewed had nothing but good to say about—

"Not here, anyway," Donna said.

15

"The judge signed a no-knock warrant," Annie radioed a low, crisp voice. "We go in unannounced and grab the target. Everyone copy?"

A dozen double-clicks from her SWAT entry officers confirmed they were primed.

"I'm moving to point."

The point position, Emily knew, meant Annie would be the first cop through the door of the dilapidated house on Burlington Avenue, on Naperville's Far East Side. First to know if Devlin Bloch would throw up his hands or toss a grenade. She leaned to Annie's helmeted ear.

"You get killed," she whispered, scared down to her boots that her best friend wouldn't emerge from this whole, "I'll quit buying you daiquiris."

Annie grinned, slapped Emily's raid jacket.

Then she pulled the Springfield Armory .45 XD Tactical from her thigh holster. She preferred a high-capacity hand-gun on point. It was handier in small spaces than shotgun or rifle, and its wide-body bullets dropped bad guys like anvils on Wile E. Coyote. She confirmed her chamber was loaded, and headed for the front door.

"Green light," Annie grunted when she arrived. She loved point. The more danger, the more alive she felt. "Launch on my five-count. Five, four, three—"

"Rabbit, rabbit, rabbit."

The call from the spotter on Bloch's front window meant the suspect was running.

"We're blown. Assume he's heading for weapons," Annie radioed, signaling her demolitions expert. "Green light, repeat, green light. Take him."

16

Front, back, and garage doors disappeared. The demo man danced a one-second jig, then rushed to his secondary position. Black-clad SWATs tornadoed into the smoke, shouting, "Police! Search warrant! Don't move! Don't move!"

Emily gripped and released her thighs, praying nobody got hurt. Especially not Devlin Bloch, the multiple-felony ex-con who lived here.

Because he could be Zabrina's killer.

Marty stared through binoculars. Branch monitored radio traffic. Nobody said a word. Emily couldn't if she wanted— her throat was too constricted.

Four minutes later, a flash of blond ringlets appeared.

It was Annie, helmet off.

Everyone started breathing.

"He's not here," she radioed, her voice tight. "We looked everywhere, including attic and basement. Bloch's gone. You guys can come in."

Branch looked at Emily, she at Marty, and all three at Annie.

They walked inside, shaking their heads.

17

"Your people were everywhere," Branch said, facial scar jumping with his scowl. "How could Bloch just disappear?"

Annie's counterstare could melt titanium. "No idea," she said. "Doesn't seem possible."

"Yet, he's not here."

"Think I don't *know* that?" Annie snapped. Then, softer, "Sorry."

Branch waved it off.

Emily left them to decide what came next.

She walked into the kitchen, wrinkling her nose at the stench. She went to the dented stove, turned off the gas under the skillet. Two walleye, so overdone they curled like Fritos.

As the bacon grease quit popping, she studied the small, cheerless room—white enameled sink, harvest-gold appliances, gouged linoleum in a shiny pink not found in nature, sheet-metal cabinets filthy with God-knows-what—and found herself agreeing with Annie. It simply wasn't possible to slip past a dozen SWATs with nightscopes, thirty backup officers, and a snuffling pack of shepherds. This guy wasn't Houdini, so where—

Creak.

She looked around but saw nothing. Probably the house settling. Her own did that constantly. Or her imagination was working overtime—

Creak.

Nope. It was both-ears real, and somewhere over her head.

She looked up.

There was a spidery crack in the middle of the grease-splotched ceiling, between two plastic "beams." It was the length of a prone man, and the only one of surrounding dozens that opened and closed like fish gills.

Shifts in pressure from the other side.

Skin prickling, she eased her Glock from her hip holster and leaned toward the debating team in the living room.

"Hey, guys," she said, keeping her voice la-di-da while putting a finger across her lips. "Bloch left us some walleye. You hungry?"

They trooped in, staring at Emily's up-stretched arm.

"Guess we interrupted supper," Annie said, spotting the fish-gilling. She pulled her gun from her holster. Marty and Branch followed suit.

"Yes," Emily said. "It's a shame he couldn't join us."

Branch squeezed Annie's arm, pointing at the narrow hall to the bedrooms.

The location of the attic hatch.

Annie hand signaled her troopers to follow. Two grabbed stepladders. The rest checked their HKs, Benellis, and Arma-Lites.

"This guy's gone," Branch said, keeping up the patter. "Let's get out of here."

"Sounds good to me," Marty replied. "You heading back to the office?"

"Home," Branch said, loosing an exaggerated yawn. "I've been in these clothes all day. I'm starting to smell as bad as you."

"Har-har," Marty said.

A SWAT held up five fingers. Five seconds till Annie popped the hatch.

"This whole situation smells bad," Emily said, locking her front sight on the crack. "I don't know how Bloch did it, but he's definitely disappeared. We need to analyze every—"

"Devlin Bloch! This is the Naperville Police! Do not move!"

It was Annie, her command bellow shaking the shingles.

"You're in the attic, over the kitchen, under the insulation! SWAT officers with automatic weapons are aiming from below and all sides! If you move, they will open fire!"

Silence.

"You have five seconds to answer me, Devlin Bloch! If you remain silent, I'll assume you're armed, and you'll be extracted the hard way! Five, four, three—"

"All right!" a voice shrieked. "I give up!"

"Do exactly what I say," Annie said. "Do you understand?"

"Just don't hurt me!"

"We won't, as long as you follow my instructions."

"I will!"

"On the count of three, get on your feet. Slowly. One, two, three."

Sheetrock groaned. Ceiling crack widened. Grease peeled away like wet bandages.

Emily leaned into the living room. Annie and two other SWATs stood on ladders, wedged into the attic hole, checking out Bloch through nightscopes. Another SWAT readied a pole-mounted floodlight. Annie positioned it, pulled the scopes, mouthed, "Go."

"Any weapons on you?" she said as two million candle-powers blasted the rafters.

"No."

"Take off your shirt so I can see," Annie said. "Turn all the way around."

Thirty seconds passed.

"Now drop your pants. Turn all the way around."

Thirty more seconds.

"Now your underwear. Turn all the way around."

"That's my dick in there, honey, not a—"

"Drop 'em," Annie said. "Now."

"All right, all right," Bloch grumbled.

Fifteen seconds.

"Pull up the Jockeys and walk toward the light. Slow and steady. If you reach for the insulation or make any other sudden moves, we will shoot you."

"I don't have any weapons. Honest. I didn't do anything," he whined.

"Sure, Dev, you're hiding in this itchy mess for laughs," Annie said. "Now walk."

Bloch put one foot in front of the other, balancing on the ceiling joists. "OK, I'm taking the first step."

"Not too fast," Annie warned.

"Sure, Officer."

"Lieutenant."

"Lieutenant, sure, absolutely, goin' nice and slow. I'm taking the second step. Now the third. Now the fourth. Now the—*yaaaaagh!*"

Marty and Branch leaped out of the way as dirt, insulation, Sheetrock, wood chips, nails, shingles, Christmas decorations, TV antenna, shirt, pants, and Bloch blasted onto the floor.

Emily was too slow, and disappeared in the whiteout.

18

"Quit fighting!" Emily roared as she grappled Bloch for control. It wasn't easy. He was so sweaty from the 130-degree attic it was like wrestling a greased pig—grab, slip, smear, slide.

"Where are you? We can't see through this dust!" Marty yelled.

"Under the sink!" she said, her head banging off the plywood door.

"Let go of me, ya psycho bitch!"

She drove an elbow into a particularly sensitive nerve.

"Ow! Police brutality!" Bloch hollered.

"Quit whining, you sissy," she heard Marty say.

Hands poked in and hauled them apart. Annie pinned Bloch to the linoleum—raising another filthy cloud—and shackled him wrist and ankle. Another SWAT searched Bloch's shoes, groin, and cheeks. "No weapons," he reported.

"You surrender?" Marty said to the coughing, flattened form.

"Uhhhnnn," Bloch said.

"Check him out," Branch said.

Two Naperville Fire Department paramedics peered into his eyes and read his vitals.

"He's fine," they declared. "Just shaken up."

"Me, too," Branch said, slapping Sheetrock off his clothes. "You all right, Detective?"

"I'll . . . be . . . fine," Emily coughed.

Branch handed her his canteen, then nodded at the paramedics to check her, too.

"Lieutenant Bates," he said at their thumbs-up, using her rank instead of "Annie" to avoid diminishing her to the suspect. "Make our guest comfortable so we can talk."

Two SWATs grabbed Bloch at the armpits and dragged him to the living room, Annie kicking a path through the trash. Branch followed with the others. Emily heard the couch groan, followed by Bloch's explosive cursing at being gouged by a spring.

Annie ducked back in the kitchen.

"Banana," she said.

"What?" Emily said.

"My daiquiris. Banana. With really expensive rum."

Emily stuck her tongue out as Annie disappeared.

"You gotta wash out that plaster dust or it'll scald your eyes," Marty said, sticking his hand in the water stream to ensure it wasn't too hot. "Don't touch the sink, it's full of boogers 'n' stuff."

She turned her head sideways under the tap, let the water do its thing. It tasted like iron, stank of rotten eggs.

Marty's cell phone rang.

"Martin Benedetti," he said, moving her head around with his free hand to rinse off all the crumble. "How can I help you?"

Ten seconds later Emily's head banged the side of the chipped enamel.

"Ow!" she said, grabbing her left ear. "Easy there, cowboy! What are you doing?"

He didn't reply.

"What?" Emily said, pulling free and wiping her face to look at him. His face was stone, his eyes hooded, nostrils flared. He stared like his dead wife was oozing from the receiver. He mumbled that he was busy and he'd call back later, then didn't close the phone.

Alarmed, she grabbed his arm and shook him hard.

"Huh?" he said, snapping out of it.

"What's wrong? Are you OK?"

His eyes were darting. His breathing was fast. His face was ashen, his lips tight.

"Yeah," he said, recovering. "Fine."

"Who was that on the phone?"

Several seconds passed. Each felt like a century.

"Snitch," he muttered, thumbing the power button.

"Marty—"

"Snitch," he repeated. "Causing a problem I'm gonna have to tend to."

He'd never used his "back off" tone with her, and she felt her anger rise. She turned away and splashed handful after handful of water on her neck and collarbone.

"Did I get everything?" she asked, feeling it run down her chest.

"Oh, yeah," Marty said, back to his normal good humor. "Pat you dry, Ossifer?"

"I'd dearly love that," Emily said, smiling through her annoyance at Marty's affectionate twist on "Officer," which he'd bestowed the first day they met. His uncharacteristic bite was probably the adrenaline flash and crash that was making them all cranky. "But duty calls."

"I suppose you're right," he said, handing her a SWAT field towel. "Best to see what the scumbag has to say for himself. We'll pick this up later."

Emily nodded, and sky-hooked the towel into the garbage can.

Roaches scattered.

19

"Who was on the phone?" Branch said.

"What phone?" Bloch said.

"The one you were talking on when we blew your doors."

"You were *spying* on me?" Bloch said, indignant.

"Of course we were, Einstein. That's what cops do with robbers."

"That's a total invasion of my personal privacy!"

"Must have taken law classes up there in Stillwater," Annie said.

"When he wasn't getting boned in the showers," Branch said, snickering.

"Up yours," Bloch said.

Branch leaned close. "That's exactly what will happen if you don't answer my question."

"I forget what it was."

"Who were you talking to on the phone?"

Bloch smirked. "Hookers."

"You were contacting escort services?"

"Till you barged in," Bloch said, settling back.

Enough dust had smeared away that Emily saw the crude tattoos adorning Bloch's chest and belly. The largest incorporated "AB," "666," and a pale blue shamrock, indicating Bloch was Aryan Brotherhood, the main white gang in American prisons.

He caught her looking. "Wanna see this one?" he asked, grabbing his crotch.

"Shut up," Branch said, bopping Bloch's foot with the cane.

"That's the best you can do, Festus?" Bloch sneered. "You wouldn't last ten seconds in the showers with me, you limp-dick cripple—"

"I wouldn't go there," Marty said, plopping down next to him. "I was you."

His arctic lack of emotion made Emily shiver. Marty used to infiltrate psycho biker gangs for a living. Violence didn't bother him a whole lot.

Bloch sensed it, too, she knew, because he didn't finish the insult. He kept up the sneer, though. For appearances.

Cops and robbers.

"So, did you find one?" Branch said.

"One what?"

"Someone to wax your wheels."

"No," Bloch said. "You interrupted my, ah, negotiations."

"So it wasn't an accomplice you were talking to?"

"Accomplice? To what?"

"We'll get to that. Let's finish your phone call first. When I check the dialing log, I'll find nothing but escort services, right?"

"Couple pizza places, too." He patted his crotch. "Rocket needs its fuel."

Annie rolled her eyes.

"What made you start running?" Branch said, switching gears.

Bloch shrugged. "I saw a lump in the yard. Moved left when the trees moved right. Didn't know it was cops, though."

Annie's scowl told Emily the team's after-action debriefing would be noisy.

"Who'd you think we were?" Branch said. "Invaders from Mars?"

Bloch shrugged. "Friends."

"You have friends that make you dive under attic insulation?"

"Why you think I'm out of prison, man? Good behavior?"

"He ratted out fellow inmates in exchange for parole," Marty said. "And his friends haven't forgotten."

Bloch's greasy smile said, *Yup.*

Branch dragged over a chair and sat in it backward, resting his arms on top. "All right," he said, caning Bloch's foot for emphasis. "Tell me about Zabrina Reynolds."

Bloch's eyes darted up and left. His body language said he was lying. "Never heard of her."

"That's funny. You murdered her this morning. Along with a sheriff's deputy"—he inclined his head at Marty—"who was a close friend of my associate's."

"I didn't whack anyone!" Bloch said, face flushing. "Who says I did?"

"Me."

"Well, you're wrong!"

"Prove it."

Bloch turned his palms up. "Man, how I prove I *didn't* kill anyone?"

"Better think of something," Marty said, scooting closer, heightening Bloch's discomfort. "You're on parole. One call to Minnesota and you're back in Stillwater, doing another dime. This time, with your Nazi pals knowing you sang like a canary. I'm sure they'd be happy to speak with you about that in the showers."

"Cops," Bloch spat. "You're all the same."

"Yes, we are. We live to rub out little grease spots like you," Branch said. He held up his phone. "Want me to call your parole officer?"

"Can't do that without a charge."

"How's assaulting a police officer?"

Bloch looked incredulous. "I wasn't fighting her, man. I was trying to escape."

"He fought me, Captain," Emily said. "No question. I was brutalized beyond imagining."

"Would you testify to that in court, Detective?" Branch asked.

"On a stack." She held up her forearms. "These scrapes are so deep they'll still be scabby at the trial." She swanned dramatically. "Oh, the shock I suffered from this animal."

Annie held up the evidence camera.

"Plus it's all on video," Emily said. "Perfect visuals for the jury." She'd actually gotten them flying off the getaway car, but saw no reason to mention that.

"Assault and battery," Branch continued. "Resisting arrest. Attempting to escape. Failure to obey a lawful police order. Felony stupid." Long pause. "Or, you can tell me about Zabrina."

"Yeah, awright," Bloch muttered.

"Say what, Devlin?" Marty said, cupping his ear.

"I said awright! I used to know someone named Reynolds. When I lived in Minneapolis."

"Where you made a nice buck as an armed robber," Emily said, thumbing through Bloch's rap sheet. "Liquor stores, minimarts, pawnshops, fast food. When they didn't hand it over quick enough, you beat them half to death."

Branch rose and limped to the cobwebbed picture window.

"The last place you robbed was a neighborhood bank," he said, staring at the overgrown willows in the front yard. "You pulled a gun, hollered 'stick-em-up.' But genius that you are, the stocking over your face had a big hole. The teller supervisor got a good look. With his photographic memory, he described you to responding police." He turned. "Down to those cute little acne pits on your chin."

Bloch scratched them, shifting uncomfortably.

"Cops nailed you a mile from the bank, cash bag between your legs. The teller supervisor testified at your trial, and you got shipped to Stillwater to play patty-cake with people of color. The teller supervisor was Zabrina's father."

"Yeah, all right. I know the guy," Bloch said. "But I didn't croak him."

"Only because you couldn't. He's been in Amsterdam the past month, on business. So you took your payback by nailing his kid," Marty said, cracking his knuckles in Bloch's ear. "Soon as you were released, you found out she lived in Naperville, put a knife in her. Then you wasted our cop during your getaway."

"I did not!" Bloch howled, so vehemently Emily sensed he was telling the truth. Then again, cons lied as easily as they breathed, just to stay in practice. "I didn't kill anyone! Not her, not that cop, *nobody*! Never!"

"So how do you explain it?" Branch said.

"It's a, whaddaya call it, a confucius!"

"You mean coincidence?"

"Yeah! It has to be!"

"We're not brain dead," Marty growled, crowding so close Bloch leaned away. "Your sheet's filthy with violent crimes. One week after your release, Zabrina eats a foot of steel. You expect us to believe that's *coincidence*?"

"Gotta be, man! I came here for the house!" Bloch insisted, stomping the carpet for emphasis. Ants boiled from the seam. Emily made a face, moved back.

"Explain," Branch said.

"Ma croaked when I was in Stillwater. This is her place.

She left it to me in her will. Ask the warden. He's the one told me. Go on, ask him."

"We will."

"When I got released, I didn't have anywhere to live. I knew people in the Cities, but I couldn't hardly stay there. Because of my, uh . . ."

"Friends."

"Yeah, that's right. Friends." Hack and swallow. "I hopped the Greyhound and found Ma's old house. Figured I'd hang here till things settled down. Then I'd move somewhere warm." He shivered. "Minnesota's so cold I crapped ice cubes every February. I'm gonna move down to Mexico. Eat me a taco every day." He leered at Annie's crotch. "A pink taco, know what I mean, blondie . . . *ow!*" He grabbed both feet, whimpering.

Branch sighed, pulling back the cane. "That is, without a single doubt, the most retarded story I've heard in my entire life, Devlin—"

"It's true! I swear it is!" Bloch said. "I gave my parole officer this address. Why would I do that if I was coming here to kill someone?"

"'Cause you're an idiot?" Marty said.

Bloch glared, then turned to Branch. "How'd you find me? Maybe that'll prove something."

Branch shrugged. "Someone told us you and the Reynolds family had history. We entered your name in the National Crime Information Center. Stillwater popped from the registry of prison inmates. We called the warden, who gave us your parole officer. He faxed us this address. We identified you through the window. You know the rest."

"See?" Bloch said. "I wasn't hiding. The warden knew I was here. My parole officer. Your computer, too. If I was gonna whack someone in Naperville, I woulda told everyone I was moving to El Paso. That proves I'm telling the truth."

Branch shook his head. "All it proves is you moved here

the week before a brutal double homicide. Far as I'm concerned, you're good for it."

"And if you haven't heard," Marty said. "We've got us an electric chair. With a governor so anxious to use it he wets himself."

Bloch looked like he might, too. "Hey! Wait! You got my sheet, right?"

Emily rattled the printouts.

"Then you know I never killed no one. Not man, woman, or kid. Sure, I beat 'em up. Just to get my green, though. I needed my green, and they had it." He pointed to the rap sheet. "Here's one you don't know about because I never got caught," he said, reeling off a date and name of a convenience store. "A rice-head behind the counter had my green. Wouldn't give it up. 'Skloo you, Chollie!' he hollers. 'My money! Get ugly face out my store!'"

He became more animated.

"I beat that ricer till his undies bled. A gun's supposed to mean something, you know. He's not supposed to keep fighting when I put a gun in his face. Just give it up."

"But he didn't," Branch said.

"Right!" Bloch said, like agreeing meant they were pals. "So I busted him up."

"And you're telling me this why?"

"To prove what I been saying—I never kill any of them. I'm very careful about that. Don't mind risking the can but I don't want no death penalty. Didn't kill anyone in Stillwater, neither. Busted up plenty of homeboys, but they had it coming. Being I was AB and they was blacker than the crack of my—"

"Finish the story about the convenience store clerk," Branch said.

"Alive when I left," Bloch said. "Not one bullet or blade, and I carried both when I did a job. Just to scare the suckers into giving me my green. I *never* killed no one, no way." He took a deep breath. "That's it. Proves my story, right? I hope I get some consideration."

"I hope you get dick cancer," Marty said.

Branch arched an eyebrow at Emily.

"I'll check out his story," she said.

Branch nodded, yanked Bloch to his feet.

"Hey!" Bloch protested. "I thought we had an understanding."

"You thought wrong. You're under arrest."

"For what?"

Branch eyed the mess in the kitchen. "Littering."

20

The Executioner stared over downtown St. Louis, pleasantly buzzed from bourbon and prime rib. Lightning white-strobed the hotel room, with violet afterglows. The picture window groaned from the cyclonic wind bursts. The Arch, that fusion of art and steel he so admired, had disappeared behind the curtain of rain.

Not to worry, he told himself. The storm would be gone by morning.

As would he.

He slid under the crisp white sheets and immediately fell asleep.

August 10, 1966

The potbellied janitor scrubbed for two full minutes, then sliced footwide streaks of clean through the suds. He checked the window for stubbornness, moved on to the next.

Folks like you made America great, thought Assistant State's Attorney Wayne Covington. *Not greedy punks like Earl Monroe.*

Tanned arms darted around his face and ruffled his Brylcreem.

"Hey, bro," Wayne said, laughing as he wriggled away from his kid brother Andrew.

"Hey yourself," Andy said, adding a noogie. "You get over there this morning?"

"Is the pope Catholic?" Wayne said, borrowing Andy's aluminum comb to slick his thick blond hair into place. Once a week at sunrise, the Covington sons gathered for breakfast at the parental Queen Anne in downtown Naperville. "Don't worry, though, Ma forgives you."

"She always loved me best."

Wayne shot him a fake punch. "A pity you couldn't join

us. Ma made griddle cakes and ham. Pineapple upside-down cake, toast, jam from her raspberry patch—"

"Shaddup," Andy grumped. "I would have been there except Brendan Stone was whining about a tummy ache. I had to go find him some Bromo-Seltzer."

"That guy sure complains a lot," Wayne said, accepting coffee from the sergeant of the twelve-man detail. The paper cup was so hot he wrapped it with a handkerchief. Better. "They don't make gangsters like they used to."

"That's for sure," Andy said. "Last night I told him criminals were supposed to be stoic so shut the hell up. Guess what he said?"

Wayne arched an eyebrow.

"He says, 'How dare you call me stoic, Officer? Everyone knows I'm Irish.'"

Wayne honked coffee out his nose, making Andy fall to the sidewalk laughing.

Earl Monroe pulled his fresh-waxed Ford Galaxie onto the gravel shoulder, kitty-corner from the motel. He waited for the dust to settle, then cranked down his window and inspected the scene with binoculars.

What a dump, he thought, vastly amused. *A silk-stocking guy like Brendan's gotta hate this.* A lumpy janitor scraped crud off the windows. A black Plymouth Fury idled nose-out from the door. Eight stocky men lined the sidewalk, jiving and joshing.

Sears Roebuck suits, Earl noted. *Black shoes, white socks, low-slung fedoras, bulging coats. Yup, they're plainclothes cops.* A mixture of Naperville and county. Exactly as his court snitch promised. Good to know the mutt was on the ball.

In a few minutes, Brendan would emerge from the motel for the ride to the grand jury. When he did, Earl would climb out of the Galaxie and wipe his hound-dog face with a big red rag. Brendan would see it and know his fate was sealed—

"What the?" he sputtered, jerking the binoculars into his eye sockets.

"Yes sir, right away," the janitor answered the sergeant. He grabbed squeegee and bucket and scuttled backward from the motel's entrance, hat flapping.

Andy ground the Fury into gear, inched backward till Sarge shouted, "Whoa." He hopped out, leaving the motor rumbling and "Yellow Submarine," the new Beatles hit, blaring.

"Awright ya damn hippie, go fetch our witness," the sergeant said, swatting Andy's arm. He didn't know how the kid could stand that cat strangle they called rock-and-roll. Kids liked a lot of crazy things, he supposed. "Rest of you, block the sidewalk with your big fine selves."

"Holy cow, Sarge," Andy said, raising his eyes to the high, thin clouds. "We expecting airborne commandos to kidnap this galoot?"

The sergeant's eye roll said he, too, thought the precautions silly, but the big cheeses wanted it that way. "Just do it."

Andy saluted, double-timed inside.

"He's a good kid, Wayne," the sergeant said fondly. "Gonna be a fine copper."

"He already is," Wayne said.

His little brother had wanted to be a police officer since he could go "bang-bang" with finger and thumb. Wayne pinned on the badge himself when the Naperville Police Department swore Andy in. The Polaroid that Pop snapped stood proudly on the Queen Anne's mantel, next to the one of Wayne graduating law school. "He already is," he repeated.

"Yeah. Your folks should be proud. Both sons in law enforcement."

"Andy's the law," Wayne said. "I'm the order."

The sergeant laughed, then laid out the route for his plainclothesmen. "All right, they're coming out," he said. "We go the moment Brendan's butt hits the seat."

"See you at the grand jury," Wayne said.

"We'll get there when we get there," the sergeant said. "Don't want to use lights and sirens. Earl Monroe still wants to knock this guy off, and I don't want to give him a target."

Wayne turned to leave but felt a twinge in his bladder. He wouldn't have time to relieve himself at the courthouse. "Where's the head on this ship, Sarge?"

"Green door," he replied, pointing with his chin. "Next to the ice machine. Can't miss it."

Wayne hurried away.

Earl thumbed the center wheel to sharpen the focus.

The coot janitor was his kid brother Daniel, brushing suds with one hand and unbuttoning his coveralls with the other. He was sweating a lot harder than August would dictate, and his jaw, carpeted with fake sideburns, moved sideways, something he did only when extremely nervous. His belly was the size of a feather pillow. That made no sense at all—Danny was thin as a whippet. He was hiding something underneath . . .

Earl's brain clutched. *He came here to "help" me with Brendan Stone!*

He recalled too late now that Danny was at crew headquarters—an abandoned gasoline station on a lonely road outside Naperville—the day the court clerk called to report

Brendan's hideout and grand jury schedule. The crew was bitching about what a commie rat fink their bookkeeper turned out to be, giving up the boss to the authorities. Earl paid no mind—Brendan's "tell-all" was a complete and utter con job. He'd tell the grand jury about every one of Earl's crimes as head of a Chicago Mob gambling-machine crew, ensuring Earl's indictment. Then he'd recant at the real trial, ensuring acquittal on all charges. Double jeopardy would wipe the slate clean forever. The idea was to make Wayne Covington, the bulldog assistant prosecutor trying to make his bones by tossing Earl's narrow butt in Stateville, look like such a sap he'd have to quit.

It all came about when Brendan was diagnosed with inoperable lung cancer. "You take care of my family when I'm gone," he'd said when pitching the idea to Earl, "and I'll take care of Covington." Earl ran it past Chicago, who approved on the spot—drowning a prosecutor at birth was a rare treat. So here they both were on a hot August morning, playacting.

But Danny didn't know that.

His brother was never in the "family business." Not now, not even when Dad ran the crew. "It's not for me," he'd said when Earl asked why. "I have different plans for my life." Even the cops left Danny alone, knowing the smart young man was on the square, and that he stopped at the garage only to see his brother. Visits Earl hugely enjoyed—he loved Danny to distraction—but never imagined would lead to something this insane.

"Where's your brains, college boy?" he spat. "You got one gun? They got twelve. And a tommy gun backing them up."

He calmed himself, trying to think.

Walk over right now, he decided. *Danny sees me, he'll back off whatever lame-brained scheme he's hatched.*

He jumped from the Galaxie and hustled across Ogden Avenue, twirling his shiny keys to attract his brother's attention.

* * *

Andy steered Brendan through the double doors, scanning for threats. So far, so good. The only people besides cops and witness was the janitor. And some cat crossing the street . . .

"Sarge!" he hollered, reaching for the Smith & Wesson under his coat.

"Earl Monroe!" the sergeant bellowed, drawing his own .38. "Halt right where you are!"

"Earl Monroe?" Wayne gasped, splashing himself as he jerked toward the bathroom door.

"You OK, Brendan? These coppers rough you up? I just came to make sure you're all right!" Earl bellowed, pushing the drama to the hilt. "You don't have to do this, you know! They can't make you testify against me if you don't want!" He started raising his hands so the cops wouldn't panic and open fire—

"Yow!" he yelled as he tripped into a pothole. He threw out his arms to save his face.

The keys flew straight at the cops.

"Monroe's attacking! He's throwing something!" Wayne bellowed as he charged from the bathroom. "Andy, get down, get down!"

Danny tore three hand grenades off his belly. Last time he'd visited the garage, he'd overheard Earl brag that he'd "accepted a crate of Kraut-blasters" as payment from a busted-out gambler who worked at the National Guard armory. He liberated four when everyone went out for a poker machine installation. As an engineering student, he was fascinated by explosives. Maybe he'd wander down to the river and blow up fish. Knock over one of the abandoned silos that dotted the Naperville countryside. Something useful, anyway . . .

He yanked the safety rings, flung the pineapple-shaped explosives, and dove behind the concrete flower planter choked with dandelions.

"Aaagh!" the sergeant screamed as shrapnel blasted his chest apart. He fell into Brendan Stone, whose blown-off head was spinning the other way.

Glass from the burning Plymouth Fury scythed the air, ripping flesh into oozy puckers, spinning one broken cop after the next onto the bird-spattered sidewalk, rooster tails of blood spitting into the wind. The motel's burglar alarm erupted, adding to the confusion.

Wayne grunted to his feet, woozy from concussion. He staggered into the smoke and flames, desperate to find his brother.

"Danny, Danny, what did you *do*?" Earl wailed, yanking his busted leg from the hole. "Brendan wasn't ratting me out, he was saving me! It was a setup! We were home free!"

He started crawling back to the Galaxie. He needed to disappear before responding officers shot him a few hundred times. From the corner of his eye he saw the janitor race around the back of the motel, unseen by the writhing cops.

He felt a little better.

* * *

Wayne retched hotcakes when he saw Andy's gums. They were dangling from his mouth by a single pink sinew, teeth poking out like cob kernels. Blood wept from his flayed body. Flames threatened to burn him alive, so Wayne wrapped his arms around what was left and pulled Andy to safety. Blood whistled through a dozen holes.

The Fury was fully engulfed. The motel windows were shattered, the squeegee melted. A couple of cops scrabbled around like impaled crabs. The rest lay silent.

Car horns erupted.

Peering through the smoke, Wayne saw a filthy lump inch across Ogden Avenue.

"Oh no you don't!" he howled.

He yanked the superheated .38 from his dead brother's hand. Ignoring the searing brand, he stumbled half-blind toward the murdering bastard, firing as fast as he could.

"Ah! Ah! Ah! Ah!" Earl grunted as bullets chunked his body. He flopped across the center line, forcing Ramblers and Chevys into screeching panic-halts.

"I surrender!" he yelled, pushing his arms over his head. "Don't shoot any more! I give up!"

"Die, die, die!" Wayne snarled, pulling the trigger over and over though the blue-steel revolver was empty. He kicked Trent, screaming curses so filthy one driver slapped his hands over his son's ears.

"This animal napalmed my brother!" Wayne shouted, wrenching from the bystanders restraining him. Others joined the free-for-all. Inhalator ambulances raced down Ogden, sirens rising. "Let go so I can wring his neck!"

"Take it easy, mister," the biggest one ordered, locking

his farm-browned arms around Wayne. "If he's the killer you say, the electric chair'll hit him like a ton of bricks."

"That's why we got Old Sparky," another farmer said, kicking the revolver away. Everyone nodded, patted the man's shoulders and back. "Don't worry. Sparky'll set things right."

SATURDAY

21

Emily laid her cheek on Marty's damp chest. It smelled like strawberries—he'd run out of Irish Spring and had to use her body wash. "First mud, now this," he'd grumbled. "Another year with you and I'll be wearing a bra."

She wiggled closer, enjoying the tiny shocks that erupted as his fingertips massaged the small muscles along her backbone.

"I feel like I ran a thousand miles," she said.

"And it's only the first day," Marty said.

"Well, technically, the second," she said, glancing at her bedside clock.

An hour ago, Branch told the detectives to knock off till seven. Their only good lead had evaporated—the cell phone log said Devlin Bloch had indeed ordered only hookers and pizza, and manager interviews proved it. Might as well catch a few hours' sleep. Bloch would stay in jail till Minneapolis found the "misplaced" files of the convenience store robbery.

She and Marty headed to her house at the southwestern-most end of Jackson Avenue. They ate cold Brown's chicken, showered, brushed their teeth, and hit the Posturepedic.

"Gets a million times harder from here," Marty said, yawning.

"Well, aren't we the little braggart."

He chuckled. "I meant the case, dear. We're back at square one. Bloch is a lug nut, but I'd bet the pension he didn't do it."

She didn't disagree.

"Plus as soon as this isn't wrapped up, we have to dance at Covington's prom."

"Oh. Right," Emily said. In all the excitement, she'd forgotten about the execution coming to town Friday, and how many double shifts it would require to successfully police. When it came to overtime at age forty-two, her spirit was willing but her body complained.

"Are you handling it all right?" he said.

"Fine," she said. "I'm all for executing monsters like Corey Trent."

He repeated the question.

"Oh," she said, catching his real meaning. "I'm fine with that, too."

"Don't fib, Detective," Marty said, wagging a finger. "The polarity of your spinal cord changes when you're not telling the truth. My fingers sense it."

"Really?"

"Nah," he said. "It's just I saw your face in the parking lot."

"I saw yours first."

Marty's sour look said, Stop dodging the question.

"You got that wired expression when I was working out your calf spasm," he said. "You thought you were dying like two years ago, right?"

Emily propped herself on one elbow and studied Marty's

face. It was all hard planes and angles, unsoftened by the kindly hazel eyes. His fleshy, exquisitely shaped lips held no hint of his usual smile.

"You're right," she replied. "So?"

"So," he said, teasing a henna highlight from her chestnut hair. "Did you think twice about pulling the trigger? Did you aim low to hit metal instead of his head? Did you hesitate, even a fraction of a second, to jump into the fray?"

"Why?" she snapped. "You going to take away my shiny little badge if I say yes?"

Another sour look.

She blew out her breath. Marty was only trying to make sure she was all right with what happened today. To do that, he had to break through her natural stubbornness.

Which was, she had to admit, not easy sometimes.

"The only regret I have," Emily said, touching Marty's muscled chest, "is the dirtbag escaped to kill poor Sergeant Luerchen."

"'Poor Luerchen?'" Marty said. "You hated Ray as much as I did."

"Yeah, I know," Emily said, sighing. "But he was one of us. He was family. He shouldn't have died that way." She kissed Marty's forehead, returned his laser stare. "I would have put all eighteen rounds in the driver's brain if I'd gotten close enough."

"You're certain."

"I am."

Marty smiled. "Then what's with your nightie?"

Emily looked down, astonished. She'd bunched the silk so high and tight it looked like a goiter on her hip.

She slapped it to her knees. "I don't know," she muttered.

"Neither do I," Marty said. "But your subconscious does. Maybe someday it'll tell you."

Then his eyes, concentrated so intensely on her face as they talked, drifted south.

"For what?" she said, knowing what *that* meant. "Dispensing your psychobabble?"

"That was free. You owe me for that remark about dirt behind my ears."

"Annie came up with that," Emily pointed out. "Not me."

"I'm not interested in Zenning the good lieutenant," Marty said.

Emily giggled, then slipped off her lavender spaghetti straps. She adored how Marty made her feel. She could crawl through ten miles of sewage and he'd be waiting at the end, eyes twinkling, telling her she was pretty.

She groaned as his giant hands worked their magic.

"Oh, Marty," she whispered. "I love you. I love you so much."

"Me, too, baby," he murmured, riding the lavender.

"I can't explain what you mean to me," she said, body tingling, breath shortening. "Falling in love with you was like being born again—oh! Damn! No!"

His eyes flew open. "I do something wrong?"

"No," she said. "I did."

She flopped backward, bouncing her head off her overstuffed down pillow. "How could I forget that?" she raged. "It's too important! What an idiot I am!"

Marty dropped his head on his outstretched arm, watching her with faint amusement. "Is this a private beat-yourself-up party?" he asked. "Or can anyone join in?"

"I forgot to put those burnt matches on NCIC."

The National Crime Information Center held millions of law-enforcement records, from fingerprints to mugshots to aliases to VINs to crime scene descriptions to the inmate locator that nailed Devlin Bloch. Any cop in America could query NCIC to see if something in one of their cases had popped up anywhere else.

She'd assured Branch she'd log the burnt matches before

heading home. An extreme long shot, she knew—they'd almost certainly been dropped by a client. But Branch's mantra was thoroughness, and she hated not having crossed that particular item off her list. Especially since without Bloch, they had less than zero.

"It's been a long day, Em," Marty said. "It'll keep a few more hours."

She shook her head.

"Yeah," he said. "I know."

He rolled off the bed and reached for his jeans.

"Oh, hon, stay here. Get some sleep. You're exhausted," Emily said, clipping on her gun and badge. "I'll drive to the station and send out the request. I'll be right back."

Marty looked at her, then the rumpled sheets.

"Think I'll tag along to ensure you don't linger, Detective," he said. "We're not due till seven, and I don't intend to spend all of it sleeping." Pause. "By the way, do we have any whipped cream in the fridge?"

"Why?" she said, heading for the stairs. "You hungry?"

"That, too," he said.

In the garage, he glanced at his watch.

"Shit. I forgot."

"What?"

"About a phone call I gotta make."

"At three in the morning?"

"It's that damn snitch," he said, not looking at her. "He keeps nutty hours."

Her eyes narrowed as she rubbed her still-sore ear. "What's really going on, Marty?"

"Nothing," he said. "This guy's causing trouble I don't want to deal with right now."

"Really? That's all? You're not in trouble or anything?"

He waited too long to reply.

Her lungs started burning from not breathing.

"I have to go do this," Marty said, heading back to the door. "Soon as I'm done I'll come to the station. Shouldn't be long. You go on ahead."

She shrugged, not knowing what else to say. She got in her car and started the engine. He went inside the house.

She waited a minute, then crept to the door. Opened it silently. Padded on tiptoes till she heard him talking in the kitchen.

"You know I'll do it, Alice," he was saying. "I'll find a way. And yes, it'll be soon. But Emily deserves to know. I just haven't found a way to tell her yet . . ."

She couldn't listen any longer.

Tears falling, she retreated the way she came and headed for the station.

22

10:10 A.M.

"Hiya, Rev!" the passing driver shouted, squinting at the glare off the church bus. "Need any help washing that road hog of yours? I can swing by home and grab the kids."

"Nah, Chet, I'm good," the minister said, waving his Windex and rags. "Soon as I finish the mirrors, I'm done."

Chet gave him a thumbs-up. "Real good luck on your trip. I mean it, Rev. Don't agree one bit with your position on that electric chair—I say kill 'em all, let God sort 'em out. But I do admire your spirit."

"Thank you, my friend. Be a nice drive if the weather holds."

"How far is it again to Naperville?"

"Seventeen hundred miles, give or take."

"Ouch," Chet said, hamming up a wince. "My fanny hurts just thinking about it."

The minister smiled. "No sacrifice too great to stop an execution."

23

"Last time I tell you to get out of your bunk," the correctional officer warned, banging the bars with his steel toe, "and read that material the warden sent you."

"What the hell's the point?" Corey Trent grunted, running his grime-caked fingers through his butt-length hair. He stunk so bad from not bathing, brushing, or wiping he could hardly stand himself. But it annoyed the screws no end. Reason enough.

"So you'll know how to be a good, honest citizen when you're released."

Trent spat, popped both middle fingers.

The CO laughed. "Fly 'em while you can. In six days they'll be as shriveled as your dick."

24

"Thinking about that baby?" Branch said as they studied lab reports. The rest of the task force was in the field, searching for clues.

Marty nodded.

"You're all right?"

"I'm fine."

"That's what I said," Branch said. "You're all right."

Marty worked awhile longer.

Then looked up.

"She called me," he said. "While we were at Marko's house."

"Uh-oh."

"Yeah."

"Was Emily . . ."

"Right next to me. I told her it was a snitch."

"She buy it?"

"What do you think?"

Branch winced.

25

"Off the ears, please," the Executioner said. "Taper the back. Leave as much as you can on top." He patted his thick-locked scalp, winked. "The ladies like it that way."

"They sure do," the barber said, jawing his Juicy Fruit. He swiveled the worn Koken barber chair toward the TV, got busy with scissors and comb. A ball game glared from the screen. Rap music blared from the speakers. The air conditioner over the door rattled and coughed, but iced the room well. "You're not from Holbrook, are you?"

"Just passing through," the Executioner said.

"I thought so. Didn't think I'd seen you around, and you don't have a tan."

The Executioner examined the barber's mahogany arms. "Dead giveaway in Arizona."

"Gotta burn the elbow that hangs out the window, at least," the barber agreed. "Are you in town for business or pleasure?"

"The latter. I'm driving to California."

"On Route 66?"

The Executioner nodded. "I've racked up too much vacation time and the boss says use it or lose it. So I decided to get my kicks. Just like the song says."

"What song?"

Now that's sad! "You're awfully young to work this late, aren't you?"

"Hah! I wish! I'm twenty-two," the barber said, snipping away. "Dad and Grandpa work days. I'm still going to school, so I take the night shifts."

"Three generations of cutters?"

The barber smiled. "Four, I hope. My wife's expecting."

"Congratulations," the Executioner said. "Hoping for a son?"

"Doesn't matter, as long as he's healthy."

"Gotcha."

The barber smiled. He finished the top, then moved to the sides. "Congratulations, by the way. You're my very last customer of the night."

"Explains why you put out the closed sign and pulled the blinds," the Executioner said, knowing very well the shop schedule. "I thought it was me."

"Nah. I've been on my feet all day," the barber said. "School, then work. The governor himself could ask for a trim and I'd still close up at nine." He squared the left sideburn, scooted over to the right. "You enjoying the drive?"

"Very much. Tons of scenery. Restaurants along the way have been good."

"Got some great ones here in Holbrook. Tell them I sent you, and they'll knock off ten percent," the barber said, naming several. "I'm Frank Mahoney, by the way."

"As in Three Franks Barber Shop?" the Executioner said, pointing to the backward lettering on the picture window.

"That's right," Mahoney said. "Grandpa, Dad, and Roman numeral."

"Glad to meet you, Frank the Third." The Executioner stuck his hand from under the cotton bib, the stripes of which matched the pole out front. They shook.

"Why are you wearing gloves?" Mahoney asked, going back to the scissors.

"Burned my hands while barbecuing," the Executioner lied. "Doctor says the gloves make it heal faster." He raised an eyebrow. "Hey, do I detect a Midwest accent?"

"You've got a good ear," Mahoney said. "Grandpa's from Illinois and still talks funny. Guess I picked up a little."

"We don't talk funny," the Executioner said. "You do."

Mahoney laughed. "That's what Grandpa says. He loves Illinois."

"Why'd he move to Holbrook, then?"

"Says all that snow got to him. He was a dentist in Springfield. That's near Chicago, right?"

"Three hours south."

Mahoney's shrug said, Close enough. "Anyway, Dad says Grandpa liked winters till 1972, then all of a sudden had enough. He pulled up stakes and moved the family here."

"Why a barber shop when he was a dentist?"

"Holbrook already had two dentists," Mahoney explained. "Plus he was tired of putting his fingers in everybody's mouth. The shop was successful right off, and Dad joined him. Then me."

"The family business."

"For longer than I've been alive," Mahoney said. "What do you do?"

"Food service executive," the Executioner said.

"Cool."

"Keeps me busy," he said, nodding toward the window. "Do you like Holbrook?"

"Well, it's the gateway to the Painted Desert," Mahoney said artfully.

"And hours from Phoenix, Vegas, or any other big city,"

the Executioner said. "I'd think it'd get pretty lonely sometimes for a young man going places."

Mahoney smiled. "You're never lonely in a small town.
Everyone stops by to stick their nose in your business."

"Touché," the Executioner said, laughing.

"Where are you staying tonight?" Mahoney asked as he
rubbed steaming white lather onto neck, cheeks, and chin.
"Best Western? Holiday Inn? Or out at the Wigwam?" He
grinned at the perplexed look. "It's a motel. Concrete wig-
wams with beds, bathrooms, and air-conditioning. I know it
sounds touristy, but it's actually cool."

"Sounds fun," the Executioner said. "But I can't. I'm
pushing through to Los Angeles."

"Tonight?"

"Soon as I'm done with you."

Mahoney frowned. "That's an awfully long drive. Nine
hours, at least. Hotter'n hell crossing the Mojave Desert in
August—even at midnight it's over a hundred. Your car
breaks down, you'll fry like bacon before the highway patrol
shows up."

"I'll be fine."

"You sure you need to push that hard?" Mahoney pressed.
"Especially on vacation and all? I'd be glad to call the Wigwam, get you the Three Franks discount."

The Executioner shook his head.

"Well, it's not my business, anyway," Mahoney said.
"Man wants to see the Mojave by moonlight, no one should
tell him otherwise."

"That what Grandpa says?"

"Nah, that's me." He bent close, touched steel to flesh.
Several dozen strokes later, he was wiping the Executioner
clean with a hot towel from the baseboard steamer.

"Terrific job, Frank," the Executioner enthused, watching
the white fog billow into in the shivery air. "Best shave I've
had since . . . well, ever."

"Thanks. I pride myself on them. The razor helps."

The Executioner reached to the shelf to examine one. He stopped midair.

"Oops, sorry," he apologized. "All right if I sneak a look?"

"Oh, sure, be my guest."

The Executioner raised the straight razor to the light, turned it this way and that. No tool marks. No burrs. Just gleam and perfect mating of ironwood handle to hollow-ground carbon steel blade. "This is a work of art," he said, deeply impressed. "And you're an artist with it."

"Thanks," Mahoney said, young chest puffing under the white smock. "That's genuine Solingen steel, all the way from Germany. Grandpa got them off the Internet. They're pricey, but they keep a nice sharp edge, which you need to clip those annoying loose ends."

"Funny you should mention that," the Executioner said, reaching to put the razor back.

"Mention what?" Mahoney said, bending to the steamer for the final hot one.

The Executioner sliced the kid from ear to ear, Solingen steel sinking so deep the edge clacked off the cervical vertebra.

"Awk . . . wha . . ." Mahoney gurgled as his eyes went full-moon.

"You're a loose end," the Executioner said, backpedaling to avoid the blood shot. "And I just clipped you. Pretty funny, huh?"

Mahoney collapsed like a brain-shot calf.

"No tip necessary, you say?" the Executioner said, snapping the kid's nose with a heel strike. "That's damn nice of you, Frank. You're a chip off Grandpa's block."

No reply.

The Executioner scrubbed the razor with blue germicide from the comb jar. It was great fun using such an exquisitely crafted weapon—everything just died better. He'd save the knife he'd mailed to himself at Phoenix General Delivery for another target.

He checked the street—still clear—then removed two matches from his briefcase.

Ten seconds later he shook them out. He walked to the TV stand and pitched them underneath.

The cut to the bone took almost no effort, he reflected as he merged onto westbound I-40 to California. Easier than the cervical lance in Naperville, and far more satisfying. All that nice frothy blood. It was primeval. The way Bowie liked.

He wished he could call.

August 12, 1966

Earl Monroe breathed as shallowly as possible. Anything else reignited the incredible pain.

Thank God he'd been hit by solid-nose bullets. He'd seen a man shot a dozen times with those and recover with bragging rights. If the cops had carried those fancy new hollow-point bullets, the so-called "Super Vels," he'd be toes-up in the county morgue.

Course, when the cops are done with me, I'll be toes-up anyway.

He took in the hospital room for the thousandth time. Cinderblock walls. No windows. Linoleum floor. Worn linen. A metal tray for his food. Another to hold his bedpan. Two IV bags, one empty, one almost, hanging from a steel hook. An ashtray full of squashed butts. An unoccupied bed to his right.

A uniformed policeman was parked outside his door. Now and again he poked his shiny head inside, but didn't say a word. Just glowered. Right now he was gone. Bathroom, snacks, or feeling up a nurse, Earl didn't know. Didn't care. The guy was a lump.

He moved his left hand under the blanket. It rattled. Same with his right ankle.

He was handcuffed to the bed.

Just like yesterday.

And the day before.

No police interrogation so far. That surprised him. Then again, the detectives were probably waiting for him to get "well" so their breaking-down would be more effective.

More fun.

The doctor was pleasant enough. Didn't curse or scowl, just checked the ankle cast, tended the bullet wounds, and chatted about weather and sports.

The nurses weren't. They pursed their lips, muttered under their breath. Anything Earl requested, they ignored. Or spat something rude, "slimeball" on the end more times than not. Jabbing harder than necessary when drawing blood, positioning the bedpan just far enough away that he'd miss and have to lay, humiliated, in soaked sheets.

The nickel-and-dime harassment that came with "cop-killer."

He winced at the burn in his chest, back, and legs, and realized his breathing had speeded up. He forced himself to relax.

The burns cooled.

His thoughts ran double-time as he analyzed what happened, and what he'd do about it. Same conclusion as yesterday. It all depended on what happened to Danny. It's not like he could ask someone. Was his brother home, eating cornflakes? Gritting his teeth in agony down the hall here? Absorbing the bad breath and rubber hoses of a police interrogation, an altogether different agony? Or laying, chilled and hairless, in the county morgue?

Earl sighed. Two days, and the only thing he knew for sure was that the detectives would come soon. Wouldn't be pretty when they—

"Damn," he whispered.

"Hi, Earl," Danny said.

"Well, that answers one question, anyway," Earl said.

"What's that?"

"If you're alive enough for me to break your neck."

Danny dragged a chair next to his brother.

"I'm sorry."

"Sorry don't cut fish with detectives, boy," Earl snapped.

"I know. I didn't mean to get you involved."

"Good to hear. Hate to see what involving me feels like," he said, pointing to his gauze patches. "These aren't good-luck charms."

"I know."

They fell silent.

"Well, anyway," Earl said, finding it impossible to stay mad at little bro. His heart was in the right place with those grenades. Even if his brain was out to lunch. "I'm glad you made it."

"Wish you had, too," Danny said. "Honest to God, Earl, I had no idea you'd be at the motel. None at all." His eyes were wide open, his mouth a downward U. "I can't explain why I did it. When I was at the garage that day, I overheard the Brendan Stone deal. Something just clicked inside me. I already had the grenades, so I put on that janitor disguise and took him out."

"Why?"

"'Cause you're my brother, goddammit," Danny said, flaring. "Why the hell else would I do something so insane?"

Earl heard the distinctive footsteps, put a finger to his lips. "Hush down. Cop's coming back. Don't want him hearing this conversation or there'll be two Monroes on Death Row."

"Death . . . Row?"

"What you think they do to cop-killers, man?" Earl said. "Throw flowers?"

Danny's face crumpled in on itself. "I wasn't thinking that far ahead."

"Clearly," Earl said.

The cop froze in the doorway, then stomped inside. "You're supposed to clear visitors with me, Monroe," he gruffed, all suspicious. "Who the hell's this?"

"My brother Daniel," Earl said. "Came to see me all the way from Purdue, where he's getting his master's degree in engineering. You weren't at your post when he arrived"—he nodded at the steaming coffee—"so I told him to wait till you returned."

The cop considered it.

"OK," he told Danny. "You can have twenty minutes. Go lean against that wall."

Danny took the frisk, and the cop left.

"You weren't thinking that far ahead?" Earl prompted.

Danny nodded. "My brain just flooded. I wanted to save you from Covington. I couldn't think of any way but the grenades. That's why I did it, and why I'd do it again." He patted Earl's arm.

"No contact with the prisoner," the cop growled from his chair.

"Sorry, sir," Danny said, pulling back.

The cop grunted, went back to his *Field & Stream.*

"It's all academic anyway," Danny said.

"Meaning?"

"You're going to be fine, Earl. I'm going to the police and confess that I did it."

"Nope."

"What do you mean, nope?"

"I mean you aren't confessing, little bro," Earl said. "I am."

Danny's eyebrows jumped.

"Not much to do here but think," Earl said, shifting the few inches the shackles allowed. "So I did. Here's how it's going to go. Wayne Covington saw me slaughter those cops. He knows it like the devil knows pitchforks, and he'll be so convincing on the stand that a jury of Quakers would draw straws to pull the switch on me. I've decided to let it happen."

Danny stared, jaw slack.

"That's right, it's gonna be me that dies in that chair," Earl said. "I'm keeping you out of it."

"You're crazy!"

"Not crazy enough to ace a load of coppers in broad daylight, pally buck," Earl said. "But since I clearly did, I gotta take my punishment."

"Earl, there's no way I can let you—"

"You got no choice, Danny," Earl said. "You're gonna walk out of here and not look back. You're so horrified at what I did that we're not brothers anymore. No further contact between us. No letters, no calls, no nothing. From now on, you don't know me."

Danny shook his head so hard his hair couldn't keep up. "I can't do that, Earl. There's no way I'll abandon you."

"You don't have a choice."

"Why the hell not?"

"Because you gotta take care of Mom."

Silence.

"Face it, Danny," Earl said. "I'm a gangster. Mom loves me, but she's not proud of me. Can't be, not with what I do. You, on the other hand, are Mr. College. You're smart, striding, gonna grab the world by the throat and shake it up. With your degree, you're gonna work for NASA or some other important program. You're the son Mom can be proud of."

"What's that got to do with the price of Sanka?"

"Everything," Earl said. "The state's gonna kill someone for this massacre, Danny. That's carved in stone—someone killed family and someone's going to pay. That someone is me, cause Covington told 'em so. Trial's just a formality."

"But if I tell Covington—"

"That will do exactly one thing—put you in the chair next to mine. Meaning Mom will bury both her sons, not just one. We can't do that to her." Earl motioned for the water jug. Danny poured a cup. Earl drank deep, smacked his lips.

"Covington's not gonna let me go," he said. "To him, I'm a stone-cold gangster who killed his baby brother. Buzzing me is personal now—a family obligation. If you tell him you're involved, he'll execute you with me. Not instead of. Because you're my, uh, what do you call it . . ."

"Accomplice?"

"Yeah. Accomplice." He cranked his head to look Danny square in the face. "One of us has to survive this. To keep the family name alive, and to take care of Mom. I can't, so you have to." He swallowed, hard. "Something else."

"What?"

"I don't want you to die," Earl said, so quietly Danny strained to hear. "I can't handle what's coming to me at State-ville unless I know you'll be all right. You're doing this for Mom and the family honor, Danny. But you're doing it for me, too."

Silence.

"Five minutes," the cop in the hall said.

"Thank you, Officer," Earl chirped.

"Don't get wise," the cop said.

Earl smirked, went back to Danny.

"So that's it," he said. "I'm taking the fall. You're going on with your life. It's gonna be a great one, and you're gonna take care of Mom. You won't contact me again. No cards, letters, or calls. Especially no visits—cops see us together after today, they'll start thinking you're maybe involved. They'll get you kicked from school, maybe drafted. They'll ruin your life."

Danny kept shaking his head.

"You got no choice," Earl snarled, full metal gangster.

"You messed up doing those grenades, and this is how you're gonna pay for it. It's my job to do this. It's yours to take care of our mother and have a life worth bragging about. Savvy?"

Danny made a little sound in his throat.

"Gonna be hell for me, too," Earl said. "We been thicker than thieves all these years, the Monroe brothers. Two peas in a pod. Not seeing you again is gonna hurt like cancer."

"Worse than that."

"Right. But we have to protect Mom. *You* have to protect Mom. Dad can't do it cause he's dead, and I can't cause I'll be there soon. It's up to you to handle it, Danny. Will you?"

Danny closed his eyes.

"Yes," he said.

"Look me in the eye and promise," Earl said.

"I'll handle everything," Danny said, staring. "I give you my word."

"That's good enough for me," Earl said. "I'm gonna make a little show for the copper. He's gonna report this visit to the detective bureau, and I want it our way. Now c'mere."

Danny stood, leaned over.

Earl patted his cheek with deep affection.

Then punched it, hard.

"You want nothing to do with me?" Earl roared as Danny stumbled back. "Fine! Who the hell needs ya? You're dead to me now, Danny! Dead! Get out of my room, you traitor!"

"You're the traitor, Earl, killing those poor officers!" Danny shouted back. "You're a disgrace to our family! Man like you isn't any brother of mine!"

"Get out!" Earl bellowed, jangling both cuffs. "Before I break these apart and throw you through the goddamn window!"

The cop chuckled.

Danny walked away.

Dying inside.

SUNDAY

26

Emily slipped into a Black Sabbath T-shirt.

"Uhn," she heard Marty say.

"Go to sleep," she whispered. "I'll be back before you know it."

"What time is it?"

She checked her glow-watch. "Four-oh . . . *man!*" She cringed at the tree limb scraping the window like Goliath's toenail. Between work and her ongoing home reconstruction, she kept forgetting to call the tree company. The limb was too thick—and too high off the ground—to prune herself, and she didn't want Marty climbing around with a chainsaw.

"In the morning?"

"Yes."

Another groan. "You don't run till five."

"I know," Emily said, double-knotting her Nikes. She was too keyed up to sleep. Two days had passed without finding a viable suspect. Or even a decent clue—if Bloch knew more about Zabrina Reynolds and her family, he wasn't saying. "Between the homicides and the execution, I've got a lot of energy to burn off—"

Click.

Marty looked like a sleepy walrus next to the bedside lamp. "Guess I'll get up, too," he said.

"You want to run with me?"

He made a face, as she knew he would. Marty derided running as a "perfectly good waste of heartbeats." His exercise was weight lifting.

Along with what they'd done for two heart-pumping hours before falling asleep.

"What are you going to do while I'm gone?" she said, smiling at the memory.

"Get us one step closer to done," he said.

She nodded. The land beneath their feet once held the two-story log home her late husband, Kinley Jack Child, built as his wedding present to her. Two years ago, it was wrecked by the serial killer who'd laid waste to the city. Unable to coexist with those ghosts, she had the house—no longer "home"—leveled and removed.

Marty talked her out of selling the land.

"Jack chose this spot for one reason," he said of the sloped, wooded lot that overlooked the DuPage River and Naperville Riverwalk. "Because you'd adore it."

"I do," she'd admitted.

"So let's rebuild."

"You and me?"

"With our own four hands. As a testament to Jack's vision, and to dance on that other bastard's grave. Living well is the best revenge, right?"

"But build a house?" she asked. "Can we do that?"

"Baby," he'd replied, enveloping her in his arms. "We can do anything."

The more she thought about it, the more she agreed.

A builder handled the foundation, exterior, and utilities. She and Marty tackled the interior, from floors to fixtures. Marty asked her to move into his house for the several years the project would take, but she didn't want to jinx their love with too rapid twenty-four-seven.

He stayed over most nights, though—his beloved beagles passed last fall from a fast-moving virus, leaving his own walls full of gloom. Together, they turned the bare bones into a home. Every tile, light, and gallon of paint were glued, screwed, and brushed on by themselves. As soon as she could flush her toilets and run the AC, she bought a king-size bed—they barely fit in a queen, let alone a double—and moved in.

When they were finished, she intended to ask Marty to unpack for good. She was ready to commit till death did they part.

"Want your ice cream?" Marty asked as they trundled down the stairs and into the kitchen.

"Just one spoon," she said about her prerun meal. "I've had way too much sugar this week."

He walked to the freezer, pulled out French vanilla. Her standard prerun meal choice.

"I'll take peach today," she said.

"Ooh," he said, spooning it into her mouth.

"I'm trying."

His nod said he understood.

"Love you," she said as she headed out the back door. Down her backyard hill, three miles out, three miles back, three cups of French roast, and a shower.

Maybe a spot more "exercise" if time permitted.

"Back at ya," he said, hefting a carton of floor tiles and heading for the powder room.

27

"Chief?" the patrolman gasped as he two-stepped away from the tide that covered half the floor. "I think . . . I'm . . . gonna . . . "

"Not in the crime scene," Holbrook Chief of Police Gene Mason said, gently escorting the youngster outside. He took advantage himself, breathing in the sun-washed air. The blood didn't bother him—he'd seen worse at highway wrecks—but the jack-o'-lantern throat sure did.

"Scare up any witnesses?" he asked, stepping inside.

"None," his lead detective said as he mapped the scene. "We canvassed twice. Except for the barbershop, all the businesses were closed by seven. And since it's so damn hot . . ."

"Everyone was indoors, AC blasting. Yeah, I get it." Mason had grown up in Arizona, but August heat still kicked his butt.

He pointed toward the service station at the end of the block. "They're open till midnight. Maybe the killer was dumb enough to buy gas."

"Forty-seven customers between six and closing, Chief," the patrolman squeaked from the doorway. Green, but game, Mason noted. Good for him. "All locals."

"You know that how?"

"The manager came down to see what was going on. I asked if he had any strange customers last night."

Mason nodded. Young Frank's parents were in Reno, enjoying their second honeymoon. His wife was in Little Rock, visiting her folks. His grandfather, who founded this shop in 1973, drove down at eight to start the day shift. He heard rap music through the door. Concerned because his grandson never left anything turned on, he peered through a crack in the blinds.

He screamed, and fainted. A passerby called nine-one-one.

The patrolman arrived with the ambulance. He saw a familiar leg through the crack, drew his gun, kicked the door.

"All locals?" Mason asked. "Manager's sure?"

"Yes, sir. I told him to write down the names before he forgot."

"Good work," Mason said.

He looked at Frank and suppressed a shudder. This was bad business. With no witnesses, maybe unsolvable. He couldn't have that. He liked the Mahoneys. And unsolved murders hurt the tourist trade.

"Go confirm everyone's whereabouts last night," he told the patrolman. "Get Billy, P.J. and Mike to help you. Then scoot out to the interstate and visit the truck stops. Copy the register receipts and security tapes."

"You think a big-rig did it?" the detective said. Holbrook, at the intersection of Interstate 40, several major highways, and old Route 66, got a lot of truck traffic.

"Doubt it," Mason said. "Most of those boys are on satellite tracker. They stop more than a few minutes, home office gets on the horn and raises hell. I'm hoping somebody cut them off and they noted the license plates." He doubted that, too, but still needed to check. "What time did you say Frank died?"

"Nine last night," answered the Navajo County medical examiner. "Give or take. They kept this place like an icebox, which slows body cooling."

"You factor that in?"

"Sure."

"Nine it is, then," Mason said. He swung back to the detective. "You hit motels and campgrounds. Get the records of anyone staying last night. In fact, go back a couple weeks. Could be a tourist did this."

"Grand Canyon's too tame so let's whack a barber?"

"Stranger things have happened."

The medical examiner said he was done with the television. Mason walked around the edge of the room, careful to step only in cleared areas. He picked up the remote control and hit the power button.

"Wow. I can hear myself think," the examiner said.

"Thought I smelled something burning," Mason said, sniffing theatrically.

"Frank woulda said something like that, you know."

"Yeah," Mason said. "I know."

The examiner looked wistful a moment, then bent to his task. Mason put the remote back atop the TV. It slipped off the hard plastic and clattered under the stand.

Mason grumbled and dropped to his knees. His bursitis flared. He ignored it. He spotted the remote near the back, slid it out.

"Hello," he said.

"What?" the examiner said.

"There's two burnt matches under here. Came out with the remote."

The examiner brought over an evidence bag. "This place was no smoking, right?" he asked.

"Without exception," Mason said, peering at the curled charcoal sticks. "Grandpa's sister was a pack-a-dayer. Died of emphysema back in Illinois. Anybody dared light up, Grandpa ripped their heads off. Even the old coots took it outside without being told."

"So what are these doing here?" the examiner wondered.

Mason shrugged. "One of those weird clues you get sometimes, I suppose." He thought it through. "Maybe we can find out. What's the name of that computer database?"

"What database?"

"You know. With the initials. Tells you if your clues popped up anywhere else in the country."

"CSI?"

Mason shot him a look. The examiner smiled.

"Let's see . . . AFIS . . . NICS . . ." Mason snapped his fingers. "NCIC."

"National Crime Information Center," the examiner said.

"Right. I'll post this on NCIC. See if there's anything about matches."

"Why?" the examiner said.

"Something to do," Mason said.

August 13, 1966

"It's your constitutional right not to speak to us, Earl," Detective Burr said. "Isn't that so, Detective Rogan?"

"He's not obliged to say a word," Rogan agreed. "That new Miranda Warning says Earl can shut his piehole tight as he wants and we can't do a thing about it."

Burr leaned so close Earl smelled the Camels on his breath.

"Then again," Burr said, "that Miranda fella isn't exactly here, now is he?"

"Not that I can see," Rogan said.

Burr put his elbow on the pulpiest bullet hole. Earl blanched white as Glue-All. His narrow eyes watered and his flat nose ran.

"You're gonna sing like a canary," Rogan said, twisting Earl's ear like a windup clock. "You're gonna tell us where you got those hand grenades, and why you threw 'em at our friends. Or you're gonna hurt so bad you'll wish you *had* died at that motel."

* * *

"I miss him, Kit. I miss Andy so damn much," Wayne Covington whispered.

"I know, honey, I know," Katherine Covington cooed, stroking her husband's broad, bent back. "We all do. Your brother was a wonderful man. A treasure."

"He was everything good in this world. Everything holy. He didn't deserve to die," Wayne said, squeezing his pocket comb till the tines drew blood. "Not burned to death in a parking lot."

"No," she said, shuddering. "No."

"Ma's a wreck. She won't eat. She can't sleep. Pop can't even talk about it. Keeps saying Andy'll be over for breakfast Tuesday so he'd better pick more raspberries."

"That poor man," Kit said. "I'll go over today, Wayne. See if I can help."

"Earl Monroe blew my brother into snot," Wayne said, breaking down. "I watched him do it, and I'll see him burn for it. I will, Kit. I promise I will."

"God bless you, darling," Kit said, weeping openly herself. "God bless you for that."

Earl screwed his eyes shut as the elbows ground into his wounds. It felt like that napalm they were dropping over in Vietnam. Those golden drips of fire that melted children's eyes.

He concentrated on his brother's face. If he was going to die here and now, at least their secret would die with him.

"We've got you cold, so you might as well talk," Rogan said, expertly working Earl's nerve endings. "Covington will testify that you, and nobody else, killed those cops and witness."

"I . . . didn't . . ."

"Covington wouldn't lie. He's Mister Clean," Burr said. "Eagle Scout. Valedictorian. Varsity quarterback, married to the head cheerleader. Straight-A's in law school. Secretary of the Junior Rotary. One of the sharpest young prosecutors this county's ever produced. He comes from an old-line Naperville family that everybody adores. He's made the front page of the paper more times than you've scratched your butt. He's a somebody."

"And what are you?" Rogan said. "A gangster who caters to degenerate gamblers. A miserable nobody with a dead gangster pa. Making you second-generation miserable nobody."

Burr flicked Earl's cheek with a fingernail. Earl flinched.

"Even Danny quit you," Burr said. "Your own brother wants nothing to do with you anymore. Know why?" *Flick.* "'Cause he's smart." *Flick.* "He knows to stay away. He knows if he hangs around you, he gets the contamination." *Flick.* "Becomes a Frankenstein like you."

"Didn't . . . kill . . . anyone . . ."

"Go ahead, stick with that story. It's working great for you," Rogan jeered, lifting his fedora to blot his shiny brow. "Only two people survived that explosion. You and Covington. Who you think the jury's going to believe? Worm Dung Earl, or Eagle Scout Wayne?"

"Face it, pally, it's over for you but the frying," Burr said. "You got nothing to lose by confessing. Save us the time and effort, and you a bunch of pain. Whaddaya say?"

Earl gathered his strength, sucked in a breath.

"If Covington's got me so tight," he wheezed. "Then why you two assholes wasting my time?"

Both detectives smiled.

"'Cause we can," Burr said.

Danny's belly burned as he stared at the *Chicago Daily News.* It was official now—mass murder the crime, electrocution the punishment.

"It wasn't him they saw, Mom," he said. "It's a case of, uh, mistaken identity."

"Oh, Danny," Verna Monroe said, eyes filling. "You're so smart, thinking up things like that. But you can't help your brother anymore. None of us can. Not with thirteen dead."

She untied her apron and smoothed her rayon dress. "I'm going to the hospital. I'll tell Earl you love him and wanted to visit, but I made you stay away." She hugged him so hard she thought he'd break. "If your father was alive, he'd tell you the same thing. So would Earl. You know it. You know exactly what they'd say."

Danny stared, torn between spilling his guts and promising Earl he wouldn't.

"Go back to Purdue," Verna said. "That's what they'd say. Return to that university life you love so much, that you're so brilliant at. Leave today. Now!"

She clapped her hands, still unable to believe her bouncing baby was a college man, one year away from a master's degree in electrical engineering. She was so *proud*.

"Once you have that sheepskin, the sky's the limit," she said, reaching for her keys. "You can join AT&T. Westinghouse. Lyndon Johnson's space program. Go anywhere, do anything!"

"What's the point?" Danny said.

Verna folded her arms around herself at the misery in his voice. She was desperate to keep the good son away from the doomed. Danny had always resisted the siren that lured the rest of her men into the rocks. It was her job to make sure he steered clear.

"You have a glorious life ahead of you, Danny," she choked. "A house with a white picket fence. A wife. Adorable babies. Everything. Don't let Earl's choices make yours—I'll be there for him no matter what. You have to walk away. Walk away from your brother. Walk away."

* * *

"What on earth are you two doing?"

Rogan and Burr straightened to see a grim-faced young doctor stride into the room, stethoscope tucked neatly in his white coat.

"Questioning our prisoner," Rogan said.

"Like Torquemada."

"Who?" Burr asked.

The doctor wrapped his hand around Earl's wrist. Weaker pulse than an hour ago. Chalkier face, sheets more rent with sweat. Bandages dented and spongy with red.

He increased the morphine drip.

"Prisoner or not," the doctor said, "this man has the right to not be abused."

Burr, forehead vein ticcing, shoved his face in close. "Tell that to the widows and kids," he snarled. "If you got the stones."

"This man is my patient, Detective," the doctor said, refusing to back down. "He has any rights I care to give him. So get out of here, both of you."

They didn't move.

"Out!"

"Earl, Earl," Verna sobbed, burying her face in her elbows. She'd driven as far as the sleepy, one-horse downtown before her vision swam so bad she had to pull over. "I don't want you to die! Not in that awful electric chair!"

She cried so hard she sucked tears into her lungs.

"Why did you do it, baby?" she gagged. "Why?"

"He was ready to confess," Burr grumbled, spitting tobacco juice as they headed for the parking lot. "If that pansy doctor hadn't stepped in, he woulda gave it up."

"No he wouldn't," Rogan said. "Earl's a tough onion. Just like his old man."

"That's the one who was stabbed, right?"

"Nineteen times," Rogan said. "By a crew from St. Louis. They wanted to expand up north, figured the quickest way to do it was whack the competition."

"So they kidnapped the old man."

"At high noon, walking to his car after installing a poker machine in a tavern. Six goons grabbed him, took him to a cornfield, beat him with ball bats. Then cut him up. They assumed he was dead. I would have too, given nineteen stabs and a broken skull."

"He played possum," Burr said.

"Yup. After they left, he crawled to a farmhouse on pure guts," Rogan said. "Nobody was home, so he busted a window and found the telephone. Called Chicago and told his bosses who did it. Then he bled out." He shook his head. "Poor farmer, coming home to that mess."

"Be hard to live there after that," Burr said.

"Farmer called the inhalator squad," Rogan said. "Too late, though. It was a morgue job."

Burr jingled his pocket coins.

"A week later, a trash hauler found the goons in a ditch," Rogan continued. "Blowtorched so bad they didn't look human. Couple of 'em got scalped. You know, like the Indians did."

"Sheesh."

Rogan chuckled. "It was pretty over the top, even for the Mob. But St. Louis didn't want a war with Chicago. They took care of the problem themselves."

"And Earl inherited the family business."

"Yup. Earl was a sharpie from the moment he popped out of Verna. Chicago figured, hell, give the kid his shot. Pays their debt to the family, and no interruption in the take."

"He did good," Burr said.

"He did great. Turns out Earl had a genius for organization. More CEO than muscleman. He quadrupled gambling-machine profits without using a tenth the violence his old man did."

"Sonny boy don't like the rough stuff?" Burr said.

"Don't get me wrong. Earl Monroe would beat the snot from Gandhi if he refused to pay the piper. But he prefers doing business with his noggin."

"Why?" Burr said.

"Practical," Rogan said. "With violence out of the picture, the politicians have no reason to conduct raids, roust the crews, or otherwise crack down. That increases profits."

"Which increases payoffs to the politicians, which lowers the heat even more."

"Which pleases Chicago no end. Earl was destined for big things in the family. Then Brendan Stone ratted him out."

"Explaining why Earl blew him into a million pieces."

"Sure," Rogan said. "Even a brainiac like Earl doesn't let a betrayal like that go unchallenged. No man can. Like I said, he's not averse to using violence."

"Averse," Burr snickered. "I keep forgetting you went to college."

"I was an English major."

"Huh. I heard you majored in snatch."

"Same thing."

They reached the car.

"Earl stood up to twelve cops and a Tommy gun to whack Brendan Stone," Rogan said, climbing in the driver's seat and popping the passenger lock. "He ate four bullets, and he knows what awaits him at Stateville. Did it anyway."

"Geez, Rogan," Burr complained, sliding in. "Sounds like you admire the cockroach."

"You know better than that. What I'm saying is, we'd have needed a blowtorch ourselves to get a confession out of him."

"So why didn't we bring one?"

Rogan grinned. "There's always tomorrow."

MONDAY

28

"Don't forget, Ray's funeral starts at noon," Emily said, having decided to deal with the Alice situation after the execution. She couldn't afford the distraction. More important, she loved Marty. To her, that meant trusting him no matter what.

"I'm counting the minutes," Marty said sourly.

"I know, I know," she said, squeezing his arm. "But we've got to attend." She looked at the powder room, the back third of which he'd inlaid so exquisitely she could cry. "Are you going to keep working while I run?"

Marty nodded.

"How 'bout I soap you nice and clean when I get back?" she said.

"I'll think about it," he said.

Emily kissed him. It felt good. "Think harder," she said, rinsing her coffee cup and heading out the back door.

He watched her sail down the hill, hair flying, arms grabbing air. God, he loved her spirit. Her intellect. The way her calves slid into her knees into her thighs into her . . .

He seriously considered chasing her down and hauling her back to bed. Then coming clean about the phone calls. About Alice. About everything.

Then thought about how she'd react, and picked up the tile saw.

29

"Four more days till you're a crispy critter."

"That's the best you can do?" Corey Trent jeered, his voice echoing in the fire-brick barrenness of Death Row. "My mama insults me better'n that."

The correctional officer jutted his bony chin. "You don't know how good you got it, punk, dying in that electric chair. Me, I'd rip off your tits and let you scream till Easter. Then pound a stake through your heart."

"I didn't kill that kid," Trent said, already bored with this conversation. He'd heard it every day since his arrest. "Or its old lady. Didn't kill anyone."

"Course you did. Your rap sheet's as long as my arm," the CO said. "In and out of prison since you could shave. Burglary, grand theft auto, break-and-enter, arson, assault with a deadly, 'bout thirty other things. Plus felonies never proved."

"Yeah, well, if you knew how to read you'd see none of them was murder."

"You stepped up. Made the varsity."

"I wasn't nowhere near Naperville that day."

"Not what Commander Benedetti said. Or the jury. Or even your own family."

The light caught Trent's steel tooth. "A psycho cop, twelve people too stupid to get out of jury duty, and I don't got no family no more, the jerkoffs. You think I care what any of them say?"

He lifted his right middle finger, which was bitten off to the first joint by a whack-job murderer he'd tangled with in the showers. "Or *you*?"

"You damn well better," the CO warned, the disrespect steaming him good. Corrigan Trent was an acid-washed freak. He'd cut up that mother like a watermelon, then killed the poor baby when Benedetti and Branch started chasing. Trent's girlfriend even testified against him, saying she'd never meant him to take her whining—"Course I want a baby, sugar, it's just that I'd get all stretched out"—seriously. Yet here he sat, proclaiming his innocence. "You got four more days on the Row. They can go hard, or they can go soft."

"Speaking of soft," Trent said, pointing to the short man's crotch.

The CO snorted. "Hard way's fine by me. Here's your breakfast. Eat up while you still got teeth." He flipped the meal through the bars, throwing short so it skittered across the dirty floor.

Trent rolled off his bunk and picked up the strangely colored loaf of . . . what, he had no clue. "The hell you call this?"

"Breakfast. Lunch. And supper."

"Say *what*?"

"It's a nutrition loaf. Latest idea from Governor Covington. He says taxpayers spend too much hard-earned money feeding you knuckleheads, so starting today, you get nutrition loaves. Morning, noon, and night." He smirked. "Except for your Last Supper, of course. Then it's anything goes. Governor's thoughtful that way."

Trent heard the rest of Death Row bitch and holler. "What's in 'em?"

"Flour, milk, and government cheese," the CO said. "Plus yeast, sugar, salt, oil, carrots, and beets. Everything's ground up, then baked. You get three loaves a day." He pointed to the sink over the toilet. "And no more coffee or pop. Tap water's good enough for taxpayers, it's good enough for you."

Trent brought the loaf to his nose. "Man, this stuff smells funky," he complained.

The CO's grin widened. "Surprised you can tell, considering how bad you stink."

"Huh. Maybe it's not the loaf, then." Trent curled his thin upper lip to his nose, breathed deep. "Yeah, that's the smell. I musta forgot to wash my face after your wife left last night. She rode my tongue like a horse, CO, tell her to stop by any time she likes—"

"Disciplinary problem in Cell One!" the CO shouted to the master controller. "Open the door!" He unholstered the "inmate compliance tool" the staff carried in lieu of guns. "Now!"

"Whaddaya gonna do?" Trent jeered as the Row whistled and applauded. "Kill me? Covington already beat you to it. Once again you get sloppy seconds. Just like from your wife."

"Shut up, Trent," a senior CO growled, putting a hand on his colleague's shoulder. "And you, go help deliver the rest of the loaves."

"You hear what he said about my wife!" the CO raged. "I'm gonna shove this stick up his—"

"Loaves," the senior CO growled. "Now."

The CO huffed off, shooting murderous looks at both of them.

Trent curled an eyebrow.

"New guy," the man replied, shrugging. "Still thinks what you say matters."

30

"Ashes to ashes," the minister said.

Rayford Luerchen's widow bawled. Pink-clad women fanned her face.

Emily bumped her shoulder into Marty. He bumped back. She kept on her game face but smiled inside. She'd attended way too many funerals in her forty-two years, and thoroughly detested them. Marty's presence—and Annie's "hang in there" wink from the other side of the flag-draped coffin—was the only thing making this bearable.

"Dust to dust," the minister said.

The Firefighters Highland Guard of Naperville kicked in. Emily cringed. Bagpipes stirred her soul but hurt her ears.

31

"Roses for Mr. Sage Farri," the Executioner said.

"Oh, how beautiful," the receptionist sighed. "Is it Sage's birthday?"

"Wouldn't know, ma'am," the Executioner said, tugging the rose-embroidered cap he'd bought to make him look like floral delivery. "I never read the cards, just get 'em where they gotta go."

"I hear you," the receptionist said. "Familiar with the hospital layout?"

"Unfortunately, no. I just landed this job."

She looked the lean man up and down. Handsome, not pretty. She liked that. No man should look better than the woman on his arm. Great build. Palms hashed with long, fine lines, like he'd worked for a living. Hair more brown then black, with a light in his blue eyes that hinted at mystery. Or more.

Whether it was a good more, she couldn't tell. He gave off both vibes.

She pointed a long, gold fingernail down the corridor. "Take this to the end. Turn right to Room 407." She put a finger across her lips. "The poor kid can't sleep at night, so he's probably napping. You won't wake him, will you?"

"Cross my heart," the Executioner said, tugging his fake goatee.

32

"Lovely service," Annie said, wiping smudges off her sword.

Emily nodded. A line-of-duty funeral, with its starched uniforms, white gloves, patent leather shoes, parade caps, sabers, bagpipers, politicians, howling sirens, and hundreds of saluting cops—many from other states, coming at their own expense to salute a fallen comrade—was a grand mixture of The Unknown Soldier and P. T. Barnum. Somehow, it worked. The comfort it bestowed on survivors, blood and blue, was indescribable.

"Ray and I had our differences," Emily said, astonished to feel herself blinking. "But he didn't deserve to die that way. Ray was one of us. He was—"

"Racist, sexist, lazy, and dumb," Annie said, unrepentant.

Emily giggled as she wiped a tear. "You really should be kinder, Lieutenant," she chided. "The man *did* get shot."

Annie's expression said she wished she'd pulled the trigger. Rayford Luerchen's cowardice two years ago had nearly gotten her best friend killed. She neither forgot nor forgave.

Something Emily found as comforting as Marty's smile. Friends were family without the genealogy.

She spotted him pacing near a limestone mausoleum that resembled a sixteenth-century castle, complete with crenellation. She started to wave, then saw he was on the phone again. He looked angry. He was slapping the golden limestone and practically barking his replies. *What on earth is going on with you, Marty?* she wondered, throat closing, legs weakening. *What kind of trouble are you in? Are you dumping me for this Alice? How do I get you to open up—*

"Dum-da-dum-dum," Annie said.

"What?"

"Bereaved at nine o'clock."

Emily turned to her left to see The Widow Luerchen walking directly toward them, determination chiseled into her heavily rouged face.

33

Johnny Sanders blew thirty-five years of dust off the clothbound, manually typed journal.

"Executions, State of Illinois, 1972," the cover read.

"Once more unto the breach," the historian said, diving in.

34

"You are Emily Thompson, are you not?" Cheryl Beth Luerchen asked.

"I are," Emily said. "I mean, yes, I'm Emily. My deepest condolences on your loss."

A regal nod of broad-brim hat. "Thank you. Rayford's passing has shaken this community to its foundation," she said. "He was a gifted policeman, and a magnificent man."

Annie bit her lip.

"Ray was one of a kind, all right," Emily managed.

Cheryl Beth's smile cracked the foundation around her Kewpie mouth. "It's gracious of you to say so, dear. I was hoping you'd be here today."

"Why?" Annie said.

Small eyes shifted. "I don't believe we've had the pleasure?"

"This is Annabelle Bates," Emily said. "Lieutenant with the Naperville Police."

Annie put out her hand.

"Oh, of course," Cheryl Beth said. "You were the girl who became so frightened in the library that Rayford had to assume command. He told me all about it."

"I'm . . . sure he . . . did," Annie said, slowly pulling her hand back.

Another regal nod.

"What did you want to see me about, Mrs. Luerchen?" Emily said.

Cheryl Beth toyed with her leather purse, which was the same midnight black as her hat. It was genuine Coach, Emily noted, not a Canal Street knockoff like hers.

"My husband told me about that terrible row you had two years ago," she said. "At the cemetery where that body was found. You called him a goat, I believe?"

Emily wasn't about to deny it—her exact phrase was, "If you and a goat were the only males left on earth, Ray, I'd hump the goat"—but there was no point in making a widow feel worse. She split the difference by shrugging.

"Don't worry, dear. I understand completely," Cheryl Beth said.

"You do?" Annie said.

"Oh, yes, Lieutenant. Rayford brought that out in people, I'm afraid." Back to Emily. "I wanted you to know I understand why you said it, and that I hold no ill feelings."

Huh! "I appreciate your saying that," Emily said, relieved. She wasn't up for fighting Ray's ghost. "Especially on a day like today."

"Thank you," Cheryl Beth said. "I also assure you it wouldn't have happened."

"What wouldn't have happened?"

The foundation cracked another eighth-inch. "He wasn't going to leave me for you."

"Uh," Emily said.

"It makes perfect sense that you'd want my husband," Cheryl Beth continued. "He was strong and virile. A leader of men. It's natural you'd find yourself intensely attracted. Especially since your husband—Jack, I believe?—dumped you so many years ago."

"Ray said . . . that?" Annie said.

Emily heard the venom and thumped a warning fist in Annie's back. *You can't win a fight with a grieving widow. Let it slide.*

"Of course," Cheryl Beth said, oblivious. "Rayford was a fine Christian man, and kept no secrets from me. He told me how Emily tried to seduce him, and how he had to dissuade her, gently but firmly."

"Gently but firmly," Annie repeated. "Did Ray say how this, uh, seduction started?"

Cheryl Beth fanned herself. "Rayford offered her some career advice. He was a natural teacher, and loved to help his fellow officers. She took it as a sign he was interested in her romantically. He wasn't, of course. He was very happily married."

"How could he not be happy with a woman such as you?" Annie purred. *"Do* go on."

Emily thumped her again.

"Things escalated. Emily demanded Rayford make a commitment. That he choose her or me."

"When was that again?" Annie said. "The day in the cemetery?"

"Yes," Cheryl Beth said. "Rayford was becoming increasingly uncomfortable with Emily's infatuation. He had no choice but to be firm—the welfare of his department was at stake. He ordered Emily to stop the harassment or he'd file a formal complaint."

"And that's when Emily called him a goat."

"So everyone could hear," Cheryl Beth confirmed.

"But you hold no ill feelings," Annie said.

"Of course not," Cheryl Beth said. "Girls always got emotional around Rayford."

"I know I did," Annie said.

She turned to Emily. "Mrs. Luerchen has been totally honest about her husband, Detective Thompson," she said, eyes glittering. "Do you have something equally honest to say in return?"

"Oh, yeah," Emily said.

She moved in close. Began to say Ray wasn't a goat but a jackass, got his badge from a Cracker Jack box, and his raisin-eyed wife was his pathetic enabler.

"I wish I hadn't called him a goat," she said instead. "I'm sorry for your loss."

Cheryl Beth patted her hand and walked away.

"'Be kind to Rayford, Lieutenant,'" Annie cackled as they walked away. "'He was one of us, Lieutenant. The man got shot, Lieutenant.'"

"Shut up," Emily muttered. "Lieutenant."

35

"All right, ladies and germs," the water crew chief said, slapping the multiton booster pump. The crane that would install it glittered orange in the hazy sun. "We need this bad boy piped, welded, and running by Friday. Folks up and down Royce Road are complaining about low water pressure, and this'll give 'em what they need."

The crane operator lifted his long metal boom to a forty-five-degree angle.

"What they need, Larry," the foreman said, laughing. "Not what they want."

36

Emily dove behind cover, rolled twice, shouldered the rifle, pulled the trigger, felt the buck, and leapt to her feet, muzzle wobbling with every wheeze.

"Again."

Roll-blam.

"Again."

Roll-blam.

"Again."

Roll-blam.

"Again."

"You're killing me!" Emily howled.

"Better here than the street," Annie snapped in the whip-tone she employed as a U.S. Army sniper instructor. "Again."

Emily did thirty to her right and fifty to her left, then collapsed.

"Well, you wanted to scratch Mrs. Ray from your brain, right?" Annie said, squatting next to her. "No better way to do that than shooting."

"What shooting?" Emily groaned, clutching the ultralight combat rifle. Annie was testing it as a replacement for shotguns in patrol cars. "I'm hopping around like a bullfrog."

She'd been plowing through task force paperwork since the funeral. Devlin Bloch still wasn't talking, and no new leads had surfaced. Then came the Luerchens. Then Marty, who'd barely said a word since leaving the funeral. "What's wrong?" she'd asked. "Nothing," he'd replied. "Just tired." Angering her because she knew it so untrue. It was one thing to keep something from her. Now he was lying directly.

Annie stopped by to update Branch on Friday's security plan. Noted Emily's hunched-over grumpiness. Conferred with him, then told her, "Follow me."

Next stop, gun range.

"This isn't frog-jumping, girl," Annie snorted. "It's high-speed low-drag tactical ninja operator training. How you gonna be Robocop if you refuse to learn the lingo?"

"Don't wanna be Robocop," Emily said. She handed over the Kel-Tec SU-16CA, then sat against the wall to flap the Guns n' Roses T-shirt. "I just wanna shoot Ray for haunting me from the grave."

Annie looked at her strangely.

"Sorry," Emily said. "Bad taste."

"No such thing when it comes to Ray," Annie said. "But I hear more than our un-dearly departed in that statement. What's wrong?"

Emily waved it off. "Nothing. Let's just get back to—"

"Tell me, Detective. That's an order."

Emily sighed, flopped back to the floor. "All right. I'm worried."

"About?"

"Marty."

A pair of traffic cops walked in. "Come back later, all right?" Annie said. They sensed it wasn't a request, and left. Annie locked the door, sat cross-legged against the wall.

"What's going on?" she asked.

"I think he's seeing someone," Emily said. "A woman named Alice."

"Oy," Annie said. "All right, tell me everything. From the beginning."

Emily shifted around. "He's been moody lately," she said. "Quiet."

"He's the strong silent type," Annie said. "About personal stuff, anyway."

"Not when we're alone," Emily said. "Not once in our two years together. We've talked about our marriages. Our spouses' deaths. Rebuilding the house. Living together, living separately, all of it." She wiped hair off her face. "But all of a sudden he's shutting himself off."

"Completely?"

"Oh, no," Emily said. "You wouldn't even notice if I hadn't told you. Ninety-nine percent of the time he's his normal happy self." She blew the drop of sweat off the tip of her nose. "But the other percent, his face gets that foggy look. Like he's lost in thought. His attention drifts. I ask him about it, and he changes the subject."

"Maybe it's the execution," Annie ventured. "He's lived with that rotten case for seventeen years, Em. Now that the end is near, maybe he's depressed."

"That's what I assumed," Emily said, shaking her head. "So I asked. He insists nothing's wrong. But I know better. He's hiding something." Her eyes brimmed, and she told Annie about the secret phone call to "Alice," the lame "snitch" excuse he'd used to cover the others, and the several unexplained disappearances he'd made in the middle of the night. "I think he's fallen in love with this Alice woman, and he doesn't know how to tell me."

She wiped her face with her shirttail.

"I fell in love with him practically overnight, you know," she said. "A year went by and it just got better. I finally started believing we were that million-to-one shot that was meant to be. Marty believed it, too."

"He still does," Annie said.

Emily fiddled with her wedding ring, then realized it wasn't there. She'd removed it a year ago, when Marty finally replaced her dead husband Jack as her heart-mate.

"But maybe we were just safe shelter for each other," she continued. "You know, an escape from all that tragedy. And now that it's over he's met someone and wants to dump me . . ."

The tears spilled.

"No way, hon," Annie said, shaking her head so hard the blond ringlets danced. "Marty's nuts about you. No way he'd take a hike, and he's too damn noble to sneak around. Besides, Branch would let me know in his special guy way if there was trouble in paradise."

"How's that?"

"'Hey, Annie, there's, uh, trouble in paradise,'" she mimicked.

They both laughed.

"So you don't think he wants out," Emily said. "Or that there's another woman."

"I read people pretty well, and I just don't see it," Annie said, shaking her head. "But you say he's hiding something. Particularly this Alice, whoever the hell she is. Hmm." She perched her chin on her small fists, thinking. "Does he refuse to talk about it? Or does he talk about it without saying anything, then move to safer topics?"

Emily tapped her nose.

"Oh, hell, my husband does that all the time," Annie said. "I have to keep steering him back to the point when he's telling me something he thinks I don't want to hear. Didn't Jack do that?"

Emily shook her head. "Jack told me everything on his mind. *Everything*. Precisely and to the point, the minute it occurred to him."

"Was that good or bad?"

"Good." Her ears colored. "Though sometimes I wished he'd just, uh, you know . . ."

"Shut the hell up."

"Yeah," Emily admitted. "When he died, I was so ashamed of those thoughts I couldn't stand myself. Now I want Marty to open up that way, and he isn't."

"Two men," Annie said. "Two ways of dealing."

"I know," Emily said. "And that's fine by me—everybody's different. But this isn't just 'dealing.' Something's bothering him terribly and he doesn't want to tell me. Something about him and this Alice."

"So bug him till he comes clean."

Emily looked at her.

"Cans of worms and sleeping dogs," Annie said. "I get it, hon. But if it bothers you this much, you need to take the risk. Can't fix a sink till you know where it leaks." She covered her mouth, yawned mightily.

"Up late last night, were we?"

Annie grinned. "If you must know, hubby was the principal and I was the naughty student . . ."

"Stop!" Emily said, slapping her hands to her ears. "That image will ruin me for life!"

Annie's laugh was full-throat. She walked to the gun safe, spun the dial, pulled out a violin case. "Because you did such a good job today," she said, flipping the brass latches, "I'm going to let you shoot my Tommy gun."

"Holy cow!" Emily said, scrambling to her feet. She'd knew all about the legendary Thompson Sub-Machine Gun—aka tommy gun, chopper, gat, and Chicago typewriter—from endless hours of watching *The Untouchables* with her dad. But she'd never seen, much less fired, Al Capone's equalizer. "Where on earth did you get it?"

"Aforementioned darling hubby," Annie said, holding it up. The 1928 Full Automatic gleamed from Cutts compensator to finned barrel to oiled walnut stock to signature drum magazine holding fifty fat rounds of .45 ACP.

"God, it's beautiful," Emily moaned, running her finger along the polished blued steel.

"I've wanted one since I was a kid," Annie said, ensuring the chamber was empty. "A genuine tommy from the Roaring Twenties, not a reproduction. Unbeknownst to me, he searched for three years till he found this. Rusty and dented, but real. He sent it to an expert for full restoration, and gave it to me last night as an early birthday present. I was thrilled."

Only Annie would prefer machine guns to diamonds! "So that's why you volunteered for the principal's office," Emily said, grinning.

"Would I wear a plaid skirt and Mary Janes otherwise?" Annie demanded. "Here."

Emily blinked in astonishment as she accepted the weapon. The Kel-Tec weighed five pounds. This beast topped twelve.

"Fourteen-point-four with ammunition," Annie said, correctly interpreting Emily's expression. "They used to make guns like Sherman tanks."

"Hurray for progress," Emily said, sighting down the barrel. "I wouldn't want to lug this an hour, let alone all day."

"Me neither," Annie said. She nodded at the Osama bin Laden target at the end of the shooting lane. "Cock the bolt and let 'er rip. Remember it's full automatic and it's going to jump."

Emily nodded, re-donned her ear and eye protection, aimed, and pulled the stiff trigger. The tommy chattered. Four seconds later the drum was empty, white smoke curling toward Osama's blown-out turban.

"Wheeeee!" she said, laughing.

"There's a lot to dislike about the old days of police work," Annie said, handing her a second drum. "Racism and sexism. Routine brutality. Lousy pay and low professional standards. But *man* they had a good time shooting." She coached

Emily through the loading procedure. "I'm going to make you an expert with Mister T."

"What's the point?" Emily said, patting her two-pound Glock.

"Same reason you carry fresh undies in your purse. 'Cause you never know."

37

"May I offer you a cocktail, sir?" the flight attendant asked.

The Executioner looked up. There'd been an opening in first class, and he'd happily upgraded. Coach was as cramped as the electric chair, and almost as deadly to the body.

"Well, it is after five," he said, nodding at the striking brunette whose nametag read JAIME. The smooth-talking pilot was James, he'd learned in the post-takeoff announcement. A cute coincidence. He wondered if they called each other Jim in the galley. "Tell me, Jaime, how much longer till we land in Chicago?"

The attendant tonged ice cubes into a glass and trickled them with Maker's Mark. The ice made a crackling sound that pleased the Executioner. "Thanks to strong tailwinds, we're ahead of schedule," she said. "We should be at O'Hare in seventy minutes, instead of ninety. If that changes, I'll let you know right away."

"No need," the Executioner said, settling back and sipping velvet. "I don't have to be anywhere till morning."

JANUARY 14, 1968

"Having been found guilty of thirteen counts of murder, the sentence of this court is death by electrocution," the judge said.

"Gee, what a shock," Earl Monroe said back.

The judge banged the gavel. The bailiffs and Covington glared. Earl didn't care.

They could only kill him once.

TUESDAY

38

Emily rounded the final curve, long legs pumping furiously. She'd decided during the backstretch to take Annie's advice, and the relief that brought made the last mile easy.

She sprinted up the long hill of her backyard. Geese honked furiously as they scattered out of her way. Emily honked back. A minute later she did a somersault on the concrete slab that would someday be a brick-and-cypress deck, then bounded through her back door.

In the gloom of a picnic shelter several hundred yards away, the Executioner smiled as he followed her through binoculars.

"The papers were right, Detective," he murmured, patting the handmade knife in his jacket. "You still take the same route every morning. See you tomorrow."

39

Johnny Sanders crunched his whole-wheat toast, blinking at the glare off his backyard shed.

"Another day in paradise," he said. Meaning it. He liked summer, even though Springfield got as sticky as Malaysia with humidity.

He reached for the mug of decaf, skim milk, and Sweet 'n Low. Poor man's cappuccino. It made almost bearable the fiber flakes his doctor insisted he start eating instead of his beloved pigs in a blanket.

He turned to the state-by-state roundup in *USA Today*, the first of two newspapers he devoured with breakfast. He'd lived a lot of places growing up as an air force brat, and enjoying seeing items from familiar datelines.

Los Angeles—LAPD refused comment on reports that roses were lodged in the throat of Sage Farri, 19, found dead in his hospital room Sunday. Farri, recov-

ering from knee surgery from a sports injury, was dis-
covered by nursing staff. . . .

"Only in Hollywood," Sanders said, shaking his head.

He finished *USA Today*, then turned to the hometown
State Journal-Register, smiling in anticipation. The reporter
had e-mailed last night, saying her story would appear today
as part of the special section, "Drumbeat to Death."

And there it was.

"A heartless pile of concrete on a moat of compressed garbage, with the narrow windows, flat roof, and crenellated snarl
of a fourteenth-century battle-castle," she called the Justice
Center. "Captain Ahab," she called Governor Covington. "The
electric chair's crash test dummy," she called Johnny Sanders.

Cool beans!

He'd leave this open for his wife and make sure the guys
at the office saw it. When was the last time a state historian
was called a crash test dummy?

"Probably never," he said to the story.

He read it twice more, then turned the page to read the
Associated Press follow-up about two fatal shootings—one
in a spa, the other in a roadside park—Friday in Naperville.

"Hey, I was just there," he told their ancient cat. The orange tabby eyeballed him, went back to gumming her tuna.

Sanders sipped a little cappuccino, read deeper.

"Zabrina Reynolds," he murmured. "Hmm. That name
rings a bell." He ran through everyone he knew—work, family, friends, church, stores, bowling league, the thousands of
execution documents he strained his eyeballs to absorb—but
couldn't place it.

Oh, well. It's not important.

He finished the news section with the obituary for Frank
Mahoney III, grandson of a popular dentist who decamped
from Springfield in the 1970s for Holbrook, Arizona.

The write-up included a black-and-white photo from a 1969 feature about Springfield businessmen who sponsored youth baseball. Grandpa Frank was one of them. He was the spitting image of his dead grandson. It prompted a pang of sympathy. For the victims, and for himself. Like the bran and skim milk, these stories were little reminders he wasn't getting any younger.

Dismissing the thoughts as maudlin, he turned to sports for the preseason reports. Springfield High football looked awfully impressive. Maybe the Senators would catch fire this year. . . .

40

"About time," Gene Mason growled.

"What's that, Chief?" his secretary asked, poking her head through the door.

"Nothing, nothing," he said, motioning for her to ignore him. "I was yelling at the feds again."

She smiled sweetly, went back to her typing.

Mason had been trying to log onto NCIC since Saturday. First the site was down for maintenance. Then it plain didn't work. Monday, he telephoned the help desk. Whoever answered said there'd been a glitch and "it'll be up and running by noon today."

Which it wasn't.

But all of a sudden it was, and he started trolling for matches.

41

"I'd put one team here," Emily said, trying not to limp as she walked along the main gate of the State of Illinois Justice Center in Naperville. "Another there, two more there. Then bring in every water cannon the Fire Department can spare."

Marty added the recommendations to his notes. "That's it?"

Emily mulled all the ways a protester could climb, tunnel, or sneak through the towering fence around what used to be the Greene Valley Landfill. Nodded. "No way they'll get past."

"They do," Marty said. "Covington hangs Cross from the nearest tree."

Emily knew about the ugly argument on I-55 because Branch told Marty, and Marty told her. "He's still miffed about a difference of opinion?"

"Of course," Marty said. "Covington's a zealot because of his brother, and sees disagreement as treason. But once Trent's buried, he'll be all smiles again."

"God save us from political manic-depressives," Emily said, rolling her eyes.

"Amen," Marty said. "As long as you're chatting up The Big Guy, ask for a thunderstorm. Intelligence predicts ten thousand protesters. Be nice to cut that in half."

"That's your secret weapon?" she asked, amused. "A rain delay?"

"Better hail than lead."

Several weeks ago, Cross asked Branch to walk the grounds of the Justice Center and poke holes in the master security plan. He also asked his two other captains, Annie, the county bomb squad, and the sheriff. All quickly complied.

Then he approached Marty.

"Find something so obvious it'll get my ass fired for negligence," Cross explained between bites of orange beef at the Chinese Kitchen.

"Hell, that's no incentive," Marty snorted. "You only got half an ass to fire."

"Said pot to kettle," Cross said. Marty had a bullet scar on his own right cheek. "So, you going to help me? Or do I tell everyone you cried like a little girl when the paramedics swabbed you?"

"I did not!"

"Well, no. But everyone will believe it anyway because it's funny." He swallowed some tea, patted his lips. "Besides, Emily's working the witness room Friday. You've got a vested interest in making sure no one gets past that fence."

"All right, all right," Marty grumbled, spearing a pair of General Tso's shrimp. "But only because you're too damn dumb to do it yourself . . ."

He'd been putting it off, though. Too busy before the shootings, then finding the cop-killer was more important. But today his thinking was muddy, his eyes sandblasted. He'd stayed up most of last night reviewing field notes and lab reports. It was slow, tedious slogging, made worse by the fact the baby kept intruding, its barely formed lips begging, "Save me!"

The shower at six and triple espresso at seven didn't help. By nine, he needed fresh air.

"Got to do something for Ken," he'd said to Emily. "Want to take a drive?"

"Can we put the top down and sing Beach Boys songs?"

"We can take my unmarked and listen to the police scanner."

"Sold," she'd said.

"You might be interested to know that Annie's recommendations match yours," he said, bringing his head to the present.

"Of course they do," Emily said. "Lieutenant Bates is a brilliant analyst and master tactician."

"And almost as big a pain in the butt as you," Marty said.

You have no idea, dear, she thought, sticking out her tongue. *But you're about to find out.*

Marty showed her the available personnel numbers. "They ain't pretty," he said, tapping the page. "Ken should whistle up the State Police right now."

Emily shook her head. "We can do this ourselves. We're stretched thin, I know, but the double shifts and vacation cancellations should give us enough bodies."

"You just peeing a circle around your territory? Or do you honestly think you can pull this off with available manpower?"

"Both."

Marty tugged at his chin, considering. Emily looked around, trying to spot the bird whose warble rose and fell with shifts in the humid breeze.

"Then that's what I'll recommend," he said, stowing the notebook. "How's your calf?"

"Still sore," Emily admitted. "I guess I pulled it worse

than I thought in the parking lot. Then Devlin Bloch fell on it."

Marty brightened. "Hey, we could charge him with that."

"What?"

"Assault and battery on police gams."

"Gams," Emily said, liking how that sounded. She'd never thought her legs slim or pretty enough to be a gam. "I always wanted those."

"You got 'em, trust me," Marty said. "Massage?"

Emily gripped the fence and lifted her leg behind her. Marty snugged it between his thighs and kneaded the kinked muscle.

"That feels great," she moaned, electric shivering extending from foot to knee. "Thank you."

"All the thanks I need is not lifting that heel any higher," Marty said. "Hear about Branch?"

Follow the bouncing segue. "No. What?"

"He needs a new hip."

Emily frowned, retrieved her leg. "So soon? Why?"

"You know how much it's been hurting him lately," Marty said, sagging against the fence. "He told the doctors, and they ran some tests. Turns out the one they put in two years ago is detaching from the bone. They want to saw it out and put in a new model."

Emily groaned. "Meaning he starts from zero, rehab-wise."

"Yeah." He bashed the fence with a knotted fist. The chain links rattled like spare change. "Or, he can leave it alone and hope it stabilizes. Entirely his choice, the doctors said."

"Some choice," Emily said. "What's he going to do?"

Marty didn't reply.

She studied the terrain. This two-hundred-acre closed landfill on Naperville's Southeast Side was a good spot for Covington's execution center. The grass-covered mountain of hot dogs, napkins, newspapers, party hats, burnt-out light-bulbs, junk mail, dead batteries, cough syrup, paint, diapers, tampons, and yellowing *Da Vinci Codes* wasn't good for much else, anyway. The methane that belched from the rotting debris fueled a locomotive-sized generator that pumped out 1,500 kilowatts of electricity. Enough to fry a thousand Corey Trents without dimming a single light in the rest of the city. The tall chain-link fence encircled the mountain, which looked like a hairy green belly bulging into the sky. Its height—190 feet above the surrounding plain—guaranteed nobody would reach the concrete death house at the peak without being noticed. The landfill fit comfortably inside the 1,700-acre Greene Valley Forest Preserve, providing a broad, leafy buffer from the rest of Naperville. Illinois 53, along the eastern edge of the property, ran straight to Stateville and its Death Row. *Eleven miles from Death to Valley*, Emily mused. *Twenty minutes, depending on traffic . . .*

"He decided to take the knife," Marty said finally. "Go through rehab again."

"Is he all right with that?"

"Got no choice," Marty said. "Lydia will rip him several new ones if he starts whining."

"I knew he married well," Emily said, standing on tiptoes and brushing her lips against Marty's sun-browned cheek. He tasted like man, salt, and Old Spice. "It goes without saying he has our support. Whatever Branch and Lydia need, we'll do."

Marty didn't reply. Just nodded absently, face clouding, attention drifting.

It's time, she decided. *Just close your eyes and jump . . .*

"What's really bothering you, hon?" she said. "It's a lot more than Branch."

"Nothing."

"Come on, Marty," Emily said. "I know something's wrong. Something bad. I deserve to know what it is."

He grimaced, then picked up a chunk of concrete. Took a running start and heaved it at the death house. It arced back to earth a quarter way up. He sighed, shoved his hands in his pockets.

"I should never have agreed," he muttered.

"To what?"

He waved his arms. "To this. To come here. To participate in Covington's stupid death dance. This execution shouldn't happen."

"Why not?" Emily asked. "Do you think Trent's innocent?"

Marty made a noise that said, *Get real*. "The bastard's guilty as hell. But that doesn't matter," he said. "Capital punishment is the crack cocaine of politics, and this so-called 'Justice' Center is obscene."

That stunned her. In their two years together, they'd never discussed the death penalty. Not even when Covington convinced the Supreme Court to overturn predecessor George Ryan's 2003 clearance of Death Row. Not even when he brought back the electric chair, scorning lethal injection as "too humane a way to dispatch our monsters." She'd just assumed Marty was as passionately in favor of it as she was.

"Some people deserve to die," she said, feeling the blood rush in her ears. "Some crimes are so inhuman that nothing less will do."

"That's what they said about Jesus," Marty said. "I rest my case."

"Charles Manson. Ted Bundy. Osama bin Laden," she shot back. "I rest *my* case."

"Mass murderers are poster children for the chair, all right," Marty agreed. "But you forgot someone equally important to the debate."

"Who?"

"Manuel."

She cocked her head. She'd been studying the nation's

most bloodthirsty serial, mass, spree, and thrill killers, from the Boston Strangler to the Bind-Torture-Kill madman in Kansas, and hadn't run across that name. "Manuel who?"

"Just Manuel," Marty said. "He was a slave, so he only had one name. He was executed on June 15, 1779. Right here in Illinois. The good citizens built a bonfire and burned him alive. Know what his crime was?"

"Homicide," she guessed. "Rape. Running away from his master."

"Witchcraft."

She blinked.

"That's right. The very first execution in the Land of Lincoln was a destitute black man we confused with the gal from *Bewitched*," Marty said. "Just one of the thousands of people America's whacked since the *Mayflower*."

"For murder. Or treason, or kidnapping," Emily said, shaking her head. "Manuel notwithstanding, I can't lose any sleep over that."

"You should," Marty countered. "Seeing how we've also executed for adultery, burglary, forgery, counterfeiting, breaking into houses, stealing horses, gay sex, helping slaves escape, the aforementioned witchcraft, and my personal favorite, concealing the birth of an infant." He swatted a mosquito, smiled faintly at the irony.

Adultery, she thought. *How appropriate.*

"That's past tense, Marty. Ancient history," Emily scoffed, temples pounding from anger. After all the death and destruction she'd suffered in her life, how could he *possibly* be one of those gutless, nothing-on-the-line Antis? "We've grown tremendously as a society. We execute only cold-blooded murderers now, not rustlers, not witches. And only if we're sure they're guilty as charged."

"Pretty sure, anyway—"

"Absolutely sure," she said, starting to pace. "It's impossible to execute an innocent person anymore. We have media.

Miranda rights. Probable cause. Dream teams. DNA. Video-taped interrogations. Juries. Judges. Appeals. Pardons. Inter-net. A thousand-and-one safeguards to make sure only the guilty are condemned."

"Yet, people are freed from Death Row every day for wrongful convictions," Marty said. "That's why capital pun-ishment is unacceptable, Em—because we're not perfect. We make mistakes. We screw up. And when we do, the *Ti-tanic* sinks, the space shuttle explodes, and an innocent per-son burns." Marty stared at the Justice Center. "With all the bread and circuses our 'enlightened' society can muster."

"Then why are you involved?" she said, pointing to the cold buff walls of the complex. "Why are you witnessing Trent's execution if it's so 'wrong'?"

"I was his arresting officer," Marty said, going rigid. "I have to be there."

"No, you don't," she said. "Branch was your partner that night, and he's not going to watch."

"Branch is in charge of security Friday. He can't be there. I don't have a choice—"

"Yes, you do!" Emily said, spitting her righteousness like buckshot. "You're a hypocrite, Marty. You could beg off from being a witness because of your precious convictions, and nobody would care. But you want to see Trent die. That makes you a lousy damn hypocrite."

"I don't 'want' to see him die," Marty snapped. "I need to see him die—"

"And so do I," she bore in. "So do the families of his vic-tims. They're entitled. I'm entitled!"

Marty scowled, started walking away.

"Oh no you don't!" Emily said, grabbing his shirt and hauling him around. His lips were flat, his face scarlet. His jaws wiggled like bags of mice. "If I'd died two years ago, are you saying you'd put my killer in a cell instead of a *coffin*?"

He waited a second too long to say no.

"I can't believe it!" she raged, stalking a circle around him. "I thought you loved me! But maybe you love Alice more. Is that it, Marty? Are you leaving me for *Alice*?"

Marty's voice strangled unintelligibly. His fingers massaging his ribs. "How do you——"

"I came back in the house that night. I heard you talking to your pretty little lady in the kitchen. After you'd thought I'd left for the station." She glared at him, slapped her hands on her hips. "Are you in love with her, Marty? Are you leaving me? Tell me everything, damn you."

"I . . . can't . . ."

"You don't have a choice anymore!" Emily screeched, pushing up so close she smelled his coffee breath. Knowing was frightening. Not knowing was worse. "If you love me, tell me what's eating you alive. Right here, right now, or swear to God our relationship is——"

"I have a son," Marty said. "Alice is his mother."

She froze.

"That's right, Emily, a son," he said, crossing his arms. "That's why I'm a witness Friday. That's why I'm a hypocrite. And that's why I'll happily dance on Trent's melted face. Because I couldn't save that dead little boy that night."

She clutched herself, gasping for air. She could have handled an Alice. Even another man. Not this. Marty had beagles. Not daughters. Not sons. No one with his DNA. His chiseled face. His square white teeth. His thick fingers. His sunray smile. His thick black moustache, which turned up at the ends like a British grenadier's. His uncanny ability to both reflect and absorb her, in conversation or complete silence——

"You bastard," she spat, turning on her heel.

"Nobody knows, Em," he said. "Only Branch——"

"Oh, this gets better and better," she snarled. "You spill to your buddy easy enough, but not the woman you love? The woman you supposedly want to spend the rest of your life with?"

"This is exactly why I didn't say anything about my son and Alice," Marty said, bouncing off the fence and grabbing her arm. "Because it would hurt you so much. But you insisted. You demanded. You said tell me Marty or I'll quit you forever—"

"Leave me alone," she said, shaking away and breaking into a sprint, barely able to see the ground through her tears. She bounced off a whippy tree, stumbled forward. It'd take an hour to run back to the station, but she couldn't stand the thought of being in a car with him. Not after he'd lied so masterfully. Not after he'd broken her heart so—

Oh, Jesus, now what?

She snatched the cell phone off her belt. "Thompson."

Her eyes widened as she listened.

"OK, Branch," she managed to choke. "I'll be right back."

She disconnected, feeling sick. She didn't want to do this, but had no choice.

"The police chief in Holbrook, Arizona, just called," she said mechanically, looking at the fence instead of him. "He found burnt matches at a murder scene. I need to return ASAP."

Marty pulled his keys. "Then we'll talk in the car. You need to hear the rest—"

"I heard everything I need to know," she said. "Daddy."

42

"Hundred and eight and climbing," Gene Mason replied. "But it's a dry heat."

Emily heard that fairy tale from every Arizonian she'd ever met. She would have kidded him about it, but at the moment, humor stuck in her throat like bad clams.

"What's this I hear about an electrocution?" Mason said.

Emily described what Covington had in mind, and how NPD intended to handle it.

"Sounds like your chief's got it covered," he said. "What's your role?"

"Standing watch in the witness room," Emily said.

"Been there, done that."

"You've worked executions, Chief?"

"Call me Gene. And yes, several. I started my career in Florida, where Old Sparky's right up there with God and orange juice. Best of luck."

"Thanks," she said. "So, I hear we've got a common thread."

"Matches," Mason said. "A pair of which I found sixteen feet from a nice young man whose throat was slit by person or persons unknown. A barber named Frank Mahoney."

"I read up on the murder on my way to the station," Emily said, having logged onto NCIC in the car as a way to avoid Marty. He kept trying to explain, but she kept shutting him down. "Tell me about the matches."

"Common kitchen type," Mason said. "Two inches long, eighth-inch square. Lit, extinguished, and deposited in the room where Mahoney was killed."

"Same here," Emily said, describing the mud spa's lobby. "I found ours behind the front door, out of the normal traffic pattern."

"Mine were under a TV," Mason said. "Deliberately placed, I believe, since the shop banned smoking." He described the sickle of Mahoney's throat. "When was your attack?"

"Friday," she said. "The shooter stabbed the receptionist, then broke her nose."

"Really?" Mason said. "Mahoney's was broken, too. We assumed naturally, from the fall."

"So did we," Emily said, perking up at the thought of another commonality. "But CSI proved otherwise. The killer stabbed Zabrina, then smashed her nose on the counter. A half hour later he gunned down a deputy sheriff who'd pulled him over for a traffic ticket."

The long silence told her he hadn't heard that part.

"Gene?" she prompted. "Are you there?"

"Yes. Sorry," Mason said, clearing his throat. "My niece was on the highway patrol. She got it during a traffic stop a couple years back. Left a partner and their two daughters. Lousy memory."

"I know," Emily said. The hateful looks she'd received two years ago from the widows of her murdered colleagues—blaming not the madman, but her, for their misery—still woke her in the little hours. "Anyway, you were saying . . ."

"Your murder occurred Friday morning. Mine was Saturday night," Mason said. "Our killer could have driven the fifteen hundred miles, theoretically, but more likely flew into Phoenix, Vegas, or Albuquerque and picked up a rental—"

"Whoa, Gene!" Emily said. "What makes you believe we're dealing with the same killer?"

The room gabble hushed.

"Wishful thinking," Mason said.

Emily shook her head, and it resumed.

"I'm reduced to that because I've got no evidence," Mason continued. "Not a fingerprint, shoe scuff, tire track, clothing fiber, or eyewitness. No suspicious cars, no prison breaks, all known dirtbags accounted for."

"What about hair?"

"That we got," Mason said dryly.

Duh, she chastised herself. *It's a barbershop!* "Are you doing a DNA analysis?"

"Already shipped to the state lab. But that'll take months. Besides, it's clippings."

"You need roots to extract DNA," Emily said.

"Right," Mason said, sounding as weary as she felt.

"I wish I could help you, Gene," Emily said. "But those matches are coincidence. I know we found them at murder scenes, and both noses were broken, but . . ."

"It's just too big a stretch to think our cases are connected," Mason sighed. "Yeah, I know. But like I said, wishful thinking's all I have left—"

"Seattle PD on Line Three," Marty grunted, pointing at the phone. "Urgent."

Emily considering flaming him for interrupting her interview. But that would be horribly unprofessional, and she wouldn't sink to the level of that awful Alice. "Gene? Can I put you on hold a minute?"

"Sure."

She punched Three as more phones jangled. The room got noisy with grabbing and answering.

"Emily Thompson," Emily said, shoving a finger into her other ear.

"Mimi Sheridan, Seattle homicide. Are you the one who posted to NCIC about burnt matches?"

Emily managed not to drop the receiver. "Yes. Why?"

"I worked a case last October. Hit-and-run near Puget Sound, middle of the day. Victim was a twenty-year-old male Caucasian. A cabbie found him in the middle of the street with a piece of broken fender through his abdomen. Kid bled out before he hit the asphalt."

"You arrest the driver?"

"Never found one," Sheridan said. "It was pitch black from thunderstorms and nobody got a description. Technically a homicide since the driver didn't stop, but everyone figured accident. Kid with an iPod, no crosswalk, poor visibility, you know how that goes."

"Sure do. So why call me?"

"I found two kitchen matches at the scene. Couldn't make them fit anything, so I moved on. I'm hoping they mean something to you."

Emily scribbled furiously. "I don't know yet. Where exactly did you find them?"

"Down his jeans."

"Whose jeans? The victim's?"

"Yup," Sheridan said. "One dropped out of his waistband when I rolled him. I searched and found a second, lodged in his pubic hair. Both burnt, like your posting said." She made a sound like slurping coffee. "That's why I remember them so well. No man sticks matches down there. Good way to start a fire in a place you don't want."

"Thompson," a sheriff's detective rumbled. "LAPD on Six. About your matches."

"Line Nine," another hollered. "Baton Rouge homicide."

Branch stiffened. Alarms clanged in her head. "Mimi, can you hold a minute?"

"No. I'm late for a stakeout."

"OK, I'll call you back after I've talked to my boss. If I'm right, you're going to want to reopen that investigation—oh, wait. Was the victim's nose broken?"

"Hmm. Now that you mention it . . ."

She took the investigator's number, told everyone to take detailed notes and callback information. Then reconnected with Mason.

"We should have been careful what we wished for, Gene," she said, staring at Marty's broad back. "Can you fax everything on your dead barber?"

43

"Everything works fine," the state executioner protested. "The final three rehearsals went like clockwork. Why mess with success?"

The electrician rubbed the copper electrodes with fine-grit garnet cloth. They gleamed like wet pumpkins.

"I want perfection," he said, blowing gently. Metal scattered like pixie dust.

"Perfection means Covington's happy," the executioner said.

"So think of this as insurance he stays that way."

Pause.

"Hand me a cloth," the executioner said.

44

"Are you sure, Detective?" Cross asked, eyebrows arching.

"No," Emily said, desperately wanting to be wrong. What were the odds of two serial killers choosing ultra-low-crime Naperville—*choosing me*—to ply their hideous trade? A billion to one? Trillion? "I'm not sure at all, Chief. But I have this feeling."

"Feeling."

"Yes." She patted her belly. "Here. Backed up by the physical evidence."

Branch passed out summaries of the phone calls. The NCIC reboot this morning had opened the floodgates.

"Where were Sage Farri's matchsticks?" a sergeant asked as he flipped pages.

"In the roses that arrived the day he died," Emily said, explaining the setup.

"Hospital security tapes?"

"Minimally useful," she said. Thanks to bad lighting and

the deliveryman's constant shifting to avoid the rotating camera, LAPD's best guess was Caucasian male with baseball cap and dark goatee. "If it helps, the receptionist said he had dreamy eyes."

When the chuckling died down, a CSI raised her hand. "How was Sage killed?"

"Ice pick into the brain," Branch said, tapping the soft part in back where neck met skull. "If not a pick, a similarly styled blade."

The CSI nodded.

"Baton Rouge, Miami, Seattle, Dallas, Kansas City, Honolulu, Naperville, Holbrook, and Los Angeles," Cross said, listing the nine in chronological order. "Starting twenty months ago. Each one had burnt matches and broken noses. Each was committed with a blade."

"Giving us a unique signature," Marty said.

"Ray's nose was intact," the sheriff objected. "He was shot, not cut, and there weren't any matches. Burned or otherwise."

"He pulled over the killer by coincidence," Cross said. "Killer shot him to escape, not because Ray was a target. Thus, no signature material."

The sheriff mulled that, nodded. "One serial's bad enough for a community," he said, rubbing his pulled-pork face. "But two? Gotta wonder what you did to irritate God so much."

What indeed? Emily thought as everyone glanced at her.

"What else do we know about the victims?" Cross said.

"All were young. None older than thirty," Emily said. "Half were natives, the other half transplants from various states. One has an Illinois connection."

"The barber," Branch said. "Frank Mahoney. His grandfather hailed from Springfield."

The sheriff snapped his fingers. "Didn't Zee Reynolds have kin here, too?"

That detail Emily didn't remember. She leafed through

her notes of the interview with the next-door neighbor, Donna Chen.

"You're right, Sheriff," she said. "Zabrina's from Milwaukee, and her family's still there. But Zabrina's maternal grandmother, Leila, was born and raised in Chicago."

"That's two Illinois connections," Marty said, looking at Emily with the doll eyes he used in breaking gang-bangers. It made her enormously uncomfortable. "Every department is sending its complete case file. We'll know soon if there's others."

"Matchsticks, noses, cuts, and age," Cross said. "Maybe Illinois. Based on that, and only that, you still believe it's a serial?"

"Yes," Emily said, feeling her neck tighten like during her fight with Marty. "I do."

"Me, too," Cross said. "Anyone think different?"

Nothing but headshakes.

45

The Executioner tilted his head, hooked the fishing line between his molars, and gentled the blade down his throat. Pretended it was raw oysters, so it'd go down easier.

The tiny handle bumped the uvula. He didn't mean to do that—it triggered his gag reflex.

He hacked, whooped, and spit.

He fished out the knife, blew his nose, swallowed some Robitussin.

"You think this is easy," he laughed, "you try it."

Bowie looked amused.

46

Branch handed over the case faxes. "Each victim is the grandchild of an Illinois resident," he said. Cross put on gold wire rims, read fast.

"So Emily was right," Cross said. "It's a serial, and it's here."

"Afraid so."

Cross flipped back a few pages. "None of the grandparents were neighbors," he noted.

"Scattered throughout the state," Branch said, tapping his copy. "Rockford to Cairo, Chicago to Moline. Nothing in common other than being grandparents of our victims."

Cross swiveled out from behind his desk. "How did they earn a living?"

"Teacher, barber, farm-equipment mechanic, and security guard," Branch recited. "Short-haul trucker, auto dealer bookkeeper, graphic artist, two housewives, and an airline pilot."

"Social and economic circles," Cross said, "that probably didn't intersect."

"My assumption, too," Branch said. "We're checking at the friend and family level."

Both knew that would take forever.

"What about the number of victims?" Cross tried. "Does that suggest anything?"

"Baseball teams have nine players," Branch said. "Can't think of anything else. Of course, nine's just the deaths we know about. Might be more."

Cross's snort said he agreed. "Let's try the matches, then," he said. "Two in every murder."

"Always in pairs," Branch said, holding index and middle fingers together. "Always burned."

"Hidden in the room where the victims were found."

"Which wasn't apparent from a quick glance. You had to look to find them. OK, we've got pairs. Hidden. Burned. Not raw wood, but burned . . . burned . . . ah."

Cross waited as Branch worked out the gaps in his leap of logic.

"This is about the electrocution," he said, thumping the cane.

"Explain," Cross said, leaning back.

"'Burn' is the key," Branch said. "The killer burns matches. We burn prisoners. The electric chair burns flesh. The chair's made of wood. So are the matches." He rose, limped the room. "I think our killer's leaving this string of bodies as a message to us."

"Or to the governor?" Cross said. "Since it's his show?"

"Or even to Emily," Branch said, "given her fame from two years ago."

"Whole lot of conclusions to draw from two tiny matches," Cross pointed out.

"I know," Branch said. "But everything that happened in the rest of the country is being duplicated here. The same exact week we're burning a killer."

"Too much coincidence to be one," Cross said, tapping

the faxes. "We'll proceed with the assumption the serial spree is tied to this execution."

Branch shook his head. "Covington's gonna have a stroke if this screws up Friday."

"Wouldn't be the worst thing to happen," Cross said.

47

Swallow.
Again.
Swallow.
Again.
Swallow.
Again.
"Ahhhh," the Executioner said, kissing the handle.

He could gulp at will now. Open his mouth, snap in the fishing line, and let the plastic hang down his throat like a pendulum.

He'd much rather have crafted the knife from steel, like all the others. But the tiniest scrap would trip the metal detectors, so he started grinding plastic. Not that flimsy milk-bottle stuff, but the expensive polymers used in aircraft wings and pistol frames.

Eight months of trial and error gave him exactly what he needed—an unbreakable polymer blade with a handle just big enough to grip. It wasn't pretty like his mirror-polished creations, but for this job, pretty was as pretty does.

He secured the swallow knife in the floor safe next to his workbench, and removed the dagger he'd use tomorrow morning. Held it to the light. The double-edge blade was perfectly symmetric. The tip drew blood with the lightest tap. The S-30V stainless steel was mated seamlessly to the high-gloss walnut handles. It balanced perfectly, fit him like a handshake.

Tingling with satisfaction, he scraped the arm patch he'd left unshaved to gauge knife sharpness. Black hair peeled away, leaving the skin underneath as smooth as glass. Not unlike Frank Mahoney's hot shave. He tested the opposite edge.

Hairs prickled and snapped.

"You shave your legs with this?" he kidded, giving Bowie a back-rattling slap. "Wait, don't answer. I don't want to know!"

He sat in the Aeron chair that kept his back from aching during his long hours at the machines. Retrieved an Arkansas sharpening stone and a bottle of oil from the middle drawer. Diamonds cut faster, but he liked the gritty smell and sound of the traditional method. He laid three fat drops on the stone, spread them with his finger. Tilted the edge to the most efficient cutting angle—twenty-two degrees—and firmly pushed blade against stone.

Skriiiiiich.

Some people likened it to fingernails on chalkboards. He found it soothing. The cows didn't, of course. Then again, he never gave them long to think about it.

Skriiiiiich.

The hair peeled perfectly.

He wiped off the slurry, huffed breath on the blade, and

burnished it on his leather strop. Put it back in the safe, dialed right, left, right, glanced at the clock. Time to call it a night. He needed to eat, shower, review the plan, and get to bed.

He had to be in place before sunup.

48

"Oof!" Corey Trent blatted as a knee flattened his belly against his spinal cord.

Own damn fault, he realized as he rolled off his bunk, going fetal to protect himself from the sand-filled socks thundering in from everywhere.

Every con swore Death Row was free of the gang beatdowns you suffered in general population. After several years of seeing it was true, he started falling asleep without his third eye watching.

Big mistake.

"C'mon, jerkoff," he heard somebody hiss. "Make another wisecrack about her."

Not gangs, he realized. *New CO from breakfast.*

Knowing that didn't make it hurt less.

Rockets exploded in Trent's brain. Something heavy smashed his balls into his shoulder blades. The disgusting nutrition loaf left his body the same way it went in. Belly blows kept him from screaming. The blanket wrapping his head would have muffled it anyway.

"Think seriously about drowning yourself in the toilet," his tormenter hissed, mashing the semidigested glop in his face. "Better than what's gonna happen to you Friday."

The rockets skidded sideways, and Trent passed out.

MAY 23, 1968

"How 'bout a cigarette?" Earl Monroe asked the passing guard. "Come on, I haven't caused you a single bit of trouble since I got here, right?"

The guard considered that. Nodded. Lit a Marlboro, poked it through the bars.

Snatched it back when Earl reached.

"Only smoke a cop-killer gets," the guard said, handing it instead to the nun-strangler across the aisle, "is what curls up from the chair."

"He wants me to run for state's attorney," Wayne said, bouncing on the balls of his feet. "He's retiring after Earl's execution, wants to give me my shot. Arranging it with the powers-that-be so I'm a shoo-in. Isn't that great, honey?"

His wife nodded.

"What's wrong, Kit?" Wayne said. He was exquisitely attuned to his wife's moods, but couldn't figure this one.

"Nothing," she said.

"Come on, doll," Wayne said, padding across the white shag carpet and perching next to her on the bed. "It's me. I can tell something's wrong. What?"

Kit sighed. "I'm proud of you, Wayne. Being elected state's attorney is a dream come true. You deserve it, and you'll be great. The best."

"But?"

She interlaced her fingers, squeezed them pink. "We hardly ever see you anymore. Me and the kids. All this Earl Monroe stuff. Even your parents have noticed—you're gone the whole day, and most evenings. Weekends included. You won't be here at all if you get this job."

"Yes, I will," Wayne assured. "I know it's been tough, my being away so much on this case."

She nodded. "I know your brother needs you, honey," she said. "But we do, too. We miss you, and we want you home with us."

Covington kissed her hand, put it against his cheek. "I'm done the minute Earl's dead and buried," he said. "Andy will rest in peace, and I'll have all the time in the world for you and the kids. I'll make it up to you then. I promise."

"I hope so," Kit said. "They need you, Wayne. So do I."

"I know," Wayne said. "Because I need you, too."

She nestled her head against his chest.

"Kids won't be home from school for an hour," he said, eyeing the freshly laundered sheets. "Want to begin making up right now?"

She nodded, eyes shining.

WEDNESDAY

49

Emily passed the Dandelion Fountain. The mist cooled her. Today's easier pace allowed her to hear the cicadas in the Riverwalk treetops, smell the moss-laden fog spooling up from the river. She loved both, but usually missed them rushing by too fast, ears pounding and lungs bursting.

Her tetchy calf did provide that one tiny benefit, she conceded—forcing her to slow and smell the roses. Which made her think about Sage Farri.

And the killer.

"Why on earth are you hunting them?" she wondered aloud. "And why did you come to Naperville? For Zabrina? Me? Somebody else? Why are you so *angry*?"

She knew the killer had a good reason. They always did, even if was understandable only to them and their buddies on Planet Psycho. Her job was to look at the situation through his eyes, see the world as he did. Then, maybe she'd get it. Understand his reasoning. See why he'd kept the remarkable secret so long, then sprung it on her so abruptly—

Forget it. The rest of the day was for death and destruction. The morning run was for her.

The Executioner heard the distant slap of shoes on pavers.

Right on time.

He poked his monocular between the two dense shrubs in which he'd cloaked himself, compared target to memorized reconnaissance. Five-six, chestnut hair that skirted the neck, oval face, large emerald eyes, sturdy body with small waist and well-defined legs and arms. Snug shorts, loose metal-band T-shirt, high-knees running style, sweating like she'd done six miles, returning home on the north side of the river, 5:45 on the dot.

He pulled his dagger from the sheath, crouched for the kill.

"Everybody ready?" the minister asked.

"Ready!" his congregation answered.

"Then let's go save a life!"

They raised the rafters with huzzahs, then boarded their long white bus for the pilgrimage to Naperville. The minister tested headlights, wipers, and brakes. The editor of the weekly paper snapped digitals. The lady who'd won the Betty Crocker regional a few years back shoveled cake at congregants who couldn't go. "With Thee in Spirit!" was written on each piece in red gel frosting. A photo of Jesus, the one with the upturned eyes and Fabio hair, was taped to a plant stake and plunked between "With" and "Thee." Well wishers buzzed like honeybees.

"Grandpa, how far is it again?" his granddaughter asked as they pulled from the gravel lot.

"Seventeen hundred miles," he said, aiming forty-eight

shiny faces at the rising sun. "And a whole bunch of prayers."

"Behind you."

Emily moved to the right. She'd noticed this woman the past few weeks, but this was the first time they'd been in the same spot at the same time.

"Hey! You're an Iron Maiden fan?" Emily said, hoping the T-shirt meant she was a fellow heavy-metal enthusiast.

"Oh, no, this is my husband's," the woman said, slowing to match Emily's cadence. "I listen to Lite FM."

Yuck, Emily thought. But started chatting anyway. The company made a nice distraction from her cold war with Marty. At work, they talked only to exchange information. At home . . . well, he was staying at his own house, not calling, not even e-mailing. She was angry, hurt, and very lonely. But she was too proud to beg him back. A miserable combination.

They small-talked restaurants, movies, and weather— "it's not the heat, it's the humidity," they agreed—then the woman asked about Emily's hair. "I really like your cut," she enthused. "Feminine *and* professional. That's hard to pull off. Your stylist is terrific."

"Thanks," Emily said. "I was lucky to find her."

"I'll say. You and I have the same length and color. I'll bet she can do mine just as great."

"Want her name?"

"Would you mind?"

"Not a bit," Emily said. Only because Paula wouldn't bump her for a new client. She'd rather lose a tooth than a stylist she trusted so completely she nodded off during the cut and feather. She reeled off Paula's number. The woman repeated it twice. "Thanks."

"Glad to help," Emily said. "You know, I run the Riverwalk every morning. Haven't seen you till just recently. New in town?"

"We just moved here from Denver," the woman said. "We're in The Cathedrals of Rivermist. Do you know it?"

Emily nodded. Chicagoans identified themselves by neighborhoods or, if Catholic like her, parishes. Napervillians identified by subdivisions. In this case, a fancy-schmancy on the city's Southwest Side. Cops couldn't afford a garage there, let alone a house.

"Hubby got transferred so the kids and I did, too," the woman continued. "I started coming here as soon as I unpacked my shoes."

"It's one of the best paths in the country," Emily said. "Smooth and well maintained, beautiful views with the river and trees. You'll like the city, too. Lots of friendly people."

"I've already met some neighbors. They do seem nice. They already invited me and my husband to join the subdivision's volleyball team."

Emily bit her lip not to laugh. Should she explain what that really meant? Nah, she decided. Let her see how wild suburban life could get.

The woman glanced Emily top to bottom, looked at her bare fingers.

"Are you single?" she asked. "My brother's looking."

"Widowed," Emily said.

"Oh! I'm so sorry."

"Me, too. He was a good guy." She made a little shrug. "But it was a decade ago and, well, time heals."

"Are you seeing anyone now?"

I don't know anymore, Emily thought. She nodded anyway, because it was easier than explaining. "But how about you?" she parried. "Do you work?"

"Stay-at-home mom. You?"

"I'm a detective," Emily said.

"Ooh!" the woman said, clapping her hands. "How exciting! Just like the *A is for Alibi* gal! You know, Kinsey what's-her-name?"

Good thing she didn't say Miss Marple! "I'm not a private eye," Emily said. "I'm a police detective. In Naperville."

"Oh," the woman said, clearly disappointed. "You know, I got a parking ticket the other day. Can you do anything about that?"

Emily rolled her eyes. Off-duty cops rarely told strangers what they did because of questions like that. Even worse was, "How many people have you killed?" She wished she'd used her standard, "Uh, I'm between jobs right now."

"Sorry, no," Emily said. "We don't fix tickets. It's a firing offense."

"Really? We never had to pay in New Jersey."

Emily made a face.

"What's wrong with New Jersey?" the woman demanded.

"It's fine," Emily said, veering off the pavers. "I'm wincing because I've got a cramp."

"Those are awful, aren't they?" the woman sympathized, stopping to jog in place. "Is there anything I can do?"

"Thanks for the offer, but no, I'm fine," Emily assured, shooing her back on course. "Don't lose your momentum. I'll stretch a few minutes and catch up."

"Please do," the woman said. "I want all the dirt on this town!"

Emily watched till she disappeared around the bend, then plopped to the grass to work her calf. A tiny part of her wished Marty was here to do it for her.

Marty stared at his TV while he ate yet another bachelor breakfast—gas-station doughnuts and grape juice from the carton. He knew how to cook. Just didn't feel like it. One of the morning show hostesses—he had no idea which, he couldn't tell one News Perky from the next—was gabbing on about "my brand-new designer boobs." From what he could gather, she'd thought her 34-Bs "too small to keep my man interested," so she inflated them to 38-DD while he was on a business trip. The boob-job version of *This Old House,* he supposed.

He shook his head. Thank God Emily had more sense than to think he cared whether hers were tiny, huge, or covered with polka dots. Just that they were his.

Were his . . .

The doughnut left a powdery mess bouncing off the screen.

The Executioner sprang as the target pulled even. He chopped his arm into her throat, clamped his hand over her mouth, and used her momentum to spin her into the shrubs.

"Buh-bye," he hissed.

The knife plunged.

The woman screamed.

Because of his hand, nobody heard.

"Get a move on," Emily ordered herself. "Massage won't catch the Unsub." Dehumanizing the serial killer with FBI-speak for "unidentified subject" made her stomach hurt a tiny bit less. She wished the cure for her and Marty was that simple.

Damned impressive, that dagger, the Executioner enthused as he scrambled up the north riverbank. *If I do say so myself.* It worked superbly on the veal calf he'd used for thrusting practice, but a human kill presented different challenges than meat that didn't move.

Like Bowie, he loved—*loved*—using a blade. The targets

knew beyond all doubt they were dying at the hands of someone who totally, thoroughly, wanted them that way.

He smiled at how well that would work Friday.

Emily's Nikes slapped cadence as she rounded the curve. The delay to work out the kink allowed dawn to brighten enough to see the river rippling. Birds flitting after insect breakfasts. A tiny figure in sharp silhouette entering the SUV atop the north riverbank.

She felt a happy shiver. Some runs were a slog, endured strictly to keep her thighs from jiggling. Today's was an un-alloyed joy, a standout. She wished she could run forever, get herself away from all the crap that was suffocating her—

The terrified shriek grabbed Emily by the throat.

She ripped the Glock from under her shirt and broke into a sprint.

The Executioner sped south on Washington Street, heading for Royce Road and home. He flipped on the radio in case they identified her right away. He hoped so. Be a kick for him and Bowie to watch the frantic coverage together.

Emily raced up to the stroller moms pointing wide-eyed at the shrubs.

"Dead," one breathed. "Dead."

Emily hissed. It was the jogger who'd minutes ago asked for Paula's number. Her head was canted, her eyes filmy. She leaked blood from a dozen cuts. A hank of hair was cut off mid-skull and stuffed into her mouth.

I didn't even ask her name . . .

She heard a freight train of steps. Nearly upon her, closing fast. She swung around, ready to trigger a killing blitz.

It was a park district policeman, leveling his gun at her chest.

"Drop the weapon!" he ordered. "Now!"

Emily froze. One wrong move and he'd mow her like hay.

"I'm a Naperville Police detective," she said, slow and calm, letting the Glock slip from her hand without moving the rest of her body. "I have my badge. Do you want to see it?"

The cop put a tree between them. The muzzle didn't waver, and he didn't reply. *Smart move*, she thought. *Bad guys will lie about being a fellow officer, hoping you'll relax long enough to jump you.* "It's under my T-shirt," she continued. "My name is—"

"Emily Thompson," the park cop said, lowering the gun. "Thought I recognized you, but I wasn't sure enough to take the chance. Sorry."

She squished into the blood to feel for a pulse.

"Anything?" the cop asked, waving back the gathering crowd.

"No," Emily said. "I hope this is random, not our serial killer—"

"Serial killer?" one mom gasped to another. "*Again?* God in Heaven, there's another monster loose in Naperville! Let's get out of here!"

Emily slapped her head, knowing she'd just screwed up bad.

"Serial killer" had just leaked to the public.

"Out of my way, you idiot!" Marty roared at the minivan in front. He spotted a gap and flooded the engine past the slowpoke.

He'd left his house a few minutes ago, heading for the station, trying to convince himself Emily was history so move on. Lots of fish in the deep blue sea, etc.

Then the emergency radio net blared an all-points on a female jogger just stabbed on the Riverwalk.

He slammed the red flasher on his roof, cranked siren to max, and lit up every police radar getting there.

50

"Don't worry about it, Em. Really," Branch said, patting her like a third grader. "A lesser cop could never screw up this spectacularly."

She winced at the sarcasm, shame turning acidic. Her slip of the lip would be all over the news the moment one of those women reached a phone.

But something worse was closing fast.

"Are you all right, Detective?" Cross said a moment later.

"Fine, Chief," she said, poking out her chin. At least she'd go down swinging. "Did you find her husband?"

Cross nodded. "With the subdivision and arrival date you provided, dispatch figured out who she is. I sent officers to make the notification." He lowered his close-cropped head, examining her like bull to matador.

Here it comes, she thought. She'd get a harsh reprimand, minimum. Removal from the task force. Even fired. She desperately didn't want that, but would understand. The media frenzy would make the investigation a thousand times harder, and she'd triggered it . . .

"Is your calf OK enough for you to work?" Cross asked.

She nodded, too surprised to speak.

"Then bump us out another fifty yards," he said, pointing to the fluttering yellow tape that squared the crime scene into a boxing ring. "The lady doesn't need an audience."

"Uh, well, right away, Chief."

The corners of his mouth twitched.

She watched Cross limp toward Branch, who was limping toward Annie, who was limping toward Marty. So much damage from the last serial. How much more could they take?

Then there was Marty. A minute ago she'd watched him thunder down Jackson Avenue, engine redlined, then brake like he'd hit a tree. He leaped from the GTO and charged down the grassy slope, stumbling several times. He pulled up short when he saw her standing around, looking fit and fine. He looked at the dead woman, back at her.

Altered course to Branch, and hadn't once looked at her.

Bet you wouldn't treat Alice this way, she thought. *Or her son.*

Your son.

The son you had with another woman . . .

Angry again, she helped the perimeter uniforms bump the tape another fifty.

"I told her," Marty said.

"About your kid?"

"Yeah."

"Why?"

"We had a fight. Big one. She demanded to know what was wrong, then said she knew about Alice. Said she'd leave me if I didn't tell her then and there. So I did."

"And she flipped."

Marty smiled thinly. "You could say that."

"Shit."

"Yeah."

"You done for?"

"Don't want to be. Might not have a choice."

Silence.

"Damned if you do," Branch said.

"Damned if I don't," Marty agreed.

Emily described their short conversation. Cross smiled at the ticket-fixing comment, otherwise just listened. She told him about the throw-down by the park officer, the victim's hair stuffed in her mouth, and the silhouette at the SUV.

"I wish I knew make and model," she said. "But it was too dark and too far away."

"It was a sharp observation anyway. Good work."

And still no mention of my screwup. Wow. To think two years ago I hated this man's guts.

She was a rookie and he was always correcting, always criticizing, always on her back to "shape up or ship out." But it eventually dawned that he spat minutiae because he cared so deeply about his people. Which made his carping, if not enjoyable, at least all right. Which made her pay closer attention to her tactics, surroundings, and attitude, which made her a better cop, which turned Cross's criticisms into comments and, more and more, to compliments.

Proving how smart I wasn't when I first clipped on this badge.

"You said something about a fanny pack?" Cross said.

"She wore one at the Dandelion Fountain," Emily said. "Blue with white stripes. No brand name." She side-stepped for the coroner and his wheelie of gear. "It was gone when I got to the body. The killer must have taken it."

"Suggesting robbery as the motive."

"Or it's the serial, and he tried to kill me," Emily said, watching Annie open her truck and hand Marty a violin case. Her ears burned. Why was her best friend trading with . . .

No. She couldn't bring herself to call Marty "the enemy." Even thinking it made her sick. That meant something, she supposed. She didn't know what.

"Why do you say that?" Cross asked.

Emily explained the jogger's comment about their similar hair. "She kind of looks like me, Chief," she said, shifting her weight to ease the bubbling in her calf. "We've got the same height, body structure, hair, and facial shape."

"Five-six, athletic, chestnut, oval."

"We're both wearing Nikes and band shirts, and the sun wasn't quite up yet. Maybe the killer was targeting me and got her by mistake."

Cross tugged on his chin, thinking.

"Possibly," he said. "He did use a knife, and the attack was brutal and efficient. But he didn't leave matches. Or break her nose."

"True."

Cross stretched. "Our serial is meticulous to a fault. If you were the target, no way he wouldn't leave his full signature. Plus, the other serial victims weren't robbed, and their hair wasn't cut off."

"So you're leaning toward a mugger," she said.

"An addict, given the frenzy of the attack," Cross said. "I'll throw your theory in the mix, because I might be wrong. But the evidence suggests you weren't the target."

Emily closed her eyes, nodded. "Someone needs a fix so an entire family dies," she said, recalling the "hubby got transferred so the kids and I did, too."

"It rains," Cross said, "even in Camelot."

51

"Got a minute?"

"Sure, boss," Johnny Sanders said, looking up from the execution documents papering his desk. "What's up?"

"Feel like driving to Chicago?"

"When?"

"Now."

Huh. In seventeen years as a state historian, he'd never been asked to go upstate on such short notice. "I suppose I could," he said cautiously.

"Good. You're appearing on *Oprah* tomorrow."

Sanders sat back, stunned. "What? Me? Why?"

"You're the crash test dummy."

Sanders felt his cheeks tingle. It was fun at first, being a celebrity—even the speaker had called to rib him. Now it was embarrassing.

"I . . . well . . ."

"Relax," his boss said, helping himself to Sanders's bowl of M&Ms. "It's priceless exposure, letting Miss Winfrey know what we do down here in the bowels of government. The governor's pleased and hopes you'll say yes."

Sanders felt sweat roll down his neck. "Why can't Mr. Covington appear? Or the director?"

"Because you're the crash test dummy," his boss repeated. "Closest thing we got to a dead man who can talk on camera."

He flipped M&Ms into his mouth.

"Oprah wants to know how you felt strapped in that burner," he said, masticating noisily. It reminded Sanders of feeding time on the veldt. "Saying good-bye to your sainted mother while the juice melts your kneecaps. You know, all that boo-hoo stuff her audience laps up."

Sanders squirmed. His only "boo-hoo" was wetting his pants when the death box buzzed. He wasn't going to tell Oprah *that*. Then again, maybe she already knew. Oprah was everywhere. "How'd she hear about me?" he asked.

"Same as us—that newspaper story."

"Oh. Right."

"I assured Mr. Covington you'd be delighted to meet with Team Oprah this afternoon. They'll put you up on Michigan Avenue and buy your gas and meals. You'll appear live on the show tomorrow morning. They'll even let you bring the wife. Whaddaya say?"

Sanders gulped.

"That's the spirit!" his boss said. "I know you'll make us proud."

52

"Heard you tripped and fell last night," the CO jeered.

Corey Trent stared at the floor, legs splayed because his balls ached so much.

"Whatsa matter, stinky?" the CO pressed, clearly enjoying himself. "No clever comeback? I'm soooooo disappointed."

Trent lifted his bloodshot eyes.

"My only disappointment's your wife," he said, voice gravelly from one of the sock-chops. "The ho ran outta gas before I could—"

"Put a lid on it, Trent," the senior CO grunted as he walked up.

"Yaz, bawse," Trent said, saluting with both middle fingers.

"Best not push that," senior said, "you don't want to be pushed back." He turned to his colleague, scowling. "Thought you knew gators bite when you mess with 'em."

The CO tensed like he was going to clobber him.

"I ain't in no cage," senior said quietly, flexing his anchor tattoos.

The CO blanched.

Then, unexpectedly, smiled.

"Guess you're right," he said, sticking his hands in his pockets. "Why waste effort on a dead man? Day after tomorrow he's a bucket of extra-crispy."

Senior slapped his back, and they moved on.

Trent shook his head.

"Hey, Core," said the arsenic poisoner two cages down.

"Yo."

"Way to punk his bony ass."

Trent laughed. "Fun slapping around the new fish."

"No finer sport," arsenic agreed. "One thing he's right about, though."

"What's that?"

"You stink like a bucket of turds. Me and the boys voted. You don't shower by six, we're gonna make ya."

The Row applauded.

53

Noon

"Sorry, dear," the Executioner said to the dead woman's driver's license, which he'd pulled from the fanny pack he'd already ditched. "But your death was necessary to make the authorities keep thinking that Emily—stop, stop, stop, stop, stop!"

He did.

Four inches from the reflective sign that shouted, "Danger! Extremely Flammable!"

Heads snapped around. The Executioner revved the engine to show he was fine.

They turned away, disappointed.

The light turned green. The fuel truck belched diesel, rumbled off. The Executioner sat, watching it grow small.

"That's twice you failed to pay attention," he berated himself, as he knew Bowie would later. "I know you're excited with Friday so close. But your brilliant plan is useless if you're not around to carry it out . . ."

Even as he talked, a delicious new twist formed in his mind.

"Risky," he decided after thinking it through. "But doable."

Fun, too.

He reacquired the fuel truck at the next red.

Checked his Rolex.

Yes. The timing would work just fine.

He flicked the license out the window, cranked the wheel, and followed.

54

"Good gravy, Wayne!" Angel Rogers sputtered. "You can't be serious!"

"As a heart attack," Covington said.

"It's insane. Unheard of. You just . . . can't."

"I'm the governor," Covington said, rolling a long, thin cigar between his fingers. "I can do whatever I want."

"Well, of course you *can*," Angel said. "I'm just saying it's a terrible idea. Insane."

"You already said insane."

"That's because it is," she snapped. "You simply cannot walk into the Justice Center on Friday and run the execution."

"I built it," Covington said. "Why shouldn't I throw the switch?"

"The media, for starters," she said, slapping his coffee table. The humidor jumped. "Every editorial writer in America will crucify you. Not to mention the late-night TV monologues."

"So what?"

"'So what' is the fact that they control the public debate. Guaranteeing the political fallout will bury you." She uncrossed her arms to smooth her jet-black hair. "I admit it's a great angle, Wayne. Personally running Corey Trent's execution is inspired. But it's not worth the downside if you want to live in the White House."

"That's because you're thinking like a press secretary."

"It's what you pay me for."

"Of course. And from that perspective, you're absolutely right—the press will accuse me of grandstanding, debasing the system, ad nauseum. But I'm not doing this for photo ops."

He stalked from behind his desk. "I'm serious about protecting the innocent, Angel," he said, waving the cigar. "I'm cleansing the world of Corey Trents, and I'm doing it with two thousand volts. I myself, not some faceless bureaucrat. I myself will throw that switch."

"Wayne . . . "

"If my taking charge makes the next punk think twice about cutting a baby out of a mother, it's worth it," Covington said. "So let the media complain. Voters are behind me on this. Not just law-and-order types, either. Since September 11, even liberals are happy I'm putting these goons to death. Even if they won't say so publicly."

He snatched up his cigar cutter.

"It's not hype, politics, PR, or spin control," he said, notching the end to suck in the flame of the wooden match. "It's *right*. I believe that to the core of my soul."

Angel sighed. "Did I ever mention how much I hate true believers?"

"The truth shall set you free," Covington said.

"Sure, in the long run," Angel said. "But you're elected in the short. Every protest sign will feature your head on Hitler's body, shoving people into ovens. In bright neon colors to show up on TV." She shuddered, thinking how awful this train wreck could be. "You do this, they'll dine on your flanks for years."

"Let 'em," Covington said, slapping his. "I got plenty. Start the press conference."

55

"Are you nuts?" Cross groaned. "That's the dumbest thing I've ever heard. Can't you lock him in his office . . . yeah, yeah, I know, his decision, not yours. Ask his nibs to call me ASAP so we can prepare." He disconnected, scowling.

"What?" Branch said.

Cross slumped heavily into his swivel chair. "Angel Rogers says Covington's going to run Trent's execution. He's telling the world now."

Branch flipped on the TV.

"Reporting *live* from Springfield," an anchor bawled, animated as a reality host. "With full Action News coverage of this dramatic . . ."

Branch thumped his cane. "He's gonna draw crazies like flies to horse flop."

"No kidding," Cross said. "We have to call the cavalry now. No choice with Wayne coming. Go ahead and notify the State Police."

"When do you want 'em?"

"By noon tomorrow," Cross said. "I'm also asking for the National Guard. Not enough cops in the world to stop ten thousand protesters if they go nuclear—"

"Chief?" his secretary interrupted, poking in her head.

"Ma'am?"

"You've *got* to see this."

"You're kidding," said the managing editor of the *Chicago Sun-Times*.

"Nope," said the news editor. "Wanna put out an Extra?"

"Is the pope Catholic?"

"Are they saying what I think they're saying?" Cross asked, looking down on the police station entrance from the upper-floor windows. To his left was Fire Department headquarters and Lake Osborne. To his right, animal control and Safety Town.

"Yup," Branch said.

Twenty-six women and a half-dozen men chanted, "Fire Emily Now! Fire Emily Now!" They were thin and tanned, with good posture, leather sandals, and cargo khakis that ended at knobby knees. They pushed strollers or lugged Baby Bjorns. The stiff wind made their signs—from "ET Go Home" to "Detective Dooms Our Precious Children"—tack like cardboard sailboats.

"Who let these idiots breed?" a traffic cop complained. "Em's the good guy, not the bad."

Cross smiled to himself. The officer was the oldest of old-school, his entire career a suspicion of "wimmen police." But Emily's gritty performance two years ago changed his opinion, and these days he was, if not Dr. Phil, at least open minded. Little victories.

"Want me to move 'em out?" Branch asked.

Cross considered it, then saw Viking, a barrel-chested paramedic who'd been here since Naperville grew corn, not condos. He was backing a truck out of the fire station attached to headquarters. It bristled with lights, ladders, and water cannons, the high-pressure pumps that knocked down fires in seconds flat.

"Don't think you'll have to," Cross said.

Viking locked down the rig and hopped out of the cab. Went to the pump controls, flipped some, twisted others. He aimed the shiny nozzles toward Lake Osborne and let 'er rip.

The wind bent the spray sideways. Water typhooned over the cop shop. Drowned khakis ran for their minivans, sputtering and screaming.

"Oops," Branch said.

The Executioner munched another bologna and cheese as he watched the coverage with Bowie. Of course Covington would be the headliner.

Friday wouldn't work without him.

56

Johnny Sanders window-shopped Michigan Avenue, killing time till his meeting with Oprah's producers. His wife was crushed to not accompany him. Both her coworkers had called in sick, so she'd been stuck. He wanted to buy her something nice, make up for the hurt.

He ducked into a jewelry store faced in white-veined black marble.

"How much?" he asked the counter man over strains of Vivaldi, pointing to the tennis bracelet he'd spotted in the window. He'd splurge because she'd adore it. Anything up to five thousand he could handle . . .

"Eighty-four thousand dollars," the man said. Matter-of-fact, like people bought a yacht's worth of baubles every day. "Plus tax. Shall I wrap it for you?"

"Just looking," Sanders said.

He continued walking north, chuckling at his naïveté, moving slow to avoid sweating up his weddings-and-funerals suit. The breeze off Lake Michigan caressed him at each cross street. Two cabs, one yellow, one white, both filthy, traded horns and middle fingers. A Chicago Police wagon serpentined down Michigan Avenue, siren blapping, blue lights flashing. Muscled Latinos dumped newspapers next to vendors— ELECTRO-GOV!—the front page screamed—and he caught whiffs of caramel corn, pizza, and Chinese. One woman screamed at another in a language he didn't know.

"Shine your shoes?" a kid asked at Ohio Street.

Sanders nodded. Nothing too good for Oprah.

He put his wingtips on the crate, let the kid rap his life story as he waxed and buffed. *What a great job*, Sanders enthused. *I can see my reflection.* The rap was catchy, even if he didn't get most of the words. All that for five bucks! Sanders gave him twenty, earning a toothy grin. Then the kid was off stalking his next tourist.

Five minutes here is a year in Springfield, he thought happily.

57

"So now I'm 'Ken' instead of 'Chief Bite Me'?" Cross said.

The guffaw on the phone was deep and genuine. "You know I can't stay mad at you."

"I liked it better when you were," Cross said. "At least you weren't handing an engraved invitation to every death-penalty yahoo on the planet."

"That's why you get the big bucks, my friend," Covington said. "I hear you called the State Police."

"I'm ramping up security now that you're coming. While we're on the subject . . ." He pitched his thoughts on calling out the Illinois National Guard.

"Sure. How many you want?" Covington asked. "A hundred?"

"Five," Cross said.

"Jesus! I don't think I've got that many in the entire state, thanks to Iraq," Covington said. "But I'll see what I can do. Anything else?"

"Yes. Get whooping cough so you can't show up."

"Same old Ken," Covington chuckled.

58

"Death Row?" the left side called.

"Hell no!" the right side responded.

"Death Row?"

"Hell no!"

"Death Row?"

"Hell no!"

"Very good," the minister said, tapping his air brakes in applause. "Let's try number seven."

"One, two, three, four! Racist, sexist, antipoor!"

"Quick, number eleven, don't peek at the sheet."

"Politicians, they don't care, if innocent people get the chair!"

Everyone cheered.

Horns sounded outside the bus. Everyone looked out.

Passing drivers showed thumbs-ups.

The minister chuckled. It was much nicer than the screaming middle fingers they usually got because of the signs on the side of the bus. The congregation whistled and double-thumbed back.

An eight-year-old girl made her way to the front, knee-long braids swaying with the ruts and bumps of the interstate. She hugged her thin arms around his waist.

"Are we there yet, Grandpa?" she asked.

"No, honey," he said, patting her head without taking his eyes off the road. The flock was precious cargo. Particularly her. "Not yet."

"Soon?"

"Tomorrow," he said. "Remember what we talked about before we left Boise?"

The girl sat on the bench seat behind him, folding her freckled face. "That it's a very long ride to Noonerville?"

"Naperville," he corrected.

"Naperville," she repeated. "And that we have to drive through Idaho, Utah, Wyoming, Nebraska, Iowa, and Illinois to get there?"

"That's right, honey. Seventeen hundred miles. Thirty hours of driving. Plus stops for meals, stretching, and the potty."

A Kenworth hauling water pipes passed on the left. The minister blinked his headlights twice. The Kenworth swung to the right, flashing taillights in thanks.

"Do you think it's worth it, honey?" he asked, curious to see what she'd say. "Spending all this time away from home? Away from mommy and your friends?"

The girl nodded. "Yes, Grandpa. The death penalty is totally creepy. I'm glad our church is protesting against it."

"And why is the death penalty wrong, honey?"

"Um," she said, sucking on her finger as she searched for the answer. "Thou shalt not kill?"

"Amen!" the bus agreed.

The minister was pleased.

And deeply afraid.

59

The fuel truck driver hustled into the office.

Four minutes later he was back in his cab, parking the truck at the edge of the concrete apron. He hopped out and unreeled a long rubber hose.

The Executioner watched.

The driver removed the cover from the fill pipe that led to the underground storage tank. He dropped the hose in the pipe and pushed a button. A pump began whirring. The Executioner assumed it whirred, anyway. Even with his window down, he couldn't hear it.

Which was very good.

The Executioner drove to the air pump. Exited the Land Rover, listened hard. Still no whir.

"How's it going?" he greeted, unhooking the inflation chuck.

"Hanging in, hanging in," the driver said. "Want me to do that for you? I'm already dirty."

"That's a mighty nice offer," the Executioner said. "But I've got it, thanks." He nodded at the back of the truck. "That's the quietest pump I've ever heard."

"Electric, with triple armor," the driver explained. "Can't afford a spark around premium unleaded."

Bingo!

"I thought tankers were miles long with fifty tires," the Executioner said, showing him the "Golly, I'm confused" face.

"Now you're talking main rigs," the driver said. "Those water buffaloes carry ten thousand gallons." He grinned, showing gapped Chiclet teeth. "Mine's only two."

"You work for yourself?"

"Yep. BP hires me to service their small clients."

They chatted about the weather and Chicago Bears prospects.

"This your last delivery?" the Executioner asked, keeping the air chuck mostly off the tire valves so he could keep the conversation going.

"One more. Then I head home," the driver said.

"Where the missus has supper on the table, I trust."

The driver's face creased. "Lost my Bess a year ago. It's just me and the cats now."

"I'm sorry," the Executioner apologized. "I shouldn't have asked. It's none of my business."

"Aw, hell, that's all right," the trucker said, slapping the side of his truck. No echo. The metal was thick, to prevent fires. The Executioner liked the irony. "Feels kinda good hearing her name in the wind, know what I mean?"

"Yes, sir, I do."

The nozzle clacked.

"Well, she's full up," the driver said, tugging the hose from the pipe. It reminded the Executioner of stripping entrails out of a steer. "Time to drive to Morris."

"What's there?"

"A plant nursery called, 'We Sell Everything but Poison Ivy.'"

"That's a mouthful."

"I'll say. But Miss Ivy pays promptly, so I say it like a mantra."

They both laughed.

"A nursery requires gasoline?" the Executioner said.

"Sure. Gotta fuel the tractors and pickups and such."

"Oh, right."

"It's a dandy end to my day, too. Plant sales in August are slim to none, so Ivy closes at three. Means I can stop for a sandwich on the way, and nobody's drumming their fingers waiting for me to show up." He removed his fishing cap, squeegeed off his dome. "I'll drive in, drop my load, take off. Handle the paperwork over the computer."

"Morris is a good place for a nursery," the Executioner said, recalling it was forty miles southwest of Naperville. "Easy access from the interstate, but rural enough neighbors don't complain about the noise."

"Only thing in five miles is a farm," the driver agreed. "And that's abandoned." He replaced the fill cover, rinsed off the hose, and closed up the truck.

"Nice talking to you, friend," he said, climbing into the cab. "Have a good rest of the day."

"You too," the Executioner said.

A few minutes later, the truck was out of sight.

Followed by the Executioner.

60

"How's the tooth?" the grandma-strangler asked.

"Wiggles some," Trent said. "But it'll heal all right."

"Cool. Be a shame losing something that first-rate."

Trent nodded. He'd implanted a stainless-steel tooth in the hole Benedetti created during the 1990 arrest. Looked cooler than hell, and burnished his rep as a bad-ass. He'd feared the COs dislodged it during the beat-down, but it turned out fine.

"So what'd you wanna talk about?" he said, stretching.

The strangler pried apart his food loaf. A couple of beet chunks flopped onto the floor. They were hard and greenish. He picked them up, popped them in his mouth. Get sick, win a stay of execution. That was the law.

"My brother got into town today," he said, looking at the toilet in case Corey was embarrassed. "Couple cousins, too. Gonna witness my burn next week. So I was thinking I could, you know, if you want, ask 'em to come by this Friday, too."

"For what?"

"For your burn, man. You said no one's gonna show for you. That sucks. You can have my family if you want. They're good old boys. They won't mind witnessing twice."

Trent was deeply touched. Couldn't say it, of course. But still.

"Naw," he said, swatting the strangler. "Be all right. Just cause my people's a bunch of pansies doesn't mean yours should do double-duty." He grinned. "Not like I'm gonna die anyway."

"Shee-it, boy, you gonna fry like hash browns," the strangler said, chewing noisily. "Just like me the Friday next. So since we're dead men talkin', I want the no-shit truth from you." His crossed eyes glinted. "Did you *really* cut that big ol' cow into minute steaks?"

"Hell, no," Trent said, still luxuriating at the feel of clean skin. He'd spent two hours scrubbing his five-nine's nooks and crannies, scissoring his hair, and shaving his ratty-ass beard. The Row applauded when he came back from the shower. "I've never killed anyone in my life."

"Me neither," the strangler said.

"So why you on the Row if you're innocent?" Trent said.

"I was framed."

"Me, too," Trent said.

They stared at each other.

Then burst out laughing.

"You really wanna know how it went down?" Trent said.

"Yeah."

"Aw right then. Here goes . . ."

Old lady wants a kid. Me, too. I don't want her messing up her figure though—that ho is hot and broke in just right. So I grab my keys and go shopping.

Few minutes later I'm at the preggo store. You know, toys and stuffed elephants and shit. Preggo's in the parking lot, waddling to a car. Like a walrus, all stuck out. Looks beat.

I roll down my window, ask directions to a church. Real polite, ma'am and miss and hope your baby's healthy. She leans close, all trusting. I whack her in head with my tire iron. Shove her in the trunk, tie on the gag, take off.

Hour later I'm at the abandoned gas station where I take my side ho's. Variety is the spice of life, right? Anyway, this place is out in the country, nothing around but crickets. Boarded up tight. I know which nails are rusted away, of course.

Haul my preggo inside. Bout broke my damn back cause that balloon of hers ain't exactly helium. I rope her hands to a busted toilet, feet to a water pipe. Stretch her like a hammock and slap her awake. Big cow eyes flicker open.

I pull the knife from my pants. It's eight inches long and thick as a—no, man, my knife. *T'other's a mile long and a foot wide. At least. Hah.*

Preggo whimpers into the gag. She already knows what's gonna happen. Since I know it too, I figure let's get it on. She follows the steel like one of them hypnotized snakes.

I cut away her panties, then the rest of her clothes. She's good-looking for a preggo, why not enjoy it? I rub her down there to open things up, then put in the blade. She's screaming like Judgment Day. Which for her, it is, I guess. I start sawing, adjusting my angle as the red squirts out. Gotta do this right, you know. Can't damage Junior.

Meanwhile, I'm slurping them plump ol' titties. Man they tasty. All fat and goobly cause a kid's in the oven. Salty like pretzels. Maybe peanut butter.

I cut straight up to her ribs, then across, then down. Her belly falls open. Kinda like the flap on long johns. Kid's right there, all webbed in like Spider-Man. I yank him out. I know it's a boy because of his johnson, though it's shrimpy as a CO's. Hah. I smack his ass to make him breathe. Saw that once on TV. Kid starts yelling like he's shot.

I tuck Junior in my coat. Don't want him catching cold. Preggo's dead, naturally. I thought about humping them tit- ties, but that would be kinda, I don't know, weird. So I walk.

Couple feet later something's tugging on me. I forgot to cut the cord! So I grab a handful and pop it off. Preggo bleats like a sheep. I hit my noggin jumping so high—it was zombie time, man. I stab her neck till she's dead dead. Then tuck the cord under the kid, so it don't leak all over my leather seats. We leave.

I'm just about to my car when the kid starts bawling. Shut the hell up boy or I'll stick you like mama, I say. He's not obeying, so I shake him. Gotta let 'em who's boss, right?

Next thing you know the little bastard's dumping on me. Damn, it stinks. He's screaming harder, too. So I smack him in the head, jam a hanky in his mouth. Now he's quiet.

That's when I hear the steps. I turn around. Two big bas- tards, rushing like nose tackles, something shiny in their hands. They're hollering, Police, freeze, don't move or we'll blast ya. Like Miami Vice *except their clothes are shitty. Turns out they're on a stakeout a couple miles away and stopped at the gas station to drain the lizard. Looked inside while shaking 'em off and saw the preggo. Heard the kid, spotted me.*

I take off. I know these woods like the back of my hand, so it'll be easy to lose two dopes who don't, right? I wish! They're gaining on me. So I bounce the kid off a tree stump. They're cops so I know *they're gonna stop to save him.*

Wrong again. Benedetti, the sheriff's guy, he stops. Starts doing that CPR. But the other one keeps running. Branch. A Naperville cop, not sheriff's. Got some goofy first name like Caesar or Detroit . . . ah, right, Hercules.

Anyway, Branch is about caught up to me. So I fall to the ground, start hollering I give up, don't hurt me no more. But

I'm hiding the knife under me. He lands on top. I snake around and sling the blade. Catch him right across his ugly face. He springs a dozen leaks, eyeball to chin. Keeps fighting, but weaker. I wiggle out of his grasp. Gonna stab him in the heart 'fore he triggers his bullets in my ass, then get myself gone in the woods.

I hear a bellow. Like Godzilla or something. I look. It's Benedetti, and man is he pissed.

I get up the knife but he don't care. Kicks my arm like a football. Knife spins into the trees, arm spins the other way. He rips out a chunk of my hair, then locks up my good arm. Snap, it's broke too. Hollers crazy stuff about my son, his son, dead sons, everyone's son. Knocks me down and starts stomping. Those boots hurt like crazy so I kick him in the nuts. It's like they're made of cement—he don't care. He's on fire. He kicks the snot out of me. Smashes my face on a tree root, knocks out my front tooth. I know I'm gonna die, right there.

Then he's off me. Branch is yelling at him, Can't do that, man, can't kill him, ain't got no weapon no more. Dumb-ass cops. I'm them, I kill me dead and stick the knife back in my hand. These knuckleheads too "moral" for that. They got "rules." I don't. That's why I always win. Always, always, always.

Only thing I regret is not having my son no more. Woulda been fun having one of them. They play ball and shit, fetch you beer when you say. Make you look good. Walk tall. But Benedetti screwed that up. Made me kill my own damn son. If he hadn't made me do that, who knows? Maybe Junior would of come by Sundays to visit his old man . . .

"Now that," the strangler said, slack-jawed and wide-eyed, "is one bitchin' good story."

Trent punched his arm. "Stick around, sonny. Sequel's better."

61

"Well, howdy, mister," the fuel-truck driver said, turning toward the unexpected crunch on the gravel. "What are you doing all the way out—"

The three-shot reply silenced the cicadas.

62

Marty dipped the sponge in the bucket of warm water. He squeezed it heavy-damp, resumed cleaning grout off the powder room floor.

He concentrated on making each wipe perfect. Press too light, the residue dried on the tiles, ruining them. Too heavy, he sucked the grout out of the joints and had to start from scratch. The hands-and-knees made him ache head to heels, and his eyes stung from the vapors. He ignored it. Finishing what he'd started took precedence.

He'd tried to catch Emily's eye when Branch told the team to knock off for the night. She didn't look up. He shrugged. Drove home to get some shut-eye.

Lay wide awake, cursing sheep.

He dressed, then fired up the GTO he'd spent a year restoring. He'd raced the amateur circuit for years, and when he was troubled by a case—or in this case, Emily—he blasted down the lonesome roads south of Joliet, stereo cranked, window down, not looking for anything or thinking of much, just feeling the wind.

That wasn't working, either.

As he rounded the old Joliet Arsenal for the turn home, he looked at the steel ring dangling from the ignition. Emily's nickel-plated house key was there. She'd painted a little red heart at the top, on both sides. Gave to him Christmas last. Hadn't asked for it back.

That means something. Don't know what. But something. Time to find out if it's still there.

He called the task force, hoping she'd pick up. They needed to talk. She didn't want to, tough. He'd force the issue. Get this thing done. Cold wars were stupid—everyone suffered, not just them. He'd seen the knowing looks from the task cops, many of whom had Been There. Emily wanted out because of the kid, fine. But she'd damn well say it to his face.

Branch answered. Said Emily went for drinks with Annie. Way they talked, they'd be gone half the night. I can find her if you want. Buy you a beer if you need.

Nah, Marty said. I'm just gonna stop at her house a while, grout the powder room.

One less piece of unfinished business.

"So Marty's a daddy," Annie mused. "And he didn't want to tell you."

"No, he didn't," Emily said, topping their daiquiris from the lipped pitcher. She was feeling the burn from the expensive rum. Nice burn. "He still doesn't."

"How do you know?" Annie said.

"Know what?"

"He doesn't want to tell you about his son."

"Because he hasn't."

"Are you giving him a chance? You've frozen him out pretty solid."

She'd pulled Annie aside at six, when Marty was at the morgue collecting Zabrina Reynolds's results. She asked about the tommy-gun transfer at the Riverwalk. Annie said Marty was borrowing it for photographs—he wrote about weapons for the sheriff's Web site—so she brought it along. Why? Emily sighed, provided the bare bones. Annie said let's get a drink when we're done. At 8:30 they headed not to Our Neighbors, the friendly local cop bar with plenty of pretzels and ice-cold Schlitz, but to Lee Ann's Mining Camp, an Alaska Gold Rush–themed drinkery that most cops slinked past for fear of getting cooties from the yuppie clientele. Perfect place for this conversation. Cops gossiped more than the oldest of old biddies, and Emily didn't want her business making the circuit.

"Whose side are you on?" Emily flared, slapping her glass on the photo-collaged table.

"Yours," Annie said. "And his." She held her glass to the light, admiring the icy yellow shimmer. "These are nice and banana-y, aren't they?"

"Don't change the subject."

"OK," Annie said, putting it down, emptying the pitcher, and signaling for another. "The subject is you, and Marty, and you love each other, and you're being total dicks about it."

Emily sputtered.

"Don't get mad at me, girly," Annie said. "I'm just telling you what I see."

"And that would be?"

"Two people who are made for each other, but too stubborn to forgive old trespasses."

"He's got a *son*, Annie," Emily said. "How can I forgive that?"

"'Cause it's part of what makes Marty Marty. You fell for him two years ago, right?"

Emily nodded.

"Loved him tender, loved him true? Never had a reason to doubt it? Knew in your bones he felt the same?"

"Yes . . ."

"Well, guess what? He had a kid then, too."

The Executioner shifted for the hundredth time, trying to get comfortable. His back hurt, his joints popped like bubble wrap, and it was hard staying awake. Killing time in the front seat of an SUV wasn't his idea of fun.

At least it was working well.

He'd buried the driver in a grove of white pines, using the rusted shovel he liberated from a tea-rose display. Tamped the backfill so the hole looked like everything else. It simply wouldn't do for anyone to discover him before Friday.

He drove the Land Rover back to the parking lot and scrambled atop the fuel truck, which he'd stashed behind the perennials barn. No need to arouse the curiosity of any passing cop. He unscrewed the inspection hatch and illuminated the tank's interior with the driver's flashlight, shirttail over his nose and mouth.

Five hundred gallons, give or take.

Plenty enough.

He gripped the ladder with both hands till his feet hit terra firma. A broken ankle would ruin everything.

He slid into the Land Rover, turned on the news, and guzzled coffee from the truck driver's thermos. Made a face at the sugar.

"Tell me something," Annie said, draining her glass. "How would you feel if Marty had died at Seager Park instead of Ray Luerchen?"

"That's the stupidest thing I ever heard," Emily said.

"Answer anyway. How would you feel?"

Emily's tongue felt thick. Booze or honesty, she couldn't tell.

"Like I'd died, too," she admitted, staring at the pitcher.

"Of course you would. And that's exactly how you'll feel if you dump Marty. You waited a lifetime for this man— don't lose him by being stubborn." Annie leaned across and punched her arm. "Just talk to him, OK?"

"Idiot," Marty spa: ng the sponge off the wall as something he'd forgott   ped into his head.

He wiped up the grouty mess and grabbed his keys. Headed out Emily's back door and trotted to the Judd Kendall VFW a block east. He'd parked the GTO there, instead of in her driveway or garage. Wanted her to come inside the house, not see his car and leave.

But the tommy gun was still in the trunk. It was irreplaceable, and he'd never have left it if he hadn't been so damn distracted.

He got to the trunk in a minute flat.

"Hey, baby, how you doin'," he purred at the violin case. Weapons were frozen music, not just flanges and pins and screws. This song was especially priceless, being Roaring Twenties, fully restored, and owned by Annie, who appreciated guns as much as he did.

He tucked the case under his arm and trotted back to the house. Poked around for a safe place to store it. "Not you," he said to the kitchen and powder room. He didn't want a grain of stone dust marring that gleaming blue finish. The foyer and family rooms were equally out—under construction or filled with tools.

Second floor.

He hustled up the sanded oak steps and put the gun and

ammo drum in the closet on the landing, under Emily's winter clothes. They'd already finished this part of the house, so the closet was nice and clean.

He closed and opened the door, admiring the squeakless hinges Emily blowtorched from a single sheet of anodized aluminum. He was good at metalwork, thanks to the endless hours restoring his race cars. She was better. His woman had the gift, the touch.

My woman . . .

He closed the door and headed back to the next section of grout.

"Party's over, hon," Annie said, belting Emily into the passenger seat of her double-cab pickup. "I'll drop you at home and pick you up in the morning."

"I can drive," Emily mumbled.

"Right. And my face is on Mount Rushmore," Annie said.

Emily hiccupped. "I'm not DUI."

"Just UI," Annie said.

"That's mere supposition."

"It's a fact, Jack," Annie said, pulling away from the Mining Camp and heading for downtown. "Lee Ann had room in her garage, so your car's safe and sound. Set your alarm when you get upstairs. Don't forget, because I'm swinging by at six to pick you up."

"Aye aye, mommodore," Emily said, saluting. She hit her nose instead of her forehead.

Annie grinned. "On second thought, I'd better call you."

Marty checked his watch. Almost midnight. God, he was tired—worked all day, worked all night. But the powder room was finished, and for that, he was happy.

"Guess Em's gonna wait till tomorrow," he muttered.

He dragged himself upstairs, every step like climbing Everest. He peeked in the closet to make sure the tommy hadn't disappeared, then walked to the master bathroom.

He washed himself of dirt, sweat, and grout spatter, then dried with her bath towel. Kept it to his face a minute 'cause it smelled like her. Hung it back on the rack, making sure the corners were lined up—she had her idiosyncrasies—and walked out into the bedroom.

"Ow," he said, grimacing.

He sat on the bed, took off his right shoe. A chunk of grout fell out. He two-handed it into the wastebasket next to her triple dresser. Score.

He tried to get up to go home, but his bones wouldn't let him.

"Quick nap," he mumbled, letting the shoe fall from his hand. "That's all I need. Ten minutes and I'm outta here."

Emily waved as Annie sped off. She opened and closed the front door, checked twice that it was locked. She wasn't drunk, not a bit. But she had to admit to a certain tipsiness.

She gathered the envelopes from the foyer floor. The day she installed the door slot, she asked Joey the mailman to make his deliveries there instead of the curbside box. He understood why, and was happy to oblige. She did, however, maintain the curb box, to fool the bad guys. Another silly superstition, she supposed. But one just like it saved her life two years ago, and as Branch said time to time, "Can't hurt, might help."

The Executioner gunned the mini-fueler under the Washington Street viaduct and into downtown Naperville. He cut west on Douglas Avenue, south on Mill Street, west again on Jackson Avenue. He stuck to the speed limit, signaled each turn. He'd memorized the information on the gas jockey's driver's license, but only marginally resembled the photo. He couldn't afford a traffic stop.

He slowed at the VFW, scouting the area. Homes, driveways, sidewalks, trees, grass. Lots of lights, but none inside the houses. Emily's included.

Nice-looking place, he thought. He appreciated artistry in industrial processes, and this had plenty. The terrain-hugging two-story featured a metal roof that looked like slate, brick cladding to match the Riverwalk pavers, contrasting limestone quoins, designer windows, and a wraparound porch. Not dissimilar to others in the neighborhood. The frame, walls, and floors, however, were poured concrete, two feet thick and sandwiched with insulation. He knew that from the *Naperville Sun* article about cutting-edge home building around town. Concrete, the article said, saved trees, cut energy bills, didn't rot, and repelled destructive critters.

Well, most, anyway.

The front of the house sat blessedly close to the street. Brass lanterns lit everything yellowish white. The entrance door looked like oak. Probably steel, given the roof. A mail slot with a shiny brass cover was cut through at waist level.

Exactly as he'd remembered from his drive-bys.

Emily walked to the powder room. She'd start the grouting before hitting the hay. The job was much more fun when Marty helped, but that wasn't possible so . . .

"I *must* be drunk," she muttered, not believing her eyes. Every line was grouted white. The exquisitely inlaid granites and marbles were sparkling clean. The floor was done, and it hadn't been when she left for work. Who in the—

She heard a titanic snore erupting from her bedroom.

"Man, oh man, oh man, oh man," she whispered.

The Executioner peered through the gaps in the garage curtains. No cars. Nobody home.

Flame on.

January 17, 1972

"Weatherman promises nine degrees tonight," Potter Stewart said.

"Nine?" William Rehnquist groused, not feigning the shiver. "Washington's a southern city, for crying out loud. If I wanted winter wonderlands I wouldn't have left Milwaukee."

Stewart's polished heels popped like snare drums as the two justices strode across the Great Hall of the U.S. Supreme Court. "Well, at least the debate was hot."

"Best I've heard in years," Rehnquist agreed. "Death penalty cases stir such passion. Mr. Furman's attorney made some impressive arguments for reversing his client's death sentence."

"Glad to hear you admit it, Bill. He's got plenty of cause," Stewart said, nodding as William O. Douglas hurried by, juggling legal pads and coffee.

Rehnquist shook his head. He'd been sworn in only ten days ago, but bowed to no one in parsing the Constitution. "William Henry Furman killed an innocent husband and father."

"Accidentally."

"He was burglarizing the man's home, Potter. In the middle of the night."

"It was still an accident. Homeowner hears a noise. Thinks it's their son sleepwalking again. Walks out of the bedroom to see what's what. Furman panics, tries to run. He trips, his gun goes off, home owner dies," Stewart recited. "Because Furman lives in Georgia, he's sentenced to the electric chair."

"Because the Georgia legislature decided execution fit his crime," Rehnquist said. "Centuries of Anglo-American legal tradition support capital punishment, and you know it."

"What I know, Bill, is that societal standards evolve," Stewart said. "We used to burn witches, flog sailors, and send our poor to debtors' prisons. We do none of that any more, because our notions of morality have changed. Become more sophisticated. It's time to declare capital punishment incompatible with 1970s America."

"I agree," Rehnquist said.

"You *do*?"

"Sure. Views do change over time. But not on capital punishment."

"I see."

"I'm sorry, Potter, but you don't," Rehnquist said. "Americans are overwhelmingly in favor of putting killers to death. That gives the Georgia legislature—all legislatures—the moral and constitutional right to impose that penalty."

"Not if we rule otherwise."

"It's not our place to substitute our judgment for theirs."

"We have to, Bill," Stewart said. "That killing was accidental. If Furman did the exact same thing in Oregon, he'd get a manslaughter conviction and fifteen years. In Rhode Island, he'd get life. Arizona, death. California, thirty years. Texas—"

"They'd hang the varmint by sundown."

They both laughed.

"All kidding aside, capital punishment is a thicket of double standards," Stewart said. "There's no rhyme or reason to how it's applied, just throw your dart and see where it sticks. States impose it so capriciously, so utterly contrary to the punishment fitting the crime, that it's—"

"Let me guess," Rehnquist said. "Cruel and unusual."

"In the same way that being struck by lightning is cruel and unusual," Stewart said, patting Rehnquist's arm. "Because dying from it depends not on truth, justice, or facts, but on where you're standing."

"Very eloquent. Do I hear the opening line of an opinion to reverse Furman's death sentence?"

Stewart smiled. "I hate to waste perfectly good prose."

"Take it easy, Wayne," the state's attorney said, offering his bulldog assistant a tumbler of Wild Turkey. "You'll give yourself a stroke."

Covington drained it in one gulp. Felt the burn all the way down. It was nothing compared with his outrage.

"Furman killed an innocent man," he fumed. "In the man's own house! Georgia properly sentenced him. How can the Supremes rule pulling the switch is unconstitutional?"

"That's not going to happen," the state's attorney said, refilling the tumbler.

Covington jumped to his feet. Until reading the summaries of today's oral arguments before the high court, he'd never dreamt his long-awaited execution of Earl Monroe might be commuted to mere prison. His boss said "no way." But if five of the nine justices bought Furman's quixotic argument that death was too cruel and unusual a punishment for causing death, Monroe could slip the chair as well.

"Quit pacing, goddammit," the state's attorney ordered. "You're making me nervous."

Covington sat, slumped, sipped, sighed.

"I'm telling you not to worry," his boss continued. "Monroe's execution is June 29. Five months from now. Much too quick for the Supremes to make a decision that far-reaching."

"Well, that's true," Covington said, rubbing the pocket comb he always carried.

"Mm-hm. By the time they do get around to deciding, Earl's body lies a-moldering in the grave. And this chair is yours." He smiled. "Just remember the old proverb."

Covington arched a tapered eyebrow.

"'Be careful what you wish for,'" the state's attorney said. "'You may get it.'"

"So what do you think, Doc?" Earl asked, swinging his black-and-blue legs. A trio of crew cuts—that's what he called the latest crop of guards, crew cuts, for their horribly unstylish buzzed heads—delivered another "cop-killer" lesson last night. He'd managed to break two of three noses, so it wasn't all bad. Didn't even get tossed in solitary. That would have meant writing up the attackers, which nobody wanted because it was, well, Earl Monroe, not a more sympathetic orphan-drowner or baby-raper. "Furman gonna live or die?"

Doc lit a pair of Camels, handed one to Earl. "Die."

"Why?"

Doc blew a stream at the infirmary window. It swirled around the thick-painted bars, disappeared toward Joliet. "Two words," he said. "Bobby Kennedy."

Earl winced. "Oh, yeah," he muttered. "What year was it again that poor Irisher got himself whacked? I lose track."

"Sirhan slew Bobby in 1968," Doc said. "Just two years after you—"

"Not you, too," Earl spat, more hurt than angry. "Thought

you were different, being decent to me all these years. But you don't believe me either, do you?"

Doc sucked the cigarette tip red.

"Darling!" Verna Monroe said. "It's so good to hear your voice! Where are you?"

"London."

"Calling long distance from England," Verna marveled. "You're attending that engineering conference, right?"

"Yes, ma'am. When NASA says 'jump,' I ask, 'how high?'"

Even with the crackle she heard the off note. "Is everything all right? Why are you calling when you're so busy?"

"No reason," Daniel Monroe said. He was rereading the summary of the Furman arguments he'd obtained from a barrister friend. "Just wanted to hear your voice. With all the traveling I've been doing, I haven't talked to you as much as I'd like."

"Well, isn't that just like you," Verna said. "Thinking of your mother when you're doing such important work for our president. But that's not really why you called, is it?"

Silence.

Verna waited patiently.

"What do you mean we've got insurance?" Covington asked.

"Sirhan Sirhan," the state's attorney said.

Covington's eyes lit up. He'd been so obsessed with what the Supreme Court might not do to Monroe he'd forgotten all about that cockroach. On June 5, 1968, Sirhan emptied a revolver into JFK's kid brother at the Ambassador Hotel in Los Angeles. The assassin was tackled by a curtain wall of

Rosey Grier, George Plimpton, and Secret Service, then charged, convicted, and doomed to breathe cyanide till his skin turned purple.

"You're right, skipper," Covington said, inner fists unclenching. "No way the Supremes boot Sirhan from the gas chamber. Not after he whacks a Kennedy."

"Not for all the tea in Red China," the state's attorney agreed. "If they're not partial to avenging Bobby, well, Charles Manson and Richard Speck are on Death Row, too."

"If the justices overturn Furman, they overturn everyone," Covington said. "The public uproar would make the Boston Tea Party look like a college prank."

"And that, my worried friend, is why Earl Monroe will die in Stateville, on time, in that great good chair of ours." He grinned. "Thank God for celebrity victims."

"You're thinking about Earl, aren't you?" Verna said. "Because of the court hearing."

"Uh-huh," Danny said, rubbing his arm. It was raining—no surprise, this being London—and his forearm ached like loose dentures. Despite his vow to Earl, he'd tried going back to the hospital to redefine The Way It Was. Earl's chief enforcer, a refrigerator-size biker named Theodore Rehnt, caught him. He drove Danny at gunpoint to Naperville Cemetery, opposite the hospital, and delivered an earful about staying away.

Then broke his arm with a lead-filled blackjack.

"Pipe down, Danny, it's a small fracture," Teddy said over his yelps. "It'll set fine. Tell the emergency room docs you fell up some stairs. They'll buy it."

He jacked Danny's other arm, but only hard enough to bruise. "Don't write to your brother. Don't call. Don't visit. Not now, not ever. He loves and misses you. But he can't see you again. He told you that the other day, and you agreed. Now you gotta accept it like a man. Beats me why Earl wants it that way, but he does."

Teddy shoved his bearlike face close. "I like you, Danny. I watched you grow up, working for your pops. But my orders from Earl are clear—next time you get beat till you flop around like Howdy Doody." He whacked the fracture for an exclamation point . . .

His shudder brought his head back to London.

"Mr. Furman's attorney made some deft arguments," he told his mother. "If the Supreme Court agrees, every death sentence in the country is commuted. It's our best chance yet."

"Yes, honey, it is," Verna said. "Earl's lawyer stopped by the house a little while ago and told me what happened. It's exciting. Maybe a miracle will occur. Maybe Earl actually won't—" She bit off the thought.

"Mom?"

"I'm fine," she said. "I shouldn't get my hopes up, is all. Hope just drives you crazy." Long pause. "There's something else you should know."

"What's that?" he said, rubbing his pounding temples. Jet lag, probably.

"If Mr. Furman doesn't win his case, I'm going to watch Earl die."

"Think Furman'll beat the rap?" Detective Burr said as he laid queens over jacks in the sheriff's locker room.

"Nah," Detective Rogan said, shoving over the pot in disgust. "The robed wonders will pick their noses, scratch their balls, then tell Georgia, 'Go ahead, y'all.' Execution is an American tradition."

"Like Thanksgiving," Burr said. "Or college football."

Rogan pointed his finger. "The Rose Bowl of frying."

They laughed. Burr dealt the next hand, Rogan the one after that.

"What if ol' Earl didn't do it?" Burr said, relighting his Tiparello.

"Like the Japs didn't bomb Pearl Harbor?"

"Yeah, yeah. I'm just saying, what if he really didn't? Like he keeps claiming? We'd be executing an innocent man."

"We just catch the fish," Rogan said. "Someone else fries 'em."

THURSDAY

63

Emily sat on her side of the bed, arms around her tucked-up knees.

She'd been loaded for bear when she walked upstairs, intending to vent her outrage over what she knew was the real problem—Marty leaving her out of that most intimate part of his life. But her dudgeon melted when she saw his size twelve feet—one shod, one bare—splayed on the pillows and his head hanging over the bottom of the bed.

She sighed, tucked a blanket over him. Headed for the shower. Dried quickly, prepped for morning, came to bed. Marty was snorting and mumbling. She kissed his head and neck, feeling so mellow from the dissipation of tension— and that boatload of rum—she didn't even mind the annoying scrape against her window screen. Time enough to fix it.

To fix us.

She fell asleep.

* * *

Johnny Sanders slept so soundly in the satin sheets that he didn't hear the phone ring.

"She's frayed," Annie sighed into the darkness. "Wary. Waiting for the other shoe to drop."

"Will she be all right?"

"Just punch-drunk. Two years ago, now this. It can get to a person."

She laid her head on her husband's chest.

"Because of the Riverwalk attack, Emily's convinced she's the real target of our serial," she said. "The woman did look like her in the dark, and he used a knife. The similarities end there, though. Her head knows that. Her heart believes otherwise."

"Wouldn't yours?"

"Sure. And I don't have half her baggage."

"You got enough," he reminded.

"Yeah, but I'm made from titanium," Annie said.

"Your head maybe. Heart's a gummy bear."

Annie smiled. He wasn't the least bit intimidated by her. Most men ran away when they found out what she did for a living. He ran toward. "Em can't stand down from red alert," she said. "That's why I took her drinking. I wanted her wasted enough to sleep."

"Rum will do that."

"Yep," Annie said, moving away to catch the AC vent. As a self-admitted heat wimp, even small body contact made her sweat. "Maybe she is fine. The things I see are extraordinarily subtle. No one else would notice."

"But you do, since she's your best friend."

"Second-best," Annie said.

"Flattery will get you everywhere, Mrs. Bates," he said. "I feel bad for Em. How can we make her feel better?"

"Catch the son of a bitch."

"Until then?"

Annie answered by covering his mouth with hers.

"The sacrifices we make for our friends," hubby murmured, pulling her on top.

Still no cars.

The Executioner trotted to the fuel truck, unreeled the hose up the driveway and across the porch. Pulled the nozzle to the mail slot.

A half-inch too big to fit.

He sawed off the nozzle with a folding knife. Pinched the rubber between thumb and forefinger, threaded it through the slot. Pushed till the end touched the floor.

Emily moaned, her rummy nightmare turning bizarre. The blank-faced killer sunk his spurs into a charging pickup truck, trying to run her over. She hurled lightning bolts at his neck. Dead beagles sang show tunes. The blood-red sky opened up, hurling babies onto the Riverwalk. She kicked the blanket to the floor, twisting side to side.

The Executioner started the pump. Unleaded premium lumped the braided hose, like a hamster through a python.

"I am so bored," Viking muttered as he broke the first of the six dozen eggs he'd scramble later for headquarters' breakfast. Ham was baking and bread was rising—he prided himself on fresh country cookin'. "Only fun I had all day was showering those losers."

"Speaking of which," said his buddy who headed the bagpipe band, "I heard they complained to both chiefs."

"Ours and Ken, right," Viking said.

"Any repercussions?"

"Yep. I have to take remedial training. Learn how to judge wind better."

"Aw, man, that's bogus—"

Viking held up a finger. "Said remediation will take place at Our Neighbors. I'll learn to gauge wind speed and direction by tossing beer at my mouth. If said beer hits, I'm remediated." He winked. "Since it's a training mission, Ken said he's buying."

"That guy's almost as cool as a fireman," his buddy said, scrubbing the refrigerator.

"Nobody's as cool as a fireman," Viking said. "But he's pretty close."

"Where am I?" Marty groaned, blinking awake.

He looked across the bed. Saw Emily.

Figured it out.

Apparently, his nap turned into an all-nighter. She came home, decided to stay. He was so tired he didn't hear a thing. *Some watchdog.* Sweet of her to not wake him, though.

He admired her legs against the navy blue sheets. Settled for kissing the top of her head. The rest would wait till after they talked.

That they would seemed settled.

He was just about asleep when something dripped in his belly.

His eyes popped open. What was it? Nothing in the room but him, Em, and furniture. No sound except the ever-scraping tree limb. No smell. Then again, for him, there never was.

He could taste it, though. Heavy and damp. Sour and viscous. Faintly metallic.

Sewer gas?

Possible, he supposed. Maybe the toilet shifted during installation. Or the wax seal cracked. Whatever. Easy enough to fix. He'd do it now so Em didn't get nauseous. He had a wrench on the Leatherman tool on his belt, and a spare seal under the sink.

He headed for the bathroom.

Time to go, the Executioner decided. The house contained enough gasoline to redefine "crematorium," and his heart was beating risk-risk-risk. He loved it. He was never so alive as when he froze the world then broke it into pieces . . .

The starter ground. It wouldn't catch.

"Come on," he said. "Come on . . ."

Maybe I was dreaming about the taste, Marty thought as he opened the bathroom door.

"No, no, no, no," he heard Emily moan.

He walked over, concerned. She was twisting and kicking, muttering "mama," "beagles," and "truck." He peered at her eyelids. They jumped like bass to bait.

Deep REM sleep, he decided.

He picked up the blanket and spread it across her. Then paced the bedroom, tasting the air like a bomb dog. Definitely no dream—the metallic was more palpable now. Emily surely needed the sleep, but if he didn't find the source in ten minutes, he'd wake her and get out. No sense taking chances. Let Hazmat figure out what it was.

Passing the window, he wondered if it was external. Riding the breeze from elsewhere and seeping through the cracks. He lifted the sash, gulped air.

Not outside.

He continued his patrol.

* * *

The hose tip retreated off the porch and down the driveway. It unlooped the curbside mailbox, straightened out behind the truck. Twenty seconds later it was even with the VFW.

The Executioner hopped out, shut down the pump, stored the hose, moved the truck another twenty yards, trotted back to the start of his long, stinky fuse.

Pulled the box of matches.

Marty padded to the first floor, awash in moonglow from the huge skylight. Emily installed it to bathe the stairs and landing in natural light. He'd been leery when she explained what she had in mind—skylights leaked when not installed perfectly—but it turned into one of his favorite features. Didn't leak a drop in even the heaviest storm—

His bare feet plunged into something cold. Some splashed up on his face.

His eyes bulged at the raw-steel taste. He knew exactly what it was.

"Run!" he screamed.

"Buh-bye," the Executioner whispered, scraping two matches and tossing them into the gasoline. Soon as it whoomped he sprinted to the truck.

"Get out of the house!" Marty roared as he wheeled away from the high-test ponding across the first floor. "Now! Out! Run for your life!"

Marty invaded her nightmare, shouting like doom. The pickup morphed into a mushroom cloud. She thrashed like a gaffed marlin.

* * *

Flames licked west on Jackson. Rounded south around Emily's mailbox, gathering speed as the fuel supply grew richer. Flashed up the driveway, across the porch, and through the mail slot, smelling the mother lode.

The Executioner raced the other way.

Marty pounded up the stairs. He had to stay alive long enough to throw Emily out the window. The concrete frame was so dense no explosion could blow it apart. The fireball would stay inside, pressure-cooking them like—

Detour.

He slammed into a wall to stop his momentum. Ripped open the closet door. Yanked the tommy gun from the violin case. Locked in the ammo drum, worked the bolt, jammed the butt in his shoulder, and ripped hellfire into Heaven.

The buzz-cloud of .45s shattered the skylight into razor rain.

He tossed the empty tommy and charged into the bedroom.

Emily's head bongo'd as she sprang from bed. "Marty! What are you—"

"Bomb!" he roared as the fire-breathing dragon below inhaled walls, floors, ceilings, furniture, tiles, tools, grout, toilets, and whipped cream, then blew its bowels in superheated fury.

Eggs splattered as something primeval kicked the firehouse. Viking turned off the gas, then ran for his turnout gear. He knew from the sound they wouldn't even make lunch.

* * *

The dragon blew through the house, up the stairs, and into the bedroom, knocking Emily into the master bath. "Marty, where are you?" she screamed as he disappeared in fire and smoke.

"This is Naperville 911," the dispatcher said coolly as all lines rang at once. "I can't hear you, slow down and tell me . . . Jackson Avenue . . . near the VFW post . . ."

She typed a series of response codes, setting off bells and Klaxons at fire stations across the city. "Explosion and fire downtown, end of Jackson Avenue, near the VFW," she broadcast. "All units respond Code Three." Lights, sirens, no speed limits.

The mapping software flashed names and addresses of nearby residents.

Biting her lip, she rang for a supervisor.

"All units, Code Thirteen," she said, switching to police frequencies. Thirteen meant a cop was under attack and death was imminent. "Jackson Avenue, Code Thirteen . . ."

64

"Marty!" Emily screamed as she kicked her way through the bedroom. "Where are you?"

Fire licked walls and baseboards, wormed through drawers and closets. Her wedding gown was a cone of glowing cinders, her mounted deer antlers, charred. Her little black dress, the one she'd dieted into so relentlessly for her first real date with Marty, was ash on a hanger. Windows were shattered, walls scorched. She saw stars through collapse-holes. Their bed was reduced to wires, wheels, and the "Do Not Remove" mattress tag.

Mayday! her head warned. *Abandon ship!*

Instead, she stepped into her work boots.

"Where are you?" she repeated, kicking aside embers. "Are you here? Talk to me!"

Still no reply.

She crunched her way to the landing.

The first floor was a lava lamp of orange and red. The stairs were gone. Tarry black smoke chimneyed up and out of the house through what used to be the skylight. She blinked at the roaring heat as her toes smacked a pile of soft.

The pile groaned.

"Sweet Jesus," she whispered, raking the haystack of concrete shards off Marty's unmoving body. Neither burned nor bleeding, she saw. Still breathing.

"Wake up, wake up!" she yelled directly into his ear. Nothing. She slapped his face, twice, hard. He moaned, but didn't awaken.

The dragon belched on her back.

"We need to get out of here," she said, contorting in pain. "You have to get up."

No dice.

She grabbed his ankles and heaved. It was brutal—he outweighed her by a hundred pounds. She heaved and stopped, heaved and stopped, dragging him across smolders and flares, bending occasionally to slap flames out of his hair.

The dragon munched at the landing.

"The block's on fire," the battalion chief reported as his command SUV screamed down Jackson. "Raise the response level to catastrophic, tell PD to evacuate downtown."

Emergency pagers sounded across four counties.

One was atop Cross's bed stand.

He dialed his direct line to the watch commander. His face hardened as he listened.

"On my way," he said.

Emily dragged Marty the final inches to the bedroom window. She pushed her head through the empty frame, hyperventilating.

No help in sight.

That would change quickly, she knew. With a blast this titanic, every fire truck in ten miles was en route. She and Marty could breathe right here till rescue—

A thousand hinges squealed outside the door. She turned to see the landing shudder, liquidate, and disappear. Flames sloshed over the threshold to ignite what was left of her Oriental rug.

FD wouldn't make it in time.

"Suck it up!" she shouted, trying to quell her panic. "You'll escape!" Easier said then done, she knew. Her escape ladder was warped useless under the fried mattress. Her sheets and blankets were gone. She didn't have any rope. Not even duct tape . . .

"Hutch," she said.

She ran to the built-in, praying her gun belt wasn't melted. She reached between two steaming piles of socks, yanked it free. A burning cinder fell on her neck. She slapped it away and raced back to Marty.

She buckled the belt around her waist. Locked one set of handcuffs to Marty's wrists. Skin steamed where steel touched flesh. She took the second set, clicked one cuff around the chain that connected his wrist cuffs, clicked the other to her belt. They would live—or die—together.

A blowtorch raked her calves.

She twisted around, yelping. Orange flames bubbled through a new sinkhole in the floor.

If they didn't get out *right now* . . .

She squatted, grabbed his neck and knees. Visualized setting a new Olympic record. Tensed her abdomen, back, and legs, said a final prayer, and power-lifted him onto the windowsill, gutting it out, going for gold.

Yessss!

Panting so hard the sill blurred, she pushed Marty to the very outer edge. She climbed over, leaned out as far as possible, wrapped her arms around the huge tree limb—*Thank you for being here! I'll never prune you again!*—then swung like Tarzan, tugging Marty till gravity took over.

The bedroom exploded.

"Mush!" Viking cried, plunging into the vortex. The hose team followed, blasting everything in sight with hydrant pressure. The water vaporized on impact.

Another hose team appeared. Then another. The foyer swirled black, red, wet, dry, flamed, and steamy as dragon fought knights for domination.

"Why aren't they out yet?" Cross demanded as he ran up. Both Annie and Branch called in on the Thirteen, saying Emily and Marty were inside the house.

The fire boss looked at him in exasperation. "The heat's monstrous. I got three teams humping hose, four more breaking walls. They're searching as fast as they can."

Cross took off for the back of the house.

65

The Executioner whistled "Ring of Fire" as he drove back to Morris. He'd dump the fuel truck in the abandoned barn near the nursery, recover his Land Rover, and head home. Bowie would laugh with delight when he heard about this brilliant maneuver.

66

Emily gripped so tight the bark flayed her palms. If they fell from this height, they might as well have died in the blast.

"We're going to make it, Marty," she said, glancing down for signs of life. All she saw were his fingers, bloated like jellyfish from his weight on the handcuffs. "I won't let you die."

The dragon snickered.

She inched them across the limb as the tip leaves ignited. Her boots fell off, then her nightgown. The gun belt sagged where the handcuff attached. Her hips screamed with each tick of the Marty pendulum.

Six feet to the main trunk . . .

Five . . .

Four . . .

Her right hand thwacked into a V-crotch.

Her certainty crumbled.

She'd have to let go to clear the obstacle. Put an inhuman strain on her remaining hand. Marty's life would come down to five numb fingers. It had to be enough.

She let go.

67

"Mr. Sanders?" the chirpy voice said.

"Speaking," Johnny mumbled, patting around for the clock.

"This is Shonda Qualmann, a production assistant with *The Oprah Winfrey Show*. Sorry for the early hour, but I need to let you know . . ."

68

"Hang on, Emily!" she heard Cross bellow as her right hand cleared the V-crotch and grabbed the other side. Ladders slammed the limb on both sides. The strain on her hips disappeared and fireproof gloves encircled her waist.

"Got you now," a firefighter said. "Let go of the tree."

"I can't," she gasped.

"You won't fall, I promise."

"It's not that. My hands are frozen."

He reached up and pried her fingers loose.

She sprawled over another firefighter's shoulder. She vaguely knew she was naked. She didn't have the energy to care. Nor did she have the foggiest clue how she'd managed to pull off this inhuman feat. Even as she uncovered Marty, and dragged him, and chained him to her waist, and swung from the house and inched across the burning tree, she knew death was a foregone conclusion. She was going through the motions for the dragon's amusement. Staying alive in Kelvin-scale heat was utterly impossible. Yet here they were. Her and Marty.

Alive.

Alive . . .

She slipped down the ladder and out of harm's way.

"God bless the Fire Department," she mumbled, sprawled on the crunchy grass with a blanket and air mask. She patted around to grab Marty's hand but it was too far away—

"It's not done with us yet!" someone yelled.

She lifted her head. The dragon was blasting through the roof, spitting cinders into the Riverwalk trees. Fires erupted like road flares.

"I think that's your cue, fellas," Cross said.

Paramedics strapped Emily and Marty onto gurneys and loaded them into ambulances as fresh hose teams attacked the woods.

The last thing she saw was her tree crackling with fire.

She wept.

69

Johnny Sanders picked up the next document. Might as well work, now that his fifteen minutes of fame had vanished. The call was Team Oprah. They'd found a soap opera actor who'd been struck by lightning and lived to tell *People*, "so we won't need your services today. Thanks awfully for understanding."

Sanders wasn't surprised. Even C-list celebrities beat crash test dummies. At least they agreed to pick up his breakfast.

He called his boss, then his wife. She was furious, vowed never to watch "that woman" again. It was sweet. He wished again he'd had the wherewithal for that tennis bracelet.

They talked awhile on Oprah's dime. Then he showered, checked out of the hotel, and parked his car a block past Union Station.

He ate at Lou Mitchell's Restaurant whenever he visited Chicago. The food was marvelous, the atmosphere lively.

The place appealed to his inner historian—the 1923 coffee shop was the iconic start of Route 66.

"More java?" the waitress asked, even as she refilled.

Sanders dripped in cream. Sighed as black turned caramel, then beige. Until the phone rang, he honestly didn't think he'd cared about appearing on national TV. Who knew he could be as starstruck as a teenager? Oh, well. Time to take off the Superman shirt and go back to Johnny Sanders, Ordinary Guy. A superhero only to his wife and, occasionally, their kids.

He skipped the parts common to all execution documents—death warrant, controlling legal statutes, staff observations, weather conditions—for the particulars of June 29, 1972. The crime. The condemned. What went well. What didn't. He shook his head. *We burned Manuel in the eighteenth century. We're burning Trent in the twenty-first. Some progress.*

The waitress gave him Milk Duds, one of the freebies Lou Mitchell's handed out. He glanced at the TV flickering over her shoulder.

"What's that?" he asked, pointing to the orange fury on the screen. "California brush fires?"

"Explosion in Naperville," she said.

"Huh! I was just in Naperville."

"Nice town," she said. "Think way too much of themselves, though. All that 'Best place to raise children' bragging they do? All I know is, I don't call Judge Judy when I lose my iPod."

Sanders laughed. "Where was this explosion?"

"Downtown. About three this morning. Blew out windows for blocks, started that Riverwalk on fire. Couple other houses burned, too. No one was hurt, though."

"Amazing," he said.

"Can't believe it myself," she said. "I was in a fire once.

Small one, but it still scares you to death." She showed him the ropy scar on her elbow. He murmured in sympathy.

"You look awfully familiar," she said. "Are you famous?"

"Not really," Sanders said. "I was the crash test dummy—"

"Yeah, that's it!" the waitress said, slapping his shoulder. "Out at that Justice Center. I read that story in the paper. Laughed so hard I couldn't breathe."

"Thanks," Sanders said.

"Sure, honey," she said, slipping him an extra Duds and palming his check. "Breakfast's on the house. We love our celebrities here at Lou's."

She strolled off, putting a little extra wiggle in her wide hips.

Who needs Oprah? he thought, savoring the moment. He watched the fire till the commercial, then started on Appendix F—the twelve official witnesses.

"Reynolds," he said. "Mahoney. Farri. Gee, those names look familiar." He watched the buses rumble by on Jackson Boulevard. "Where did I just see them . . ."

His cup slipped from his hand.

"Honey, are you all right?" the waitress said, hurrying over with a rag and horrified expression. "That coffee's scalding! Did you burn yourself?"

He had. He didn't care.

"Tell me the fastest route to Naperville," he said.

70

"Big guy's coming along," Dr. Winslow assured as she bandaged Emily's hip gash. She'd inspected the resident's job, pronounced it sloppy, resutured. "He keeps asking to see you."

"Can I?"

"Not yet," Winslow said. "You're going to rest here another hour. I'll bring you coffee and a magazine. Hope you like *Parents* or *Field & Stream*. It's all we've got these days—"

"Forget it, Barbara. I need to see Marty. And get to work."

Winslow glared, and Emily knew resistance was futile. The good doctor wouldn't think twice about locking the door to enforce her medical decisions.

"All right, you grouch," Emily grumbled.

"I am rubber, you are glue," Winslow said. "Besides, Marty's got a knot on his head. I want to be sure his scans are clear before you visit."

Emily nodded. "Any other injuries?"

"The usual for your merry band—burns, cuts, and bruises. Nothing serious, though." Winslow pointed to the padded examination table. "All right, you know the drill."

"You should buy me dinner, all the times you've seen me naked," Emily grumped, lying back and opening her cotton gown.

Winslow snickered, began probing the scarred-over holes and cuts.

Emily yipped.

"Did that hurt?"

"Your hands are cold."

"Sissy."

Six probes and a cheek pinch later, Winslow told her to get dressed.

Emily reached for the bit-snug jeans Annie and Lydia Branch brought over. Her entire wardrobe was ash, so they'd cadged the manager at Lands' End into a pre-hours shopping spree. The sizes were correct, but that didn't mean much in women's clothes—"ten" might mean eight, twelve, or maternity billowed.

Annie also included a Cylinder & Slide Glock 17 with holster, belt, and spare ammo. She didn't trust Emily's cooked equipment, and would lend from her custom armory "till you get to the toy store." A fire marshal found Emily's badge in a mud puddle. It was scorched and dented, but functional. She'd been tempted to accept Cross's offer of a new badge, but decided she wanted this one instead.

"I'm really sorry about your house," Winslow said, walking to the sink. "You and Marty worked so hard on it." She had, too, spending more than a few nights with them bending conduit and taping Sheetrock. "Think you'll rebuild?"

Emily's eyes filled. Not with sadness, but fury. The devil who attacked her—and her man, and their home, and the savior tree—was going to meet a very nasty end. She'd promised herself that dangling from the limb, and intended to deliver.

"I don't know, Barbara," she said. "I really don't. This is the second time, you know. It's a great location and means so much to me. But maybe it's jinxed beyond hope."

"Evil spirits?"

"Something like that."

Winslow nodded. "I get that. But don't do anything rash. It'd be such a shame to feel driven out by that scum." She washed, toweled, and wiped the sink. "If you decide to sell, let me know. I'll buy it as an investment. You can buy it back if you ever change your mind."

Emily thanked her profusely, then pointed to her scars. "Speaking of rash and scum . . ."

"Those look great," Winslow said. "All healed up, and fading nicely. Is the one on the calf still bothering you? It bites back when I press."

Emily thought about saying no, so the truth didn't get to NPD's medical board. But she wouldn't lie to Barbara. The medium-tall brunette with the dusting of freckles and big, caring eyes was a friend as well as Edward Hospital's chief of emergency medicine.

"Yes," Emily said, feeling the tug when she flexed her foot. "It hurts when I do this."

"Then don't do that," Winslow said.

Emily rolled her eyes. "I could have said that and I didn't even go to medical school."

"Me neither," Winslow said. "I just like to stick needles in people."

71

"Quit yelling. In case you hadn't noticed, I'm in the chair next to yours," the Executioner said, downing his bourbon in a single gulp. He deserved Bowie's tirade, but was tiring of it.

"I know I shouldn't have deviated from the plan," he said. "But I thought the house was empty." Another fill and gulp. "They made it out alive. Both of them. So stop worrying. Nothing will stop tomorrow. Nothing. All right?"

Bowie grinned from ear to ear.

72

"Aw, come on," Sanders groaned at the unending line of cars. I-88 was a parking lot thanks to lane reconstruction, and he'd been stuck much too long. "Let's go."

He did. Another three feet.

He swerved onto the shoulder, ignoring the shouts and horns. He'd take the next exit to Ogden Avenue, drive west till he hit Naperville. He wasn't worried about tickets.

He'd get a police escort when they heard what he'd found.

73

Cross dragged over a chair. Branch said his hip was fine. Cross tapped his gold badge, which read CHIEF.

Branch sat.

"Emily should be here soon," Marty said. Saying it aloud made him happy. A few more times and he'd float like on morphine. "Doc's got her in lockdown to rest."

Cross knew that because he'd arranged it with Winslow. Emily was a thoroughbred, and as such, needed the occasional forced cooldown to not cripple herself. "We just came from her room. She looks good. Came through it like a champ."

"Course she did," Marty said, though he wouldn't actually believe it till they were face to face. He took a deep breath, let it out. "OK, tell me."

"The house was bombed," Branch said.

"How?"

"Gasoline," Annie said as she tied a fist of get-well-soon

balloons on the window latch. "Fire marshal figures a hundred gallons give or take, given the size of the explosion."

"How did it get inside?"

"Pumped through the mail slot," Branch said. "The point of origin was the front door."

Marty thought about that, nodded. Made sense. The slot was the only accessible opening on Emily's first floor, as her windows were locked and her exhaust ducts too high to reach.

"Next time we'll stencil a fake one," Marty said, walling off the destruction to allow full concentration on the work ahead. "How was the gas delivered?"

"Most likely truck," Branch said. "People eating downtown around the time of the blast reported a small fuel tanker driving south on Washington."

"Markings?"

"None reported."

"Plate?"

"Partials from six different witnesses," Cross said. "None the same. Task force is running every combination, and rousting fuel suppliers to conduct an immediate inventory."

"Checking sales, too?"

"New and used," Cross said. "Wholesale and retail."

"Good," Marty said, for lack of anything better. He remembered the blast. Nothing after.

"Was anybody hurt?" he asked, holding up his wrists. They were black as shoe polish, with mustard-yellow dots throughout and purple flares off each side. "Besides me and Em?"

"Cinders ignited five houses," Annie said. "But FD got everyone out. Including Shelby."

"Outstanding," Marty said, genuinely pleased. The yellow Labrador retriever lived a few doors down. He'd helped save Emily two years ago, and Marty had barbecued him a twenty-pound prime rib as thanks. They'd been pals ever since. It helped immeasurably when his own dogs died. "He's got more lives than Garfield."

"Yep," Annie said. "So zero casualties other than your thick head."

She danced away from Marty's swat.

"We found two burnt matches," Branch said. "On Jackson, where the gasoline fuse started."

"The what?"

Branch explained.

"So it's our serial killer," Marty said, feeling murderous despite the compartmentalization. "And he clearly wants Emily dead."

"Or you."

"Me?" he said, startled. "How you figure?"

"You were there," Cross said.

"Yeah, but how would the bozo know that? It's Emily's house."

"The man does his homework," Cross said. "Knows you stay over most nights."

Marty thought about the rich irony in that, shrugged. "Well, yeah, I'd much rather he target me than her," he said. "But I just don't think that's the case. Among other things, Emily being the target explains the Riverwalk knifing."

"Emily's look-alike," Cross said.

"Mm-hm," Marty said, biting his lip. The wrists really smarted. If they were only strained as Doc insisted, he'd hate to feel broken. "When the victim's identity made the news, he realized he botched the kill. He needed to take out Em some other way. Something equally ballsy, to send whatever message he's dreamed up. So he pumps gasoline into our house—"

Annie smiled at "our."

"—then lights the liquid fuse. Since there's no body, he escaped."

"Meaning he's still out there hunting," Branch said.

"The better for us to . . . catch him," Marty said.

They nodded, knowing exactly what the pause meant.

"How did she and I get out?" he continued. "Were we blown clear?"

"Not exactly," Cross said.

He described Emily's rescue moves.

Marty's jaw dropped. He tried to speak. No sound emerged. He tried again.

"Good God," he managed, completely stunned. "How is that even *possible*?"

Cross massaged his backside, mentally cursing the errant shotgun blast that removed half of it two decades ago. "Motivation and adrenaline," he said. "When I worked patrol in Vegas, I came upon a fresh accident—a kid pinned under a minivan near his home. His mom came charging down the street, bent over, and lifted off the van. Lady was a ninety-eight-pound weakling—her words—yet she was so buzzed from her child in danger she lifted that van like it was nothing."

"I hear ya," Marty said, still shaking his head. "But what Emily did was . . . is . . . impossible."

"Good thing it wasn't, bucko," Branch said. "Or you wouldn't be here taking up space."

"Speaking of burned," Annie said, "how did you *get* into that tree?"

"Didn't you hear Ken?" Marty said.

"That's how Emily evacuated you," Annie said. "Not how you guys survived the blast to begin with." She wrote "100 gal. gas" and "1000 tons concrete" on the nurses' whiteboard. "This plus that equals instant death," she said, tapping the numbers. "How did you avoid that fate?"

"You," Marty said.

Her eyebrows lifted.

"Soon as I stepped in that gasoline pool, I knew there'd be an explosion," Marty said. "No other reason for it to be there. The fireball would cremate us if it didn't have a place to exit before it reached the bedroom. So I created one."

"How?"

"Your tommy gun."

She stared.

"Heat rises. So I machine-gunned the skylight," Marty explained. "Created a chimney. Most of the blast vented straight up and out the hole. Reducing the fireball just enough to save us."

Stunned silence.

"Talk about impossible," Cross said. "You're a whole lot smarter than you look."

"Thanks," Marty said. "I think."

"That's the best sacrifice that burp gun could have made," Annie said, kissing Marty's forehead. "Saving Emily's life."

"Hey! What about me?" Marty demanded.

"I *told* you not to scratch it," Annie replied.

74

10:17 A.M.

"You know how this makes me look?" Covington snarled through the cell crackle. "Blowing up two cops on the eve of my execution and I can't do a thing about it? That's pathetic, Ken. Catch that animal and catch him now. Before I become the punch line on late-night TV."

Cross looked at the phone in disgust as he sped south on Illinois 53. Intelligence reported a big wave of buses exiting I-88, so he was heading to the Justice Center to make sure the National Guard understood his rules of engagement. The thought of an irresistible force—roiling protesters—meeting the immovable object—soldiers with live ammo—made his teeth hurt. Covington was turning it to root canal.

"Good thing they didn't die," Cross said. "You'd look even worse."

"That's for goddamn sure," Covington said, not getting the sarcasm but mercifully losing steam. "Hey, did Emily really drag Benedetti out on that limb?"

"She did."

"That's one silver lining, anyway," Covington said. "I'll play that up at my press conference this afternoon."

"You do that," Cross said.

"Helluva cop you got in that woman, Ken. Maybe I'll steal her for my security detail."

"Maybe I'll stick you in that electric chair," Cross said.

Covington laughed.

Cross didn't.

Lockdown expired, Emily practically skipped toward Marty's room. She couldn't wait for the big reunion. They'd clear the air between them, then go nail the—

"Where are you?" she wondered to the rumpled bed.

"Getting more head scans," Winslow said, appearing from around the corner.

"Why?" Emily said, frozen as Fargo in December.

"Computer crash," Winslow said, looking disgusted. "It ate Marty's results along with a few dozen others. He's at the head of the line, but it'll still be an hour. Maybe two. Sorry."

Emily thawed. "At least he's all right."

"Absolutely."

"I'm heading to the station, then. The more of us working—"

"—the quicker you catch the guy," Winslow said. "By all means, go."

Annie had retrieved her car from Lee Ann's and parked it in the south garage, so Emily headed for the exit. "Call me the minute I can see him?" she called back.

"The second," Winslow said.

"Want a break from the road?" the choir director shouted over "Crown of Glory."

The minister nodded and pulled onto the shoulder. They

switched places. He stretched as the bus rejoined traffic, then headed to his granddaughter, who was sitting by herself in the back.

"How you doing, kiddo?" he asked, snapping the purple rubber band in her ponytail.

"Fine, Grandpa," she said, looking up from SpongeBob Jesus. "But how come you aren't?"

That startled him. "What do you mean?"

"You're sad," she said. "I can tell."

"Really? How?"

"Your eyes get all shiny," she said. "And your mouth goes like this." She crooked each little finger and pulled down the corners, flattening her cheeks.

"That's a very interesting observation," he said.

"Thank you," she said, her sit-in-place curtsy exposing her knobby knees. She tugged her pink dress over them. "How come you're sad, Grandpa?"

He sighed. "Well, capital punishment is a very sad thing. We're doing the Lord's work, driving to Naperville to protest this execution. But that doesn't mean it's fun."

"No, it isn't," she said, pouting. "I want to go home."

The comment puzzled him. With the toys, coloring books, candy, and ceaseless doting from charmed older congregants, she'd been Little Miss Sunshine since Boise.

"Why would you want to turn around, honey?" he asked. "You know how important this trip is to everyone."

"Because I don't like it when you're not happy, Grandpa. It's icky and I hate it."

He smiled. "Me, too."

She put her hands on her bony hips. Same way her mother did when annoyed with Reverend Daddy. "Then why go there?"

He closed his eyes, having asked himself that a hundred times since they left the farewell party. "Because I have to," he said, hugging her close. "No matter what."

"Why does it make you sad?"

He steepled his fingers, blew out his breath. "Remember Uncle Earl? He was my brother, and he loved me, and he was really unhappy he couldn't live long enough to meet you."

"Sure!" she said, clapping. "I love Uncle Earl! Is that the surprise you told us about in Boise, Grandpa? Is he going to be in Naperville tomorrow?"

"Well, no, honey. He's in Heaven. But we're going to Naperville *because* of him."

"What do you mean?"

"Uncle Earl protected me from some very bad men when we were little. But I didn't protect him back. I was scared they'd hurt me, too, so I didn't help." He studied her a long time. The choir switched to "Amazing Grace." "You always help your brother when he's afraid, right?" he continued. "When the thunderstorms come and he shakes and cries?"

She nodded.

"Well, I didn't help Uncle Earl like that. I was too scared. I didn't have a brave big sister to show me how to be courageous."

She screwed up her face, considering. "That's why you couldn't help Uncle Earl?" she asked. "Because you were afraid of the bad men?"

"Yes," Daniel Monroe said.

He still was.

So much had changed since he threw those hand grenades. His brother was dead. His parents were dead. The cemetery where they rested had been dug up for the expansion of Chicago O'Hare Airport. Their boyhood home was a six-lane highway, the abandoned gasoline station where Earl's crew hung out, a bustling suburban minimart. All he had left were memories. And the dull ache in his arm where Teddy Rehnt blackjacked him to enforce Earl's will . . .

His granddaughter was motioning him to lean over. He complied.

"It's all right, Grandpa," she whispered with Skittles breath. "I'm afraid, too."

"Really?" he said. "Of what?"

"The lightning." Her hands shook. "It scares me to death. But my brother's more afraid than me, so I just close my eyes and sing campfire songs, so he isn't."

"That's the bravest thing I've ever heard," Danny said, throat cementing. "I wish I could have done that for Uncle Earl."

"Are there still bad men in the world, Grandpa?"

"Yes, honey, there are."

"Are they in Naperville?"

"Yes. They're the ones conducting this capital punishment."

"Are you afraid of them?"

"A little, honey."

She threw her arms around his waist. "Don't worry, Grandpa!" she cried, chopping the air with her hands. "I'll protect you! I learned kung-fu in gym class. Bad men can't hurt you when I'm around, 'cause I'll karate their noses off so they can't smell where you are!" More chops. "Yah! Hwah! I'll fix 'em!"

"I know you will, baby," he said, kissing her flaxen hair. It smelled like peanut butter. He loved this little girl so much it made him weep sometimes. She was clearly God's way of saying, "It's all right, Daniel. You've suffered enough for your sins."

But he still couldn't forgive himself. He became so guilt-racked after burying Earl and Mom that he resigned NASA for the ministry. He took over a penniless but proud church in Boise, married a good woman, begat a daughter, who begat his granddaughter, all the while hoping a life of good works would slay the beast within.

It didn't.

"Nobody would protect me better, darling," he said. "But

we're on this pilgrimage so *I* can stop the bad men. So *I* can make things right, by not being afraid. It's what I have to do."

He thought of the steel lump in his bathroom bag. The kraut blaster he hadn't thrown at those police officers because the first three worked so ruthlessly. Yes, he was guilty, and he was goinig to pay for it tomorrow.

But so would Wayne Covington. If the governor hadn't resurrected that burning barbarism and named it "justice," perhaps he would have stayed silent, marinated in his own guilt juice till the day he died. But Covington did. He dug up Earl's coffin and let the evil out. The man deserved what was coming to him.

One more day, my friend. Get ready.

The nemesis CO whistled "Tomorrow" as he walked past.

Corey Trent twisted his face into a scowl. It masked his interior grin.

One more day, asswipe. Get ready.

75

10:22 A.M.

A thoroughly embarrassed Emily was shushing the applause from the lobby-desk officers when she heard her name.

She turned to see a tall, lean man staring like her nose was on fire.

"I'm Detective Thompson," she said cautiously. "And you are?"

"Your serial killer."

She tackled him as the desk cops yanked their guns.

"No! Wait!" he yelled as they crashed to the floor. "I mean, I'm here *about* your serial killer! My name is Johnny Sanders. From Springfield. I'm a state historian—"

"The crash test dummy," she said, immediately placing the face. She checked his ID, assured the blue flood that the man was legitimate, and helped him to his feet.

"Sorry about that," she said, breathing hard from adrenaline swoosh. "Between the killer and the fire downtown, we're a little jumpy."

"Sure, sure, I understand," he said. "I'd knock me down, too, the dumb way I worded that." He brushed off his slacks. "I was in Chicago this morning on a work assignment. The moment I realized I had important information about your serial killer, I drove out here."

"What is it?"

He told her.

Everyone froze.

Emily forced the frog out of her voice.

"Find Branch and Cross," she told the desk cops. "Hurry."

76

"Tell them, Mr. Sanders," Cross said.

"Johnny," Sanders said, swiveling his chair toward the jumble of cops, clerks, CSIs, computers, coffee cups, bagel crumbs, and whiteboards, which were collaged with maps, diagrams, morgue photos, lists, addresses, phone numbers, and a handwritten sign that read ABANDON HOPE ALL YE WHO ENTER HERE. He blotted his high forehead with a linen handkerchief, glad his wife packed extras.

"I'm a State of Illinois historian," he began. "Several months ago, I was assigned to digitize our execution records. All of them, 1779 to present."

"Why?" a detective asked.

"Federal grant," Sanders said. "The Justice Department is paying the states to put their old paper records online. So I review each document, track down missing pieces from public and private sources, and digitize it for the Internet."

He held up the sheet of paper that caused his lap burn at Lou Mitchell's. "This is Appendix F from the execution held

June 29, 1972, at Stateville. When you see it, you'll know why I came here."

Emily passed out copies. Hands slapped desktops and foreheads.

"Damn! It's our serial victims," a detective said.

"Correct. We finally have our common link," Cross said. "Go ahead, Johnny."

"Yes, sir," Sanders said as Branch handed him water. "A few days ago, I was at home in Springfield, reading the morning newspapers. I saw the obituary for Frank Mahoney. The barber whose throat was cut in Arizona?"

Heads nodded.

"Another story mentioned Sage Farri's death in Los Angeles and Zabrina Reynolds's here in Naperville. At the time, they didn't mean anything to me."

The cops drummed fingers, inhaled coffee, studied the handout.

"At breakfast this morning, I reviewed the next document on my list," he said, rattling Appendix F. "It contains the names of the twelve official witnesses to that June 29 execution. They share the same last names as the victims of your serial killer."

"What's an 'official' witness?" a computer tech asked.

"The ordinary citizens who volunteered to witness the execution as representatives of the people of Illinois," Sanders said. "There's twelve, same number as on a jury."

"In addition to the reporters and relatives?"

"Yes, ma'am. An entirely separate group."

Cross took over.

"Johnny saw the names, remembered the newspaper stories, put two and two together. He drove here to let us know." He flicked his foam cup into the overflowing wastebasket. "Every victim is the grandchild of a person on Appendix F. Name for name."

"Why didn't this F pop up when we ran the victims before?" a CSI asked.

"It's never been digitized," Sanders said. "It gathered dust in a records warehouse for more than three decades. That's what my project's about. Making documents Internet friendly so you guys can search them from anywhere."

Branch thumped his cane. "Thanks to Emily's burnt-match posting on NCIC, we've already backgrounded eight of them. Now we'll get the rest."

Cross extended his hand. "Thank you, Johnny. I'll inform the governor personally how vital your help was in finding this killer."

Sanders beamed.

"The officer will escort you to your car," Cross said, waving over a uniform. "As I mentioned earlier, keep this information to yourself. Tell no one. If reporters call for comment, plead ignorance. It's crucial we keep the killer in the dark about how much we've learned."

"I will, sir," Sanders said, flushing from the applause. "Just catch this maniac." He recalled the roses in Sage Farri's windpipe. "Nobody should die like that poor boy in LA."

The officer touched his arm, and they walked out.

"Questions?" Cross said.

The CSI raised his blue chin. "Sanders said twelve witnesses. Only eleven on this handout."

"That's 'cause you ran out of fingers," the detective said.

"I still got this one," the CSI said, raising it.

Emily smiled. Wisecracking eased the strain of killer hunting.

"I left it off for security," Cross said. "I haven't told him yet he's a target."

"Told?" the CSI said. "He's alive? We can save Twelve from this freak?"

"If we don't," Cross said. "Everyone in this room can start looking for a new career."

Deep breath, blowout.

"Starting with me."

June 29, 1972

Hello?" Danny Monroe said, frowning as the word echoed without response. It was unlike Mom not to be on the stoop, purse in hand, when he pulled into the driveway. "I'm here!"

No sound but the ticking of the grandfather clock.

He and Verna were driving to Stateville Prison this morning—her to witness the execution of her eldest son, him to wait in the car, per his long-ago agreement with Earl. For years he'd tried to talk her out of it, but she remained adamant that "my baby not die alone."

"We're going to be late!" he said. "Come out, come out, wherever you are!"

Still nothing.

Shrugging, he checked each room as he made his way to the back of the house. Window air clicked off, on, off. Dust motes drifted over the snowflake shakers Mom collected on family vacations. Yellowed snapshots of him and Earl grinned from faded eggshell walls.

Everything normal. Nothing out of place.

Just Mom.

He poked his head into the bedroom he and Earl shared as kids. It was cramped for two growing boys, but a lot more fun then when Dad put on the addition and they got separates. He smiled, remembering their all-night whisperings about girls, parents hollering to get to sleep before you-know-who got their butts you-know-what . . .

"There you are," he murmured to the sleeping beauty curled on Earl's old bed. She was in her Sunday best—pearls, heels, hose, hat. Her omnipresent purse leaned against the maple headboard, handles up like rabbit ears. She hadn't slept an hour the past three nights, she'd confessed, even with the pills her doctor prescribed. He knew how she felt. She must have laid in Earl's spot "for one quick minute" after getting dressed, and that was that.

"Up to me you'd sleep all day," he sympathized, walking around the bed. "But you'd never forgive me if I let you miss Earl's—"

Blood dripped from her left wrist. Her favorite kitchen knife quivered point-down in the beige shag. Her face was bleached, her fingers stiff, her delicate features collapsed. Her pill bottle was empty on the bedstand, next to a half-drunk glass of water.

"Mom!" he cried, grabbing her up and shaking her hard. Blood from the carpet pool squished into his shoes, splattered his clothes. "Oh my God, wake up! Talk to me, please!"

She was cold as soft-serve.

He ran gagging to the bathroom.

"What in the hell is *this*?" Earl Monroe asked, lips curling in disgust.

"Fresh underwear," the prison doctor said.

"Looks like a diaper to me."

A barely noticeable shrug. "If you like."

"I don't. Man, I can't wear diapers to my—"

"You ain't a man," growled the crew-cutted guard in the corner, unfolding his arms with undisguised menace. "So put 'em on."

Earl snickered. "Whaddaya gonna do if I don't, sweet cheeks? Kill me?"

Crew cut flicked his head. The other muscled guards moved in, happy for the chance to pound the scumbag into compliance one last time.

Doc held up his slim brown hand.

"He'll cooperate. Won't you, Mr. Monroe?"

The condemned prisoner grinned. "Sure, Doc. Since you called me mister and all."

"Time to go watch a monster fry," Wayne Covington said.

"Be strong, darling," Katherine Covington said.

"Got no choice," Wayne grinned, kissing her. "Andy will swoop down and kick my keister if I'm anything but." He walked out, twirling his car keys.

Something in her pinched expression made him come back.

"I promise this is the end," he said, squeezing his wife's hands. "The long hours, the time away. It ends today. No more obsession."

"I hope so, Wayne," Kit said, more sharply than she'd intended. But it had been a long, lonely six years. "Your family needs you back."

"Whatcha got?" the Supreme Court clerk greeted his compatriot. "Baseball pool?"

Compatriot held up the envelope. "The Furman decision."

"Already?" Clerk said, blinking. "I didn't expect that for months."

"No one did," Compatriot said. "But five minutes ago, the chief justice called me in and said disseminate this PDQ."

"So what'd they decide? Thumbs-up? Or down?"

Compatriot unwound the envelope string, looking around for justices who'd kick him back to freshman law for peeking. "Only one way to find out."

In the end, I simply didn't have the courage, read the note she'd taped to the bathroom mirror. *Earl needed me at that dreadful place today, and I couldn't go. I couldn't watch him die. Not my firstborn, not that way, burning to death in that hideous electro-chair.*

You think I'm strong, Danny. I'm not. I couldn't be there at the end for your brother, or for you. For that I'm truly sorry. I left this note in hopes you'll understand why I couldn't face you this morning. I'm ashamed at how you'll find me, and I wouldn't blame you for hating me forever. I pray you don't. I hope Jesus doesn't either.

By the time you read this I'll be with your dad. In a few hours, Earl will join us. Do not despair at our deaths, darling. You're a wonderful man. Kind, brave and unafraid. Get married, have children, continue your important life. Think of us when you're able. Because of you, the family name will have pride and honor. Not the shame Earl and I brought to it. And at the end of your days, you'll join us in this better place.

Your loving mother, Verna

Danny cried so hard he hiccuped.

Earl dropped his prison-issue trousers, then slid down his boxers. Flashed crew cut with an Elvis wiggle-waggle of the hips. It drew a hate-filled scowl.

He chuckled, then stepped into the crudely sewn "underwear." It was thick as one of his mother's quilts, and dyed the same dirty gray as the trousers. He tugged it over his bony knees and into his torso, making sure nothing pinched.

"Gawd!" he complained, waving his hand like airing out a bathroom. "What's that stink?"

"Aftershave," Doc said. "We don't have any more deodorizer."

"You're kidding, right?"

"Governor's been busy burning up your friends," crew cut said. "We're fresh out."

Doc's look said, Shut up. The guard did.

"I had to use Hai Karate," Doc said. "It'll do fine."

"Diapers and aftershave," Earl said, shaking his head. "And they say *I'm* evil."

He pulled up the trousers, then tucked in his T-shirt. A good buddy in the laundry shrunk it extra-tight to show off his muscles to the witnesses. No use wasting all that barbell work.

Ding-ding-ding-ding-ding.

The *Chicago Sun-Times* copy boy trotted to the Associated Press teletype, which condensed the planet onto six-inch-wide rolls of paper.

"SCOTUS/FURMAN/TK," the bulletin read.

"Hey, Red," he said, ripping it off for the front-page editor. "Supreme Court's gonna release that Furman death penalty decision."

"Good," Red said, stuffing his pipe with burley. "I need a new lead for Kup's edition."

"Be funny if they banned it, huh?" the clerk said. "What with the fry job at Stateville?"

"Freakin' hilarious for Earl," Red said, flaming the bowl.

*   *   *

Danny stepped out of the pink-sloshed bathtub and walked into the bedroom. He pulled a black suit, white shirt, regimental tie, and socks from Dad's closet, thankful Mom hadn't had the heart to throw them out. They fit surprisingly well. He'd have to go without underwear. He couldn't wear another man's shorts. Not even Dad's, not even under this circumstance.

"Don't worry, Mom, it'll be all right," he said, slipping his feet into a pair of waxed Florsheims. Another perfect fit. "I'll take care of everything."

He kissed her cheek and pulled Earl's keys from her purse.

Time to do what she couldn't, and he hadn't.

"'Scuse me a minute, boys," Doc said.

He walked to the bathroom and guzzled vodka from his pocket flask. This burn was harder to deal with than the others. He liked Earl. They'd have been friends if he wasn't a cop-killer. But he was, so there you go.

He wiped his mouth and went back to work.

The court clerk crossed his arms, tapped his foot.

"Don't get impatient with me, young sir," the head of the duplication center said, glaring over her glasses. "I'm repairing the mimeograph as fast as I can."

"Sorry," the clerk said. "But if I don't get this decision out soon, the chief's gonna haul me up the flagpole and see who salutes."

Earl glanced at the clock as his cell door unlocked for his lawyer.

One hour.

"Anything?" he asked.

The lawyer grinned.

Danny pulled off Illinois 53 and into the Stateville park-ing lot. Gravel dust swirled around the fresh-waxed Ford Galaxie. He didn't see Teddy Rehnt. He wasn't surprised—in his gruff way, the enforcer was as close to Earl as he was, and taking this equally hard. Danny didn't blame him a bit for skipping the circus.

Tingling and lightheaded, he locked the car up tight. Walked away. Returned a minute later to recheck each lock—no sense losing Earl's Galaxie to a thief. Realized he was dawdling.

He headed for the entrance.

"My legal eagle says the court might actually call this off," Earl told Doc. "He's wetting his pants he's so excited. What do you think?"

"Warden Gabriel will stand next to the telephone during the process in case that very thing happens," Doc said.

His hangdog expression said not to count on it.

"Let's just keep a good thought, then," Earl said as the es-cort team marched up. Eight of them for one of him. *I still got it, baby.* "And if it doesn't work out, hey, everyone dies, right?"

Doc shook his hand. Several crew cuts hawked and spat, disgusted at the deference.

"See ya in the next," Earl said, winking at Doc, then hold-ing out his arms for the manacles.

They chained the condemned prisoner tight, then marched him down the vaulted hallway and through the steel door that marked the end of Death Row.

* * *

"What the hell are you doing here?" Detective Burr said, planting his hand in Danny's chest. "Thought you and brother were splitsville."

Danny cast his eyes down, pup to alpha. "I don't have a choice, sir," he said. "My mother intended to be Earl's family witness, but she came down with pneumonia last night."

"Pneumonia?"

"That's what she says. But it's probably just worry," Danny said. "Long and short is my mother can't be here for her son, and begged me to do it instead. What choice did I have?"

Burr searched his face.

Danny shrugged, hoping "her son" instead of "my brother" reinforced his expression of helplessness, duty, and anger at having this odious chore dumped in his lap. He'd practiced on the drive here, and hoped it would be enough.

Burr looked at Rogan.

Rogan nodded.

Burr lifted his hand.

"Thank you for understanding, sir," Danny said. "It's not that I want to be here, but . . ."

"Hey. Family. Whaddaya gonna do, huh?" Burr said. He patted Danny's shoulder and pointed to the main door. "Through there."

A guard frisked Danny twice, then escorted him to the witness room set aside for relatives of the condemned. Danny looked around. A scatter of empty chairs, a window, and him.

He sat in the second row, shaking so hard he thought he'd vibrate apart.

Earl wrinkled his nose at the continuing assault of Hai Karate. Prison electricians bustled about, checking power lines and connections. He'd tried chatting up the first one, but the guy only blinked, like a hoot owl. The second one turned away after mumbling he wasn't allowed to talk to condemned prisoners.

He gave up.

The biggest annoyance wasn't death, he decided. It was his freshly shaved skull. It itched like lice bites, and he couldn't scratch it—his head, chest, waist, thighs, shins, forearms, and biceps were cinched to the oak with leather straps. Even if he managed to free a hand, his head was covered by the skullcap that contained the entry electrode. All he could do was rub the arms of the chair real hard and hope it fooled his skull.

"Danny's a good kid," Burr said, lighting another Camel. "Sucking it up to help his ma."

"Yeah," Rogan said. "I guess we all got our crosses to bear. His is Earl."

Kit Covington danced an imaginary partner through her bedroom, swirling and twirling, happier than she'd been in six years. Her man would be in her arms tonight, his tour of duty over. As soon as Wayne cleared the driveway, she dropped the kids at her mother's, stopped for a manicure and wax, then shopped for the perfect lace negligee. In every war, the victor got the spoils. She was his.

"Finally," the court clerk muttered.

He grabbed the damp purple mimeos, hustled to the press room, and threw them on the release table. The milling news hawks snatched them like free pretzels.

The UPI bureau chief whistled, then pounced for his phone.

* * *

Earl hummed tonelessly, gazing at the curtains that separated him from the carton of eggs who'd watch him sizzle like Oscar Mayer's bacon. *You want me to die because you think I did it. What the hell do you know?*

The thought held no rancor, though. Earl stopped being angry the moment he decided to keep his mouth shut about who'd really killed those cops.

He wasn't nearly as scared as he thought he'd be. He knew why—he'd kept Danny safe. That's why he took without complaint the food, the beatings, the humiliations, the bullshit solitary, and now the two thousand volts. So his brother would live. He smiled, proud of himself. *Even though I'm sitting, I'll die on my feet. Not a bad way for a man to go out.*

A crew cut sauntered into the death chamber and pulled the restraints even tighter. He knuckle-clanked the skullcap twice, whisper-cursing Earl in richly creative shades of blue mixed with the names of the dead cops. Earl didn't respond. What was left to say?

The crew cut left.

He glanced at the clock over the curtains. It was twice the size of the one outside his cell. Had three hands instead of two. The extra, fire-engine red against the black of the others, hopped a precise distance every second. It made no noise but he heard every tick.

He tried to swallow when it landed on six. Couldn't.

No spit.

Ding-ding-ding-ding-ding-ding-ding-ding-ding-ding.

Flash.

The copyboy raced over. The quarter-mile of presses in the basement were already spitting out Red Streaks.

"It's Furman!" he bayed across the newsroom.

*   *   *

The curtains drew back like it was movie night. Earl peered through the glass. Twenty-four eyeballs stared back. None was familiar.

A second, smaller, curtain shimmied to his right. Earl looked sideways, expecting to see Mom.

"Danny!" he shouted, equally stunned, overjoyed, and gut-shot. "What are you—"

"Mom just couldn't do it, and asked me to come instead," Danny shouted back. "I'm here for you, brother. The Monroe boys will ride this fire to the end."

The intercoms clicked off, turning their talk to pantomime.

In the adjoining anteroom, a rigid copper switch, burnished bright for conductivity, slid into a willing prong. Dynamos kicked to life under Earl's slippered feet. Danny felt the vibration and stifled a gasp. The public address crackled like AM in a thunderstorm. Earl locked eyes with Danny, thinking how happy he was Mom stayed home 'cause he sure didn't want her seeing this. Danny stared back, thinking of when those grade-school bullies knocked him off his Schwinn Black Phantom and said it was theirs now, punk, and Earl got it back, and Dad swabbed ointment on Earl's ripped knuckles, not asking a single question, just patting his eldest son's head. The official witnesses bit their lips and held their breath. Covington zithered his pocket comb, thinking of Andy and raspberry jam. Doc's nostrils flared from hard breathing. Crew cuts cracked their knuckles. Most stared with unvarnished glee. Some looked away, mumbling. Earl rubbed the chair like God gave a damn. Danny said anything that came into his head, just talking, motioning, moving toward the glass. The guard warned him to sit. Earl kept nodding, picking up a few of the lipped words and guessing the rest. The warden watched the hotline. The governor ignored it. Mom turned a degree colder. The red hand joined the blacks at twelve.

And the lightning bolt hit.

"Gwaa!" Earl puffed as the electric chair groaned like a peep show. If the restraints hadn't been sufficiently tight, the surge would have flung him against the window, bug on a Peterbilt. His joints twisted, his backbone collapsed.

Four seconds.

He turned the red of boiled lobster. Spittle leaked from both corners of his grimace. His eyes banged Tilt with each shift in the alternating current, wildly spinning the witnesses. Danny punched one thigh, then the other, then the first, then the second.

Twelve seconds.

The two-thousand-volt hotshot, designed to instantly blow out the central nervous system but hardly ever did, dropped to five hundred for the secondary burn.

Springfield dentist Frank Mahoney felt his spine tingle as the condemned's eyes bored in. "Did not," they seemed to whisper. "Did not did not did not." Then they rolled up, like those zombies on late-night TV. He fumbled for the airsick bags the warden promised. Leila Reynolds, a bookkeeper for a Chicago auto dealer, handed over two of hers.

Sixty seconds.

Tertiary burn.

The official executioner was a Stateville groundskeeper who needed the stipend for his kid's braces. He cranked the voltage back to two thousand, exactly as the manual dictated. White lights dimmed to bronze throughout the prison as the dynamos suckled electric milk. Three thousand convicts flung curses, food, and feces.

The lightning hit again.

Bones snapped as Earl's fingers twisted into square knots. If he hadn't clipped his claws to the quick last night, they would have driven through his palms, Jesus nails. Skin blistered under the electrodes. Blood misted through his protruded lips.

"The condemned prisoner has bitten through his mouth guard," the executioner said for the benefit of the tape recorders logging the event. "Cleaving his tongue and causing extensive bleeding that the witnesses can see. We need to reinforce it for next week's burn."

Danny, barely breathing, clenched his hands till finger bones crackled.

Ninety seconds.

Quadriary burn.

Glowing maroon blotches spread across Earl's face. His skin slid around, and his eyeballs wormed from their sockets. Pinkish foam dribbled from his nose as capillaries burst. T-bone and sweet potato from last night's Last Supper bubbled down his chin.

One hundred twenty seconds.

"I'm so sorry, Earl," Danny whispered. "I'm sorry, I'm sorry, I'm sorry . . ."

As WGN Radio telegraphed updates, Teddy Rehnt crossed his arms one way and his legs the another, face contorting, eyes burning, wondering who he could maim for this.

Greasy smoke erupted from the skullcap, followed by metallic blue whomps of flame.

"The doctor should include electrode integrity in his final examination," the executioner intoned. "The guards missed the gapping of the skullcap, and it's causing a severe arc."

Four witnesses gagged. Three sat unimpressed, one trembled like aspic. Frank Mahoney fainted on Leila Reynolds's shoulder. Brewster Farri, a John Deere mechanic from Moline, thrust his fist in the air, shouting, "Amen!"

Wayne Covington laughed.

Danny Monroe stared unblinking through the windows. These people were barbaric. That anyone with a soul could volunteer to witness this cattle slaughter was beyond comprehension.

Two hundred forty-seven seconds.

Earl's body temperature had risen to slow-oven. His muscles crawled like spiders. His gallbladder poached in its own bile. His skin took the sheen of old ham. The grounding electrode burned a hole in his maniacally twitching left calf—

"Oh no," the executioner gasped as the telephone rang.

Three seconds later the grim-faced warden drew his finger across his throat.

The executioner yanked male from female, uncoupling the dynamos, brightening the lights.

"The Supreme Court just struck down capital punishment," he heard the warden announce over the PA system. "All executions nationwide are canceled. The court ruled five to four that state execution statutes are applied too unevenly to be constitutional . . ."

Doc rushed into the chamber, heart rabbiting. He grabbed Earl's wrist to search for a pulse. He yelped, yanking his hand back from the fry-pan heat.

"Undo those straps," he ordered. "He might still be alive."

The crew cut stuck his hands in his pockets.

Doc pushed him aside and placed his stethoscope, careful to keep fingers well above the steel listening bell. He tried chest, neck, and wrist, then shook his head four times.

Too. Late. He's. Dead.

The curtains closed.

Frank Mahoney blinked awake.

"I guess I fainted," he murmured, looking sheepish.

"I'm afraid so, dear," Leila Reynolds said.

"What happened? Is it over?"

"Mr. Monroe is gone," Leila said, patting his arm. "Better you didn't see it."

Brewster Farri chattered about the skull flames. "Weren't they amazing?" he said to the other witnesses, who'd lined up at the exit. "Those reds and yellows? And that crazy blue? Wow. My kid would've loved that. Looked like the Fourth of July, doncha think? Huh? Doncha?"

Covington stayed in his seat, steepling his manicured fingers, mesmerized by the steam that curled from Monroe's ears.

"I got ya, Earl," he whispered, recalling how the bastard's grenades had so shredded Andy's face that Pop had to bury him closed-casket. "I promised I'd burn you, and I did."

Danny walked out, climbed in the dusty Galaxie, gave Stateville the finger, and headed home for their dead mother, the ochre sky streaked with tears.

FRYDAY

77

"Don't say a word," Emily murmured as she shut the door. She removed her jeans, top, and shoes, and snuggled under the hospital sheets. Thanks to her chat with the night nurse, no one would stop by to record Marty's temperature. "Not even a syllable. Just rock my world."

"The plan must be perfect if *you* can't find anything wrong," the Executioner said, grinning.

Bowie grinned back.

Pleased at his approval, the Executioner stretched, then did thirty-five jumping jacks, push-ups, sit-ups, and knee bends.

He repeated till his muscles shivered.

Then took a shower.

2:49 A.M.

"Are we in Naperville, Grandpa?"

"So it would seem," said the Reverend Daniel Monroe, parking the bug-smeared church bus in the slot indicated by the traffic warden. His wide-eyed congregants stared from the windows.

Noise buzzed like locusts. Buses, trucks, cars, RVs, motorcycles, horses-and-buggies, and a bicycle built for two vomited protesters toward the chain-link fence. Hundreds of cops formed a loose ring around the base of the hill. National Guardsmen in desert camo filled the gaps. They looked like Robocops with their padding, helmets, and guns. Fire engines idled inside the fence, waiting to stiff-arm crashers. TV slow-danced the crowd, thrusting erect lenses toward willing mouths. Shirts ranging from "Have *My* Baby, Corey!" to "Naperville: Catch the Buzz!" sold fast, as did five-dollar water. The Justice Center—which Danny found grim enough in abstract but totally inhuman now—glittered large and lonely atop the garbage hill.

"Golgotha," he whispered.

2:51 A.M.

"What's happening?" Dr. Winslow asked, stifling a yawn. She'd been paged at home because two of her ER docs called in sick.

"Nothing," said desk supervisor Jeanie Gee. "Had a flurry from two gravel trucks colliding, but that's sorted. One funny thing, though."

Winslow raised an eyebrow.

"A patient ordered three cans of whipped cream from food service. I checked his orders. No dietary restrictions, so I sent it up to his room."

"Is the patient by chance Martin Benedetti?" Winslow

asked, recalling Emily's call around two seeking "hypothetical medical advice" for a "hypothetical patient." Amused, Winslow said the "patient" could be "active" if he or she didn't hit his or her head.

"That's right. The guy from the fire," Jeanie said. "How'd you know?"

"Lucky guess," Winslow said.

2:52 A.M.

"Bird Nest to Castle."

"Go ahead, Nest," said SWAT Lieutenant Annie Bates.

"Everything's good down here. How's it look from the top?"

Annie slapped a mosquito, made one more binocular sweep of the vast crowd.

"We're surrounded, the poor bastards," she said.

Branch snorted. "We must be in clover if you're making jokes."

"Roger that," Annie said. Branch was running the combined forces from the bunker near the main gate. She roamed the wide, flat roof of the Justice Center with her weapons specialists and spotters, anticipating problems. "The folks are great. No one appears angry, and there's no fighting. Just singing, chanting, and praying."

"A respectful riot?"

Annie chuckled. "Never been in one of those," she said, repositioning three sharpshooters to other parts of the roof. "But I'll give alms to all their gods if it stays that way."

3:01 A.M.

"That was . . . swampy," Emily breathed, rubbing his pillow on her drenched face.

"Least I can do for you saving my life," Marty said, stroking her hair. "Friends?"

"Friends," she said, putting out her hand.

"We can do better than that," Marty said, flicking the top from the Redi-Whip.

3:14 A.M.

"All right, Bowie," the Executioner said, holding up the checklist he'd been preparing for two years. "Let me know if I'm missing anything. Gun, swallowing knife, honey, keys, letter . . ."

3:22 A.M.

"If I'm your birthday cake," Emily purred, licking melted whipped cream off her hand, "where's the candle?"

"You already blew that out," Marty said.

She started giggling. A few seconds later, he joined her. It turned into full-blown laughter, which they muffled in the sheets.

"Since we're friends again," she said when she could talk again. "Tell me about your son."

His breath caught. Then released.

"What do you want to know?"

"Everything."

He sighed. "Not much to tell."

She gave him the hairy eyeball.

"Honest," Marty said. "There isn't. That's one of the problems."

"But you do know Alice."

He nodded. "Her name was Alice Caldwell. She was my first true love."

"I had one of those," she said. "Didn't go further than kissing, though."

"We did," Marty said. "We fooled around after prom. Didn't go all the way, but let's just say I slid hard into third base. A few months later, she tells me she's pregnant."

She winced.

"Tell me," he said dryly. "Her folks were deeply religious, so they decide she's going to have the baby whether she wants to or not. In February, she delivers a bouncing boy."

"Happy Valentine's Day, Daddy."

Marty chuckled. "He was all spit and vinegar, with hazel eyes and a full head of hair."

Like you, Emily thought. "Was he healthy?"

"As a lumberjack. Huge lungs on that kid." He said it a little proud. "Hospital thought there was an earthquake one night, but it was him, crying for mommy's attention."

"All you boys do," she teased. "So, you saw him?"

"I did," Marty said. "I even got a photo. Curled-up little Polaroid of him and me. Have to dig it out now, since you know."

"I'd really like that," Emily said, meaning it. Annie was right. Even though that boy was another woman's son, he'd been born to Marty, too. That made it part of him.

Part of her.

"So why was Alice calling?" she asked. "And why did you return her call that night?"

"My son needs an operation. He's got a brain tumor."

Her breath sucked in like a vacuum.

"It's OK," he said, squeezing her hand. "Tumor's benign. Just in a very tough place to get out, which makes it an extremely expensive surgical procedure. He can't afford it."

"He doesn't have health insurance?"

"No. He started his own business a few years ago and couldn't swing the premiums."

"How much does he need?"

"Quarter million. Maybe more."

"Ouch."

"Yeah," Marty said. "Alice doesn't have it, so she called me. I have no idea where I'm going to get it. With the mortgage, my house isn't worth that much. I'll have to borrow it, I guess." He shook his head. "I wish I'd told you about all this, Em. I really do."

"So damn selfish," she murmured.

"Yeah, I was," he said.

"No," she said. "Me. Giving you such a hard time. I issued an ultimatum. You told me. I bit your head off, Wicked Witch of the West. I'm really sorry, Marty."

He squeezed her arm. "Me, too. For hiding him from you so long. Truth is, I was scared."

"Of losing me?"

"Of losing us," he said.

She kissed his chest.

"Losing that, too," he said. "Anyway, to finish the earlier story, Alice took off. Her family, our son, everyone. One week after the birth."

"Did you try to track them down?"

"No," Marty said, reddening a little.

"Why not?"

He shrugged. "I was sixteen. Had no interest in playing house, and my folks sure didn't want me saddled. Seemed a blessing in disguise at the time. Now it's a dull ache in the back of my head. Never hurts, but never goes away. Alice's phone call turned it into a full-blown migraine, worrying about a boy—well, a man, now—I only know from a photograph."

How could you give this man up, Alice? "What's your son's name?" she asked.

"Don't know," he said.

That startled her. "Didn't Alice name him at birth?" she asked, sitting cross-legged.

"She wanted to wait, see what sounded good. Then they disappeared."

"Huh," Emily said, marveling at the coldness of that act. *I should talk.* "Did you ever think of a name for him?"

"Me?" Marty said. "No."

"Want to now?"

He blinked, pulled back a little. "What purpose would that serve?"

"None," she said, the idea warming her. "Just think it'd be nice, that's all. I don't want to keep calling him 'Baby X.'"

"Huh. Well, I don't know." He dug whipped cream from her ear. Licked it. "Maybe. Let me think on that. If we give him a name . . ."

"He might become real. Not just a photo anymore."

Marty nodded. "I don't want that causing a wedge. You're too important to me."

Emily kissed him full on the lips. "It won't," she said. "Not ever again. I promise."

They fell silent.

Comfortably.

"You did a great job on that powder room," she said. "It was exquisite."

"Course it was. Thought of you while I did it."

She squeezed his arm.

More silence.

"Wonder if the boy has brothers and sisters?" he mused. "If he likes beagles . . ."

Another thought occurred as he talked. She debated bringing it up. Decided honesty wasn't just the best policy, but the only.

"Is that why you beat Corey Trent so viciously?"

"Come again?" Marty said.

"Think about it," Emily said. "He murdered a newborn in front of you. A newborn boy. The reaction you had was so out of character for you, maybe your own boy was on your mind. Remember what you said during our fight?"

He shook his head.

"'That's right, Emily, a son,'" she quoted. "'That's why I'm a witness Friday. That's why I'm a hypocrite. And that's why I'll happily dance on Trent's melted face. Because I couldn't save that dead little boy.'"

"Have I mentioned how distressing your memory can be?" he grumbled.

"Useful, though," she said. "So?"

He considered it. Blew out his breath.

"Maybe you're right," he said. "It was the rottenest thing I've seen on the job. Even those psychotic bikers I lived with never did anything that inhuman."

She took his hand. "Want to tell me?"

He nodded, settled back in the pillow.

"We were out in the sticks to see an informant," he said. "Me and Branch. One of those joint investigations you cook up. I'd drunk a lot of coffee, had to take a leak."

She moved closer.

"Branch was driving. He found a boarded-up gas station. I hopped out, did my business. Peeked inside as I zipped up, saw a butchered young woman."

"Whose baby had been stolen."

"Didn't know that then," he said. "Just that she was dead and her end of the umbilical cord was ripped out. We looked around. Heard a wail. Spotted a shadow running for a car."

"Corey Trent."

"Yup. We chased him. Younger then, so we moved lickety-split. We were closing in fast, so he took the kid by the ankles and swung for the fences. Figured we'd have to stop."

She knew that from the reports. Hearing it firsthand made her ill.

"No God that night, that's for sure," Marty said. "Branch

kept chasing. I stopped. It was a boy. Hazel-eyed, full head of hair."

"Like your son."

"Yeah." Long pause. "Boy laid in that dirt like a seed sack. Gurgling. Crying. Bleeding out of his mouth and ears, busted all to hell. Then he quit breathing." She felt his heart race. Gripped his hand tighter. "I did CPR. Didn't help. That boy died in my arms, and Corey Trent did it."

"So you went crazy."

"The state's attorney ruled I applied the appropriate amount of physical force to effect the arrest of a fleeing homicide suspect," Marty said.

"You went crazy."

"Yeah," he said, smiling thinly. "I broke both Trent's arms. Kicked the hell out of him, snapped off that tooth. Would have killed the bastard if Branch hadn't pulled me away. To this day I wish he hadn't." He traced a finger from eye to chin. "That's how Branch got slashed, you know. Trent had a knife."

Emily nodded, recalling the captain's omnipresent scar, which wiggled when he clenched his teeth. "That's another reason you went crazy," she said. "Because he's your best friend."

"You are," Marty said. "But he's my brother. No way I let that slash go unanswered."

"I wouldn't either, if he was you."

Marty's nod said, *I know*. "We arrested him. He went to jail. He pays tomorrow."

"Today," she said, glancing at her watch.

"Even better. It's closer to noon." He snorted at her unasked question. "Yes, I hate the death penalty. Yes, they should ban it. Yes, I'm happy Trent's getting it. Yes, I'm a hypocrite."

"And I'm the hypocrite's biggest fan," she said, kissing him.

Marty reached for the second can of whipped cream.

"Ah-ah-ah," she said, rolling into the bedside chair and slipping on her clothes. "We already had dessert. It's time for the main course."

"What's that?"

"We identified the serial killer."

"What?" Marty said, bolting upright. "Why didn't you mention that when you walked in?"

"I missed you," she said.

He thought about that, chucked her chin. "I like the way you think, Detective. Now spill!"

3:23 A.M.

"Awfully darn good how you worked out that bus swap, Reverend," a congregant said. "We'd have never gotten here otherwise."

"The Lord provides," Danny said, smiling. "But it's nice having earthly help, too."

3:24 A.M.

"His name is Daniel Monroe," Emily said. "Brother of Earl Monroe, a minor-league gangster executed in 1972 for—"

"Blowing up cops," Marty finished. "And the grand jury witness they were guarding."

"Branch said you'd remember," she said. "Did you know Daniel?"

"Never met the man. Or Earl. But the crime was fairly fresh when I joined the sheriff's. The old-timers ground that tragedy into us rookies—that this is what can happen on even the dullest assignment, so pay attention."

She thought of Rayford Luerchen.

"When did you figure it out?" he asked.

"Last night," she said. "We've been nailing down details ever since."

"And you're able to come here why?"

"You complaining, big boy?"

"Not hardly," he said, squirting whipped cream into his mouth. "Ro a-red."

She squeegeed a glob off his lip. "At one-forty-five, Chief Cross said those of us working the execution should get a few hours' sleep," she said. "I told him I'd stop on my way home, let you know what we found. He said take my time because you're pretty slow on the uptake."

"Remind me to kick his half-an-ass later," Marty said. "After buying him a martini."

"Flatterer," Emily said, feeling herself blush.

"What about motive?" he asked, back to business. "I get Danny whacking the warden or guards to avenge Earl. Our victims weren't even born, though. Why them, why now?"

She fished Appendix F from her purse.

"These are our serial victims," she said. "Zabrina Reynolds, Frank Mahoney, Sage Farri, and so forth."

"And?"

"They're also the grandkids of the twelve official witnesses to Earl Monroe's execution."

Marty whistled. "Talk about revenge being best served cold. Danny waited three generations to avenge his brother."

"Not just Earl."

He arched a single eyebrow.

"Verna Monroe was supposed to be the family witness that day."

"That's Danny and Earl's mom, right?"

"Mm-hm," she said. "But Danny went to Stateville. He told the case detectives, Burr and Rogan, that she'd gotten ill that morning and begged Danny to attend in her place. They discovered later Verna with her wrists slashed."

"Danny's one sick puppy," Marty said, rubbing his own. "Murdering his own mother."

"He didn't. He's the one who found her," Emily said. She explained what Rogan told her from his Florida retirement home, and how Johnny Sanders's bombshell helped them re-create that long-ago Execution Day.

Marty shifted to his other hip. "No wonder Danny went nuts," he said. "Finds his mom in a pool of blood, watches his brother fry, sees twelve rubbernecks watch like a day at the races. So Danny delivers his own death penalty."

"Because they murdered his brother," Emily said. "Symbolically, if not literally."

"Right. The big question is, Why now?" He scratched his heavy stubble, thinking. "It would have made sense killing those folks in the seventies. But he let it go. What changed?"

Emily played air piano. Movement helped her think. "Something profound," she said, finishing the Minute Waltz in thirty. "Drastic enough to trigger a nationwide serial spree—"

"The chair," Marty said, snapping his fingers. *"That's* the trigger."

"How?"

"Earl was Illinois's final execution," he said. "The Supreme Court banned them nationwide that same day."

She strained to remember the law lectures from the academy. "Uh, *Furball versus Georgia*, right?"

"Furman. The Supremes issued the ruling right during Earl's electrocution."

She made a face. "Talk about rotten timing."

"Yeah. Then four years later the Supremes said whoops, executions are constitutional after all, so y'all go ahead," he said. "Illinois obliged, but in the interim decided to mothball the chair for lethal injections. Needles were more warm 'n' fuzzy than flaming eyeballs."

"Don't start."

His grin said, Who, me? "Danny came to grips with Earl's death because the electric chair had been scrapped," he said. "We know that because he spared the twelve witnesses. Then Covington gets elected and brings it back."

Emily sprang to her feet. "The exact *same* chair, too," she said, pacing. "He retrieved it from Stateville for his new center. Announced it to the planet, and none too subtly."

"'Rabid dogs must die,'" Marty recalled from the campaign trail.

"'Condemned prisoners have no souls,'" she said. "'Fry 'em like onions.'"

"The chair, and Wayne's hyperbole, was such a staggering insult, so personal, that Danny snapped," Marty said. "Now he wants to kill the people who watched his brother die. The ones who stood shoulder to shoulder while Covington killed Earl."

"But they're dead," Emily said. "Or otherwise unreachable. So he takes out their families. Like the witnesses and Covington took out his."

"Speaking of Covington, I assume he knows?"

"Chief Cross told him."

"Only good news in this mess," Marty said. "At least he'll stay out of Dodge."

She sighed.

3:47 A.M.

"Goddammit, Wayne, don't be an idiot," Cross snapped into his cell. "Tell Angel Rogers to issue a press release saying you caught the flu and—"

"Show fear to a predator, he tears your throat out," Covington said. "Face him down, let him know you're in charge, he cowers and slinks away."

"This isn't George of the Jungle," Cross said. "Danny

Monroe is the brother of the man you electrocuted thirty-five years ago. He won't be impressed you're alpha wolf."

"So find him."

"We're trying," Cross said. "He left Idaho with a busload of congregants—"

"Congregants?"

"Danny's the minister of a small church in Boise. According to their cops, he's a wheel in the Idaho anti-death-penalty movement. Branch just talked to his wife. She says they're traveling here to protest the reintroduction of the chair. They don't have cell phones, so she can't contact them. He's undoubtedly here already, with the bazillion other buses. We're checking every license plate, and I've circulated Danny's picture to all hands."

"Needle in a haystack," Covington said.

"A lethal needle, Wayne. He's here to kill you."

Covington harrumphed. "And that man calls himself a good Christian."

"So do you," Cross said.

3:52 A.M.

"It's much too early to be awake," the water crewman grumped.

"Cry me a river," the crew chief said, passing over coffee. "We need that pump running and our butts out of here by noon. Or be stuck in execution traffic till our pensions kick in."

4:02 A.M.

"Just follow the yellow brick road," the uniformed cop said, pointing to the bright yellow glow-sticks marking the path to the chain-links. Branch decided to line the fence with holy protesters, figuring they were less likely to start trouble. The strategy was working, the cop saw. These folks fell over themselves to be polite.

"Thank you, Officer," Danny said, gripping his grand-daughter's hand. That congregant was absolutely right—to be here at all was a miracle. The transmission blew in western Iowa, and the lone garage didn't stock bus parts. The tow driver sympathized and said his pastor might lend his bus to the cause. Danny met him, arranged the swap—"I'll fix yours while you're gone, and we'll trade back when you return," the pastor promised, glory hallelujah—and they were back on the road. "Everybody, listen to the policemen. They're here to help us."

The cop saluted with his ax handle. "Thanks, padre. Have a good day."

"I intend to," Danny said.

Patting the grenade in his jacket.

4:09 A.M.

Corey Trent belched. Backed away from his own breath. Last night's Last Supper—corn dogs, Twinkies, and Dr Pepper—was giving his belly the yips. Better than nutrition loaves, though.

"Doing all right in there, son?" inquired a Justice Center security man.

"Couldn't be better," Trent said.

4:15 A.M.

Emily shivered. The hotel's air-conditioning was atomic.

She slipped on undergarments, bulletproof vest, uniform, and twenty pounds of gun, knives, handcuffs, and other tools

of the trade. In the hollow on her neck, under her hair—
*where Danny Monroe shoved that ice pick into poor Sage
Farri's brain*—she taped a spare handcuff key. On her chest
went the battered but proud badge. Finally, she sat on the
bed and double-knotted her boots.

Her cell sang "Paranoid." She rolled backward and
snatched it off the bedstand.

"Look both ways before you leave the room," the familiar
voice rumbled. "Check the car for tampering. Spot anybody
suspicious . . ."

She didn't mind Marty's lecture. He did it for love, not
because he thought her dense.

"I really wish you could be there," she said when he finished.

"I tried," Marty grumbled. "Barbara vetoed it. Says the
rocks in my head need to settle. She even called the sheriff to
make sure I don't play hooky. Chicks are evil."

"You're just figuring that out?"

She played I-L-Y on the keypad, disconnected, and tucked
into breakfast. French vanilla ice cream, not the spinach
quiche and cantaloupe she'd ordered from room service. She
needed comfort food today. Seeing Corey Trent die would be
satisfying—particular after hearing those sickening details
from Marty—but nauseating. She ate five tablespoons,
called it a day. Tomorrow she'd eat that *and* half a steer.

Finally ready to leave, she plucked Marty's photo from
her wallet and slipped it into the pocket of her vest.

Her final backup.

4:40 A.M.

"So whaddaya think? Gonna have a riot?" the state trooper
said.

"Hope so," the Guardsman replied.

"Me, too," the trooper said, popping his gum as he scanned

the floodlit sea. "This kumbaya stuff is boring. They issue you girls real bullets this time?"

The Guardsman snorted. When his unit was deployed to O'Hare Airport in the wake of September 11, the troops were issued rifles but not ammunition. To make sure nobody got hurt. Osama probably wet himself laughing when he heard that.

"Real as a heart attack," he said, patting the thirty-round magazine in his full-auto M-4 combat assault rifle. "This governor's a grown-up."

4:48 A.M.

"No hints of trouble, and the crowd's still happy," Annie reported. "But what are those folks doing? Ten rows to your left?"

Branch craned his neck. "Sticking flowers in the Guards' rifle barrels."

"Groovy," Annie said. "Castle out."

5:01 A.M.

The Executioner pulled the Land Rover into the parking lot at Safety Town, the child-size Naperville that sat kitty-corner from the police station. The chartered bus to the Justice Center idled quietly in the humidity, several dozen employees ready to board.

5:02 A.M.

"I can't see anything, Grandpa!"

Danny swung her up on his shoulders. "Better?"

"Wheee! I'm halfway to Heaven!" she squealed.

5:03 A.M.

The Executioner gargled a double squeeze of honey, tucked the bottle in his glove box, removed the knife from his jacket, tilted his head back, clipped the fish line between his molars, let the plastic slide into his throat. The handle touched the uvula.

No problem.

He grinned. Like good bourbon and bad women, knives were an acquired taste.

5:04 A.M.

"Change already," Emily snapped at the light. She was mere yards from Safety Town. Might as well be miles. "My bus leaves in six minutes."

The light didn't care.

She looked both ways, floored it through the red.

Nobody to write tickets, anyway.

5:05 A.M.

Marty power-surfed the channels, absorbing updates from "Mount Deathmore," the nickname du jour for the Justice Center.

The night nurse walked in, looking beat. They traded sympathies about his head, her bunions, and how everyone but cops and nurses got to sleep at home nights. She checked his monitors, flicked the IV to ensure smooth dripping, headed out.

She stopped at the door.

Turned, shuffled back, pinched his cheek, and left.

5:07 A.M.

The Executioner walked to the bus. He'd miss the Land Rover. It had performed well. He wondered when they'd find the fuel truck driver. Probably when their trees started to smell funny.

"Good morning, sir," the Justice Center security guard greeted.

"And the same to you," the Executioner said, handing over his letter of invitation. "The governor mentioned something about a preboarding search?"

The guard held up his wand. "Just like the airlines, we're checking everyone for weapons." He tapped the plastic bucket. "Keys, change, and other metal objects, please."

The Executioner dropped in everything but his tiny gentleman's knife. "What about this, Officer?" he inquired, displaying the red herring. "It's my good-luck charm."

"Mmm, that's a beaut," the security man said, admiring the intricate inlays of onyx and titanium. "But it's not allowed. Run it back to your car if you like. Or I'll hold it for you, give it back after the event."

"The latter. I'm too lazy to go back to my car," the Executioner said, handing over the knife. It would make the guy's day when he realized what he had.

The metal detector moved around his body. No bleeps. A pat-down followed. The guard looked in his mouth—more diligence than the Executioner expected—but didn't notice the monofilament hidden by teeth and tongue.

"Welcome aboard," the guard said. He sealed the knife in an envelope and handed over a receipt. "We leave for the mountain in three minutes."

5:10 A.M.

"C'mon, baby," the next in the bathroom line whispered when "Occupied" became "Open." "Let's join the mile-high club."

"You *are* high," she giggled. "But I'm game."

5:11 A.M.

"Wait for me! Wait!" Emily cried as she tumbled from her car.

Brake lights flashed. The security guard came out.

"Hi, Emily," he said, checking his manifest. "How's things?"

"Hurried," she huffed.

The guard knew her well, but checked her ID anyway. "You're you," he said. "And authorized for weapons. Welcome aboard."

She scrambled up the steps.

5:13 A.M.

"How come that Porta-Potty's rocking, Mommy?"

"Earthquake," Mommy said, hurrying her son to another line.

6:14 A.M.

Kit Covington stared at the plasma TV hanging between the bedroom mirrors. The longer she watched, the deeper her melancholy became. Despite Wayne's solemn promise that this was the end of his obsession with death, it was clearly just the beginning.

7:24 A.M.

"Approaching the mountain, Governor," his bodyguard said.

"So I see," Covington said, chest tightening. It was one thing to know intellectually someone in this crowd intended to kill him. Quite another to feel it. For the first time since dragging his brother from that burning Plymouth Fury, he doubted himself . . .

Cowboy up, pal, he chided. *You're doing this for Andy.*

The motorcade turned up the hill.

7:25 A.M.

"Covington's on the mountain!" a protest leader announced after the long squawk from his walkie-talkie. "He's driving up the back way, the coward!"

Jeering spread like radiation.

7:28 A.M.

"What are hell are they chanting?" Covington asked, the limousine's armor muting the words.

"Fe fum fo fi," his bodyguard said. "Corey Trent, he should not die."

Covington rolled his eyes, misgivings forgotten.

7:52 A.M.

"Come here often, sailor?" Emily said as she walked the concrete ramparts. The crowd's roar, barely a whisper inside, thundered like afterburners up here.

"Only to pick up guys," Annie replied, binoculars sweeping. Even at highest zoom she couldn't see the end of the bus line. Twenty thousand seemed conservative now. Guardsmen piled out of Humvees. Network anchors mouthed "heartland" and "rock-ribbed" and "the common people." Humidity percolated, water reached fifteen a throw, and toilet lines grew triple deep.

Yet not a wink of trouble. She'd seen more violence at her son's Little League games.

"How's things downstairs?" Annie asked.

"Dull. Only a few witnesses have arrived, so I thought I'd visit," Emily said. She cupped her ears, trying to catch their words. "What's that they're chanting?"

"Wayne's World," Annie said, grinning.

7:59 A.M.

"We shall overcome," Danny sang with the rest of the congregation, the grenade as heavy on mind as pocket. "We shall overcome."

8:07 A.M.

The Executioner walked into the washroom and entered a stall. Instead of relieving himself, he fished the polymer knife from his throat.

"Perfect," he whispered, wiping it down with tissue. It passed the pat-downs and metal detectors with aplomb, and now was the fox in the high-security henhouse.

He peeled and flushed the protective tape from the blade. Hit the handle again for the stubborn scraps. Anchored the knife into the cloth sheath sewn onto his right shirttail, which was accessible through slits in both trouser pockets. He stood, tucked, belted, and washed.

A minute later he was drinking coffee from the refreshment bar and chatting with three witnesses. The steam from the cup reminded him of the puffing towels in the barbershop.

He smiled.

"Remember that time on Wayne's boat?" one asked the other. "K.J. got so seasick that . . ."

The Executioner reviewed the schedule as he listened.

Covington would start the press conference at 11:00 sharp. The witnesses would enter the viewing room at 11:30. Security would remove Corey Trent from his cell at 11:35, have him strapped and capped by 11:45, open the curtains at 11:50. The dynamo would finish powering by 11:55, Covington would direct the reading of the official death warrant, Trent would say any last words, and the chair would deliver justice.

That was the official plan, anyway.

The Executioner's was different.

8:14 A.M.

"Nope," said the Naperville patrol officer as she examined the Iowa plates. "Wrong state, wrong number, wrong church, wrong type of bus."

"Just like the first hundred," her partner said, typing plate and description into his PDA and flashing it to the intelligence unit. Intel would contact the registered owner to ensure the bus wasn't stolen and was supposed to be in Naperville.

"Cheer up," the officer said. "Only two hundred to go."

"Glory be," her partner said, rolling his eyes.

9:01 A.M.

"Hello, hi, great to see you," Covington said, shaking hands with each Justice Center staffer. "I really appreciate what you're doing for the good people of our state."

Emily, back from the roof, kept her head in motion and her ears open. Covington had plenty of bodyguards, but this was her room, in her city. Nobody would be hurt on her watch. Not that there was any serious danger of that—Daniel Monroe's presence out there ensured the castle was locked down tight. Her expression stayed serious, "game face" as much a weapon as gun and pepper spray. But she was excited inside. It wasn't every day you met a governor.

9:11 A.M.

"Twenty thousand?" Marty said.

"And growing," Branch said.

Marty tented his hospital sheet, power-flipped the channels.

"Emily's fine," Branch said.

"I wasn't thinking about her at all," Marty said.

"Right," Branch said, sucking the crème from his Boston. "And I hate doughnuts. Gotta go act like I know what I'm doing. Talk to you later."

Marty disconnected the call, deeply troubled.

9:45 A.M.

Danny left his granddaughter with his most eagle-eyed congregants, then joined the elders on the far side of the bus corral. He'd dreaded this moment since leaving Idaho. But these people were family, and needed to know.

10:00 A.M.

"All right, Trent," the senior guard said, holding out the condemned's T-shirt, slacks, slippers, and deodorant-infused adult diaper. "Time to get dressed."

"Sure thing, boss," Trent said, jumping to his feet.

"Did hell just freeze over?" one guard said to the other as Trent dropped his drawers.

"Why?"

"He didn't give us static. Stateville says we'd have to Taser him to get his clothes—"

"Uh, hey, fellas?" Trent asked.

The guards looked.

Trent was stroking himself at them.

"That's better," the guard said, cracking up.

10:07 A.M.

"Let 'er rip, make sure she's working," the Royce Road water crew chief said. "Then we're gone."

The engineer pushed the starter. The massive booster pump kicked to life.

10:30 A.M.

"And that's what I must do," Danny finished. "Questions?"

"My God, Reverend," one breathed. "You really murdered all those policemen?"

"Yes," Danny said. "And Earl took the blame. He died so I might live."

"Your brother's a saint," said another, looking to the sky.

"No," Danny said. "He wasn't. But he's the best man I ever knew."

"There's no other way to resurrect Earl's good name?" the choir director asked.

Danny shook his head. "I'm a killer. So is Governor Covington. It's time we paid for that. This is the only possible way." He rubbed his face. It felt a thousand years old.

"I understand if you need to turn me in right away," he said. "But I pray you don't. I need to bring down Covington to pay for the blood on my hands. This is my Golgotha."

He paused.

"And his."

10:42 A.M.

"Boss?" the walkie-talkie crackled.

"Go ahead," the crew chief replied.

"I'm in a driveway east of your location. Water's pouring like Niagara. It's coming from the ground and inside the house. I rang the doorbell, but nobody's home."

The crew chief stomped in frustration. "Extra pressure broke something."

"My guess. Lots of old pipes in this sector."

The engineer silenced the pump. The crew chief grabbed his radio.

"Send a water evacuation team ASAP," he told the public works dispatcher. "And police to open the door."

10:45 A.M.

"He congratulated me for pulling you out of the house," Emily said. "Then he shook my hand."

"I hope you washed after."

"Very funny."

Marty smiled at the phone. "All's well on Deathmore, I trust?"

"So far. Ten of my witnesses are here. The others are at Safety Town, waiting for the bus. Chair's ready, and so is the staff. The protest is noisy, but nonviolent. Danny Monroe's nowhere to be found. Tell the truth, I'm bored."

"Beats the alternative," Marty said.

"Love you, too," she said.

They hung up.

He looked at the phone, then at the television, debating.

10:47 A.M.

Danny Monroe floated as he walked toward the police command bunker. To his astonishment, the elders not only blessed his plan, but vowed to stand with him.

"There's no escaping 1966," one said. "What you did was horrific. But you're no longer that man. God changed you for the better." She opened her arms. "We love you, Danny. We'd be honored to stand by your side at the press conference . . ."

"Thanks, boss," he murmured to the sky.

The sun seemed to wink back. Danny smiled. Probably a cloud.

"Where do you think *you're* going?" Dr. Winslow demanded.

"To do my job," Marty said, tying his shoelace.

"Trent will perish just fine without you," she said.

Marty shrugged, headed for the door.

Winslow planted a hand in his chest. "The sheriff excused you from witness duty. You're trying to rescue Emily." She nodded at the TV. "Aren't you?"

"Never entered my mind, Doc. This is strictly about me and Corey Trent."

"I worry about her, too, Marty," Winslow said. "But I know she'll be fine. You're not. Just because I let you play horsey before doesn't mean you can handle the stress of an execution. You still need several days' rest."

Marty took her lightly freckled wrist, gently pushed it to the side.

"I'll call the sheriff," she called after him.

"Tell him I said hey," Marty called back, waving.

10:57 A.M.

"Three minutes, Governor," the director said. "Take your position."

Covington strode to the press pool in the north wing of the Justice Center. His speech was in his pocket, but he wouldn't need it. He knew every syllable by heart.

10:58 A.M.

"This says he can," the ACLU lawyer barked, rattling the judicial notice allowing his client, the Reverend Chris Andersen, to use his prop at his press conference.

"It's the stupidest thing I've ever heard," Branch said. "People will stampede."

"Not my problem," ACLU said. "I have the court order, and I demand you obey it."

Branch read it twice, shook his head in disbelief. Gave it to the city attorney. She read it thrice. Called the courthouse, talked to the chief judge.

"It's legitimate," she said. "We have to honor it."

"It's a big mistake," Branch said.

"I know," she said. "But his honor disagrees."

"Gotta call Ken on this," he said.

"No argument here," she said.

"I demand immediate recognition of this court order," the lawyer said.

"I demand you shut up," Branch said.

Cross answered on the first ring. Listened intently.

"Not a chance," he growled. "Confiscate it on my authority."

Branch did.

"Be right back, Reverend," the ACLU lawyer said. He unleashed his cell, stepped outside.

Four minutes later, Branch's cell rang. He listened, face tightening.

"Well?" the ACLU lawyer said.

"Make sure it's empty," Branch snapped to the head of the bomb squad.

Who ran it through the explosives sniffer, then past his German shepherd's highly trained nose. The sniffer didn't beep. The shepherd yawned.

"Just a metal shell," the bomb guy declared, sticking a pencil up its hollow bottom. "No explosives. Definitely a prop."

Branch handed the grenade to Andersen. "I hope you know what you're doing."

"So do I," said the Reverend Daniel Monroe. He didn't enjoy deceiving the officer or the lawyer about his name, but had no choice if he was going to bring down Covington. "So do I."

"Geez, what happened?" the city attorney asked when the door slammed shut.

"We got bigfooted," Branch said. "By the chief justice of the Illinois Supreme Court."

"Wow," she marveled. "When's the last time Ken didn't get his way on a security matter?"

"Never," Branch said. "Then again, this whole damn thing's Bizarro World."

10:59 A.M.

Emily headed for the witness room to search the chairs a third time. Considering that not even a housefly could get inside the Justice Center without pat-downs, she found the precautions overly dramatic. But orders were orders.

11:00 A.M.

"Three . . . two . . . one . . ." the press room director mouthed.

"Good morning," Wayne Covington said, heart soaring from the Zen purity of this moment. "I'm Illinois Governor Wayne Covington, and today the spiritual heirs of Abraham Lincoln gather on these fruited plains to visit justice upon a man who gives none."

"Oh, barf," the *Chicago Tribune* reporter groaned.

"Must be his own speech," the *Daily Herald* reporter agreed. "Angel Rogers would drink hemlock before she'd write that."

Covington shifted to camera two.

"His name is Corey Trent. He kidnapped and disemboweled an expectant mother. He ripped away her baby boy. He broke the baby on a tree."

He felt the poisonous anger from 1966. He fought it. Nothing could mar the tempo of the most important speech of his life. He forced himself to focus. Felt the red tide retreat.

"In fifty-nine minutes I'll rid the planet of this beast. If another takes his place, I'll exterminate him, too. I'll use the electric chair, not lethal injection. Monsters don't deserve to merely fall asleep and not wake up. They need to boil and bubble, because they steal our innocence and never give it back. I know this personally, profoundly, and all too well."

He felt the aluminum comb in his pocket. Scorched and twisted, half its teeth missing. His only connection to the never-aging corpse in the family plot. His personal rosary from 1966.

"His name was Andy Covington," he said. "He was my kid brother . . ."

11:06 A.M.

"A hand grenade?" the State Police commander sputtered. "You outta your mind, Branch? Did Ken sign off on this?"

"He had no choice," Branch said. "Just like the rest of us."

11:07 A.M.

"Naperville Police," Officer VapoRub announced through the door he'd just lock-picked. "We're here to help you with the flood. Is anybody home?"

No answer.

"Hope this guy's insured," he said, shaking his head in sympathy as he splashed through the ankle-high water. "Fixing this mess will cost him a fortune."

"Us, too, after he sues," the director of public works said. "Got four more just like this on Royce Road. Old plumbing that popped when the pressure boost kicked in." He stuck his head out the door. "OK, guys, we'll start in the rec room. Pray it's dry."

The evacuation crew hefted tools, hoses, and pumps, and headed down the stairs.

11:08 A.M.

"Are they insane?" Annie said.

"Yes," Cross said. "But that's beside the point. Make sure your people know."

"Understood."

She clicked to the tactical frequency. "Castle to all units. A minister will conduct a press conference shortly at the main gate. On orders of the Illinois Supreme Court, the minister will use a deactivated hand grenade as a prop. The bomb squad confirmed it's inert. Repeat, inert. Do not shoot when you see it. The minister has permission to use this grenade as a prop. Acknowledge verbally, not with clicks."

Everyone checked in, and Annie went back to her binoculars, swearing.

11:09 A.M.

"Not again!" the Guardsman groaned as last night's catfish supper made its fourth encore. He raced for the Porta-Potty, M-4 flailing against his chest, praying he'd make it. He'd already ruined two good sets of cammies.

"Listen up, ladies!" a sergeant bellowed as he stormed from the command tent, not noticing Catfish running away. "Some crazy preacher's holding a press conference at 11:45. Gonna wave around a deactivated grenade as a prop. One of those pineapple jobs from World War Two."

The troops began muttering. Only an idiot waved a grenade willy-nilly. Too much possibility of being zapped by friendly fire.

"What can I tell ya?" the sergeant said, shrugging. "Man's got a court order. So don't shoot the sumbitch. Keep your fingers on yer peckers where they belong."

They saluted with one hand and grabbed crotch with the other, laughing.

Marty checked the Caller ID as he stepped off the shuttle bus. Sheriff's number. Winslow called him as promised. He didn't blame her—he'd have done the same in her position. But he had different priorities. *I tried to answer, honest,* he said to the phone. *But the reception's so lousy. All that thick concrete.*

He walked inside.

11:10 A.M.

"So what do you do?" the Executioner asked the seventh witness.

"Operations manager at Southern Illinois Airport," she said, bright red talons pinching the handle of the teacup. "My husband teaches physics at Carbondale High."

"Are you friends as well as financial supporters?"

"Certainly," she said. "We see Wayne and Kit all the time." She tilted her head, let her bangs brush her eyebrows. "And how about you? What kind of work do you do?"

"I'm in the food business," the Executioner said.

"Pastry chef?" she teased, smiling at the Danish in his hand.

"Cattleman," he said. "I supply custom steaks and roasts to restaurants around the world."

"Really?"

"Mm-hm," he said. "I started at the bottom, on the cutting-room floor. Now I own the place. When chefs from New York to Paris need the perfect cut of Midwest beef for an important client, they call me." He flashed a radiant smile. "The last inaugural showcased my work. The First Lady was very complimentary."

"How interesting!" she said, moving closer. "Wayne throws parties for his friends all the time at the Mansion. How could I possibly have missed you?"

"My travel schedule allows little time for socializing," the Executioner said. "I'm forced to keep in touch the old-fashioned way."

"Contributions," she said.

The Executioner winked. "I got involved with Wayne two years ago. I was deeply impressed that he was building this Justice Center with only private funds. So I wrote him a check for . . ."

He named the figure.

"No wonder you're here today," she said, curling a strand of hair around her finger.

"I'm sure there was no connection," the Executioner said, "between my modest fund-raising efforts and Wayne asking me to read the death warrant at his kickoff execution."

"Just like I'm here because I know how to spread salt on runways," she said, holding his forearm a moment longer than strictly social. "Perhaps we should have lunch when this is over. Talk about politics."

The Executioner smiled. "Nothing I enjoy more than a long discussion."

11:11 A.M.

VapoRub felt like he'd been zapped with a cattle prod.

By the expressions of the pump operators, they did, too.

He swept his eyes across the twenty-by-thirty-five rec room. The walls were covered with cork, and square-eyed from casement windows. Glossy acoustical tile and full-spectrum fluorescent tubes brightened the dark brown carpet. The steel bench that filled one end of the room was jammed with milling equipment, cutting oil, arc welders, grinders, polishers, and other tools, powered by a bank of one-ten and two-twenty outlets. A Wells Fargo floor safe sat at right angles to the bench. A leather razor strop hung off the back of the Aeron chair.

The photographs dotting the cork were framed in lacquer black. They showed cattle in various stages of rendering, from the bolt gun that stunned them senseless to the white-coated knife teams that sliced off everything but the moo. Each photo dangled from a worn-out knife hammered into the cork. A photo collage over the workbench showed Emily Thompson, Martin Benedetti, Wayne Covington, and a dozen other people.

"And that's not even the bizarre part," VapoRub mumbled.

That particular honor went to the granite slab in the center of the room.

Which contained an electric chair.

Nine feet high.

Six feet square.

Made entirely of stainless-steel Bowie knives.

"They're welded together," the water crew chief said, squatting for a closer look. "There's hundreds of 'em. Finger-size to monster." He pointed to the wired device on the eighty-knife seat. "Any idea what this is?"

"Telephone answering machine," VapoRub said, opening his cell to call in the cavalry. He didn't know if this was related to the execution, but no other explanation made sense. "Vacate the house. This is now a crime scene."

11:16 A.M.

"Governor George Ryan was misguided when he released all those monsters from Death Row," Covington said to camera three. "So I put them back. The result is this magnificent center, and the justice it will deliver to Corey Trent today."

Breathe, swivel, continue.

"Some of you may wonder, Why Naperville?" he said. "Why not some poor town in rural Illinois, out of the public eye?" He nodded. "Well, I'm happy you asked."

11:30 A.M.

"Please fill each row before starting the next," Emily said, escorting the official witnesses to the chairs facing the nine-by-twenty viewing window. Her excitement over meeting Covington had long evaporated. While she was still happy at Trent's impending dispatch, this wasn't a celebration. A baby was still dead—

"Marty?" she said, shocked, as she spied him in the back. "What are you *doing* here?"

"Need to see this through," he said.

"Did Barbara approve your leaving the—never mind," she said, fearing the answer.

Marty winked, then went to the back row to sit.

Right on time, the Executioner noted with approval.

11:31 A.M.

"We got a hit," the intelligence officer said. "Danny Monroe switched buses in Iowa." He reeled off the new plate and description.

"Find it," Branch ordered.

11:33 A.M.

"Naperville is the envy of the nation," Covington said to camera two. "With its strong schools, proud businesses, close-knit families, and stunning lack of crime thanks to the ever-vigilant cop on the beat"— a salute to Ken for putting up with all this—"Naperville is the zenith of the American dream. So when people ask, Why Naperville? I ask, Why not?"

The reporters snickered.

"You laugh!" Covington thundered, seizing the opportunity to ratchet the drama. "You think I'm ashamed to put an electric chair in the nation's most celebrated suburb? Well, I'm not. I'm honored. As are the people of Illinois. We built a cathedral of justice on a mountaintop, and the world turned out to worship."

He pointed toward the ululating mass at the base. "I didn't select a lonely hamlet that reporters deign not visit. I selected Naperville, dead center of the American experience." Passion foamed out his lungs and over his lips. "I will never shirk my responsibility to visit justice upon America's evil-doers. Never. Never. *Never.*"

He touched the flag pin on his lapel.

"So it gives me great pleasure to announce that I'm going to build on today's success, and next week's, and next year's, and bring the Justice Center concept to the rest of the planet. It will take decades, and all the energy I can muster. But I will never rest. Never falter. And one day I'll look back in pride and say, 'We did it, Andy. The Covington boys won.'"

11:34 A.M.

"Morris Wolf, please."

"May I ask who is calling?"

"Katherine Covington."

"Right away, ma'am," said the chief receptionist of Chicago's most powerful matrimonial law firm. "Please hold."

She muted Wayne as she waited.

"Kit?"

"Hello, Morry," she said. "How's your squash game?"

"Rusty," Wolf said. "Business is booming and I don't have time to practice. I've got Wayne's speech on CNN."

"Then you know why I'm calling."

Wolf cleared his throat. "You're the two loveliest people I know. Are you sure you want this?"

"Yes," she said, staring at the TV. She loved her husband. The thought of living without him made her physically ill. But dead people didn't fight fair—they took and took and never gave back. She could no longer compete. Neither could the kids, who'd finally quit asking where Daddy was tonight. "File the papers."

"Now?"

She sighed. "Wait till Monday. Wayne deserves his Sunday *Times.*"

11:35 A.M.

"Dead man walking," the head guard announced as they shuffled Corey Trent from the cell.

11:36 A.M.

"Just leaving Monroe's hideout," Cross told Branch as he raced toward the Justice Center. "It's a small split-level on Royce Road. Not too far from the gravel quarry. Neighbors see the owner occasionally, but have never met him."

"Who found the place?"

"A water crew checking a flood. They asked us to open the house because pipes had burst. They found an electric chair in the rec room. It's made of arc-welded Bowie knives."

"Bowie . . . knives?"

"Hundreds of them, perfectly milled," Cross said. "So highly polished the chair's one big mirror—you could shave in front of the thing. Monroe's an expert craftsman."

"Explains his expertise with the cutting."

"Something else," Cross said. "A telephone answering

machine was on the seat. It's filled with messages to some-one named 'Bowie.'"

"That's two references to Bowie," Branch said. "Why does that sound so familiar—oh no."

"I've already alerted Annie," Cross said.

11:37 A.M.

"Turn this way, Reverend . . . a little more . . . perfect," said the NBC field producer. His lawyer source at the ACLU promised "a speech that'll blow up the planet." The producer hoped so. Tiddly-winks had more violence than this crowd. "Stay like that. Speak loud and clear. Don't squint when the camera's on. We go live at 11:45."

"We're gonna be on TV, Grandpa?" his granddaughter asked, eyes dancing at the thought of all her friends watch-ing.

"Going to," Danny corrected. "And yes, honey, we are. The television people want me to talk about someone spe-cial."

"Who?"

"Uncle Earl," he said.

11:44 A.M.

"Are you sure you don't want to pray, my son?" the priest asked.

"You ain't my daddy, ass-eyes," Trent snapped, bucking against the harness leather. "Get the hell out of here before I kick your sissy ass."

There's the man we know and hate, he saw the guards think as they hustled the priest away. Exactly as he'd hoped. Too much niceness would raise suspicion.

11:45 A.M.

"Three . . . two . . . one . . ." the director mouthed.

"Good morning," Daniel Monroe said, clutching a Bible. He wore funereal black, a minister's collar, and a cross. His granddaughter played at his feet, and his congregation hummed around them. "On June 29, 1972, a young man named Earl Monroe died in the Illinois electric chair. But he didn't commit the crime."

The NBC producer scowled. *This* is why he convinced network to cut away from the electric chairs line-dancing at the east gate? An innocent-man blubberfest? Sheesh. He'd give this clown fifteen seconds, then cut back to the dancers.

"The man who threw the switch is here today. His name is Wayne Covington, the governor of Illinois. He killed a completely innocent man in 1972, and I have the proof here with me."

Protesters rushed over to listen, followed by network anchors. The congregation switched from humming to "Onward Christian Soldiers."

God, I'm good, the producer thought triumphantly.

"Crowd's changing all of a sudden," Annie told Branch as she snapped off an alert to all commands. "Aggressive body language. Angry expressions. Recommend Condition Orange."

"What is this mysterious proof, you ask?" Danny continued, heart banging so hard it threatened to blow his chest. "Very simple—it's me. I blew up twelve Naperville and county policemen in 1966. I blew up the witness they were guarding. Earl Monroe didn't do it. He simply took the blame, to keep me off Death Row. My name is Daniel Monroe. I'm Earl's little brother. I'm here today to confess my sins, and clear my brother's name."

Branch stared at the television in the bunker.

"I murdered them all!" Danny thundered, full-metal preacher. "I, myself, and no one else! I was the motel janitor! I threw those hand grenades! I killed thirteen innocent men! And Wayne Covington, the governor of Illinois, was my partner in crime!"

"That's our guy," Branch radioed main-gate forces. "Get him out of there quick and quiet before the crowd decides to protect him."

He turned to the white-faced ACLU lawyer. "You have no idea how much I'm gonna enjoy telling everyone you personally vouched for this cockroach."

11:46 A.M.

"Mr. Governor," CBS interrupted, jumping to her feet. "A man at the base of the mountain has just accused you of murder. He says on June 29, 1966, you killed an innocent—"

11:47 A.M.

"Ohhhhh, man," Catfish groaned. He'd sat here nearly an hour and still wasn't done. But high noon loomed, and he was a professional.

He emerged from the Porta-Potty, embarrassed to look at the next person in line. He unslung his M-4 and trotted toward the main gate, wondering what all the commotion was.

11:48 A.M.

"He said *that*?" Covington said, staring down the reporters. "How dare he! His brother committed that horrible crime, and got exactly what he deserved. Just like Corey Trent will in twelve minutes."

11:49 A.M.

The three official executioners marched into the anteroom, tugging black hoods to collarbones. In the death chamber, the electrician made sure the copper electrodes were welded tight to Trent's head and left calf, then walked to the back and inserted a key in a wall plate. The center's director inserted his own key on his side of the chamber. "Three, two, one . . ."

Twist.

The simultaneous move started both the generator and the fail-safe program that ensured the power wouldn't stop even if the generator was subsequently destroyed.

The electrician left. The director pushed a button. The blue velvet curtains whirred apart, exposing the viewing window. Trent spit eye-acid at the witnesses. They stirred uncomfortably, glad the window was bulletproof.

The Executioner waited, each second exploding in his brain.

11:50 A.M.

"I'd like you at my side for this, Emily," Covington said.

The governor's offer was as welcome as it was surprising—she ached to see Corey Trent up close. See if breathing the same air could make her understand his unspeakable evilness. But she shook her head. "I'm sorry, sir. My job is to guard the witnesses."

He nodded at his bodyguards. "They'll take care of your folks," he said. "I need you in there with me." He moved closer, dropped his voice. "We're two of a kind, you and me. We know what it's like when family dies. How it feels to lose half your soul. You deserve to be there."

His bright eyes weren't for show, she knew. He was thinking about his dead brother Andy. It made her think of those she'd lost. Of the murdered baby. Of Marty and his heartache.

"Equally important," Covington said, louder now, spell broken, "Mr. Hill here asks for your armed presence. He's afraid of big bad Trent."

"Wayne's the one who's scared," the Executioner parried. "I'm just his beard."

Covington gave him an affectionate arm-pummel. "We'll make our exit immediately after Leonard reads the death warrant. Please, Emily, say yes. We'll be out before you know it."

Emily glanced at her sergeant, who nodded.

"Deal," she said.

11:51 A.M.

"You heard right—Danny claims Wayne killed an innocent man," Cross told the chief justice as he floored his cruiser up the mountain. He could barely hear over the wall of sound. "The extraction team's nearly to him, but the damage is already done. The crowd's turning fast. Shut this circus down, Your Honor. Before I have to start shooting."

11:52 A.M.

Danny thrust the grenade over his head. The already riled crowd recoiled in fright.

"This is one of the hand grenades I used to kill those innocent men," he announced. "Don't worry, this isn't real. There's no powder. It's harmless as a tin can." He pointed to his granddaughter, who stared up at him as if deity. "I would never put this darling child, or my congregants, in harm's way with something real. This is only a symbol."

The extraction team pounced.

11:53 A.M.

Catfish burst through the front line, adrenaline scouring his brain, eyes darting everywhere, ears blasted by the frightened roar. "Grenade!" he screamed, swinging the M-4 onto the terrorist's chest. "Everybody down!"

"Abort! Abort! Abort!" his sergeant yelled, charging like a fullback.

Catfish caught a flash in his peripheral vision. Uniform. Sarge. Waving. Abort.

He eased off the trigger as his cammies filled anew.

"It's the bad man!" Danny's granddaughter shrieked. "I'll save you, Grandpa!" She wriggled out of his grasp and plunged into Catfish. "Wah! Hyah!" she yelled, chopping the giant's legs. It wasn't falling so she threw an elbow into its kneecap.

Catfish buckled, howling. The M-4 burped full auto.

"Condition Red," Annie spat. "All commands, all nets, Condition Red."

The Executioner unrolled the official document. Thanks to the eye-popping checks to the governor's "Dreams of Justice" fund, Covington asked the man he knew as Leonard Hill to be the chief witness and read the death warrant to the condemned. "Mr. Hill" gratefully accepted. It gave him the entrée he needed into this holy of holies.

"Corrigan Bowie Trent," he intoned, nearly drunk with the thrill. So close now. So damn close. "Having been found guilty of murder and infanticide, we the people of the sovereign State of Illinois hereby sentence you to . . ."

The M-4 burped twenty-six bullets before Catfish unjammed his finger.

"Reverend!" the choir director screamed.

"Grandpa!" his granddaughter screeched.

"Medic!" Catfish yelled. "Medic!"

The crowd exploded like an anthill stomped.

"Riot, riot, riot," Annie said. "Launch gas, ready on water. Sharpshooters, lock and load. If they reach the moat"—a fence one hundred yards off the castle walls that bristled with warnings of lethal force if breached—"you have a green light to open fire."

Tear gas vomited from the roof cannons. Twenty seconds later the lower hill was covered with white chemical fog and screaming, retching protesters.

"You're accused of murder, Wayne," Cross said, voice tinny through the intercom. "A riot's under way. Twenty thousand people will hit this place when the fence fails. I'll have to open fire, and a lot of them will die. Innocent people, Wayne, the kind you *don't* want to kill."

"Forget it," Covington snapped. "Trent's dying on schedule."

Cross slammed his hand on the bulletproof glass. "Get on

the goddamn loudspeaker and tell the crowd this is over. It's the only way I can save them. And you."

"He's right, Governor," Emily said. "Time to end this."

"Yeah, Wayne-o," Trent hooted. "End this."

Marty's head was throbbing. But not enough to keep him from noticing that chief witness Leonard Hill was sliding behind Emily as Covington argued with Cross. That was weird. Civilians in high-stress situations almost always froze in place. When they did move, it was jerky, hurried, panicked. This Hill fellow crept smooth as silk.

He moved himself to the second row.

Danny Monroe smiled up at the mountain as medics labored to stanch the flow from the bullet stitch. His granddaughter was right all along. This wasn't Golgotha.

It was Heaven.

11:54 A.M

"Gas isn't working fast enough. Fire water cannons," Annie ordered the Fire Department.

An ocean's worth of high-pressure water blasted the protesters. Thousands flew like tenpins. The rest rammed the chain links en masse. Not to resist, but to escape.

"Fence is starting to buckle," Annie told Branch.

11:55 A.M.

The executioners hovered over the buttons. Trent cursed Covington's wife, children, friends, and manhood, then started in on Emily. Cross cajoled and threatened from the other side. Covington threatened back. Marty started for the viewing window. Covington's bodyguards escorted the witnesses back to the refreshment area. Hill kept creeping. The executioners said they were ready. Emily fidgeted, impatient to leave before the lightning hit.

"It's time to go, Governor," she said, tapping her watch.

"Not till Trent is dead," he replied.

"That wasn't the deal."

"I changed it."

She walked to the door, pushed the handle. Locked.

"Only the chief executioner can open it," Covington said. "And he's busy."

"This has gone on long enough," Emily said, angry now. "We're leaving."

"We're staying, Detective. I'm going to spit in Trent's face when it begins to smoke."

More cursing from the chair.

11:57 A.M.

"This is an official court order," Cross said, waving the fresh fax from the Illinois Supreme Court. Hill moved past Emily. Marty relaxed a fraction. "Cancel this execution immediately or I'll do it for you."

"I won't," Covington snarled. "And you don't have the authority to overrule."

"Watch me," Cross replied. "Mr. Director, turn off the power."

"I can't," he said.

Cross whirled on him. "What are you talking about?"

"System's in fail-safe," the director said, chin divot quivering. "It won't accept a shutdown order until 12:30. That's to ensure the execution proceeds even if there's a power failure. Or a terrorist attack."

Cross spotted the bright yellow hotline. "Suppose he's in Springfield and calls you. How do you handle a stay then?"

"Simple. We don't push the buttons."

"Explain."

"The generator charges the burst-battery. But the executioners release it by pushing all three buttons at the same time." He pointed at the anteroom. "They're the fail-safe to the fail-safe."

"If they don't push, nothing happens?"

"Right. The power's still there, but it doesn't flow to the chair."

Cross went back to the intercom. "Executioners. Can you hear me?"

"Loud and clear, Mr. Cross."

"The Illinois Supreme Court canceled this execution. As the chief law-enforcement officer of this city, I order you to step away from the buttons and leave the anteroom."

"Right away."

Get ready . . .

"Belay that!" Covington roared. "I'm the governor, and I'm overriding the court! Stay at your posts and push those buttons!"

Get set . . .

"Detective Thompson," Cross said.

"Sir?"

"Place the governor under arrest for failure to obey a lawful police order."

"Yes, sir," Emily said, reaching for her handcuffs.

Go.

Hill snapped a kick into Emily's left leg, spinning her to the floor howling. His arm snaked around Covington's throat and cut off his air supply. As the governor choked and spittled, the polymer swallowing knife whipped from Hill's pocket onto Covington's neck.

"What the hell are you doing?" Marty roared, banging on the glass.

"Saying hello to my long-lost brother," Hill said, pushing in the tip. Blood trickled from sliced capillaries. "How you been, Corey?"

"Not bad, Jason, not bad," Corey said. "I hear you're friends with Wayne."

"Yup," Jason said. "Having a lot of money does that. You want out of that chair?"

"If you wouldn't mind."

"Lieutenant Bates," Cross radioed as he studied the surreal exchange.

"Go ahead," she sputtered as shifting winds whipped the roof with cannon water.

"The governor is bowing to the wishes of the people and canceling this execution. Get it on the public address. Then bring your explosives team to the chamber. We have a situation."

"You said your family disowned you," Covington gurgled as the chokehold loosened.

"I lied," Corey Trent said. "You of all people should know us filthy psycho killers do that."

The knife went a fraction deeper. More blood dribbled.

"Let him go," Emily ordered, drawing her Glock and aiming it at Jason.

"You shoot," Jason said, "Your precious governor dies, too."

Emily breathed and released, tightened her grip, steadied her aim. As soon as Jason's head cleared Covington's, she'd take him out—

"Detective," Cross said gently.

"Sir?"

"Ease off just a little, would you? Wayne will gripe forever if Jason's brains land on his suit."

The light tone told her he had a plan and was playing for time. She hoofed out a breath, took her finger off the trigger.

"So what do you want?" she asked Jason.

"You," he said.

"So I assumed," she said, recalling the firebombing and Riverwalk knifing. "But why?"

Jason grinned, pointed at the enraged giant on the other side of the glass.

"Him," he said.

Loudspeakers thundered. Nobody understood. Then one man caught on.

"We won!" he shouted. "Pass the word, the execution's canceled!"

"I'm sorry, Grandpa," his granddaughter bawled at the disappearing ambulance. "I let the bad man hurt you. I let him, I let him."

"No you didn't, baby," the choir director said, hugging her close. "Grandpa's going to be all right." Danny was seriously injured but stable, thanks to the solid-tip bullets and quick action from the army combat medics. "You deflected all the other bullets. If it wasn't for you, honey, he'd be dead. Your karate chops saved his life."

"Really?" she said, brightening.

"Absolutely. We'll go visit Grandpa as soon as the doctors fix him up." She didn't mention he'd probably be arrested for mass murder. One mountain at a time. "Your mama's taking the next flight from Boise and will be here soon . . ."

Catfish watched, stone silent, hardly breathing, till a water cannon swept him away.

Annie led two explosive entry teams—NPD and army—toward the witness room. Tactical boots pounded the concrete. Cross met them outside, explained the situation.

"The man with the knife is Jason Trent," he explained, pointing him out on the closed-circuit monitor. "He goes by Leonard Hill."

"The chief witness is Corey's brother?" Annie asked, stunned. "How'd he get inside?"

"Trojan horse," Cross said. "Hill wrote many a fat check to Wayne's private electric-chair fund. As thanks, Wayne invited him as a witness today and asked him to read the death warrant. Essentially, he brought in his own executioner."

Annie's lip twitch said, Play with matches, you get burned.

Cross didn't disagree. "Like his sisters and parents, Jason publicly disowned Corey after the 1991 conviction, and broke off all contact. No visits, letters, calls. Nothing through Corey's lawyer, either—we checked. Jason fell off everybody's radar screen."

"But now he's back. To save a man he hasn't seen in nearly two decades," Annie said, mulling and discarding rescue options. "In an action he knows may kill them both. Why?"

"Brotherly love," Cross said. "Madness. Ego. Revenge. Suicide by cop. Take your pick."

"All this to kill Covington," she muttered. "Would have been easier to shoot him at a parade."

"I don't think it's about Wayne."

"Who, then?"

"Marty. Jason hasn't given details, but I'd bet my badge he's here to avenge Marty's putting Corey in the chair to die. I believe he'll kill Emily and Wayne, and make Marty watch."

"Bastard."

"Jason wants Marty to suffer the rest of his life," Cross said. "What better way than humiliating him with all those serial killings, then murdering Emily and the governor?"

"Emily's armed. Can she take him out?"

"Had her finger on the trigger. I backed her off. Even with an eyeball shot there's too much risk of Jason slitting Wayne's throat. We have to dig them out another way."

"The chamber doors and windows are bullet- and bomb-proof," Annie said. "The entire electrical system is triple armored against terrorist assault. The burst battery has even more armor. The air scrubbers in the chamber prevent using knockout gas."

"If this was easy, I wouldn't need you." Cross explained what he had in mind.

Annie's grin was wolfish. She snapped off a salute and rapid-fired orders.

"You know what the worst part is?" she said as the troopers checked equipment and radios.

"What?"

"Devlin Bloch's innocent. We have to turn him loose."

Cross snorted, and the teams moved out.

"I'm really, really unhappy you did this to my brother," Jason said.

"Then he shouldn't have killed that mother and child," Covington snapped.

Jason opened a half-dozen capillaries.

"Keep in mind you're alive only because he is," Emily warned, releveling the Glock.

"Dead bitch talking," Corey sneered.

"I thought you wanted to kill *me*, Trent," Marty said, slamming the glass.

"Same thing," Jason said.

11:59 A.M.

"Castle to Bird Nest."

"Nest," Branch said.

"Rioters are in full retreat," Annie's deputy reported as the crowd flailed away from the mountain. "Water cannons and announcements are working. We won't have to shoot."

"Roger that, Castle," Branch said, relieved. He'd rather die himself than have to massacre twenty thousand unarmed civilians who weren't guilty of anything but being scared. "Nest out."

"All right, Emily," Jason said. "Unbuckle my brother from that chair."

"No."

Jason sawed deeper. The governor whimpered as blood soaked his bespoke shirt. "Do as I say, Detective. I dissect cattle for a living, and you know exactly what I did to those twelve grandkids. With knives I crafted myself. Slicing Wayne-o ear to ear won't bother me a bit."

"How about a bullet in your eye?" Emily said, shocked to find herself so calm. Annie's lessons were really paying off. "Think that would bother you?"

Jason laughed. "You remind me of the cows who try to trample me when they realize I'm going to turn them into minute steaks. Same result, too." He squeezed Covington's neck till his face turned purple. "Now slide your gun to me and undo those buckles."

"Go ahead, Detective," Cross said. "They aren't going anywhere."

She nodded, understanding he still needed time. She put the Glock on the floor, kicked it Jason's way, and started unbuckling the heavy leather.

*   *   *

The demo man bomb-puttied the chamber door, from the side the Trents couldn't see. "I'll attach every bit of explosive I've got, Lou," he whispered. "But it won't be enough. This was designed by the folks who built Fort Knox."

"We're gonna give you a helping hand," Annie said. "Rest of you, this way."

Corey sprang from the chair, sank a fist in Covington's belly.

"You'll have to finish that later, brother," Jason said over Covington's groan, keeping the polymer blade tight. "Power's only good till twelve-thirty." He looked at Emily. "You. In the chair."

Fear soaked her pants.

"Hey!" Marty roared through the glass. "You said you wanted me. So do it, you coward. Kill me and let her go."

"You beat my brother half to death," Jason said. "Broke his arms, gave him that steel tooth. Then put him in this slaughterhouse. Killing you would be too easy a punishment for your vast crimes. Instead, you're going to watch Emily snap, crackle, and pop in Old Sparky. Just like you'd planned for my brother."

Corey giggled.

"I knew you'd like the symmetry, bro," Jason said. "Strap her in."

"Shoot the bastards, Em," Marty said, vision swimming. "Both of them. Now. Covington created this mess. Let him take the heat for it."

"I have to protect the governor," she said, the back of her knees slippery with sweat. "You know it."

"Dammit," Marty said, gritting his teeth and forcing his head to clear.

Corey shoved Emily in the chair. Buckled the straps so hard her hands and feet puffed. Ripped out a lock of chestnut hair. She wanted to yelp but wouldn't give these two cacklers the satisfaction. Corey locked the skullcap on the bare spot—"don't worry, hon, blood improves electrical conductivity," he said—then he ripped away a trouser leg and locked the exit electrode to her calf.

"*Love* that bullet scar," he leered, dry-humping her knee. "Makes me wish we had five minutes. That's all it'd take, babe. Five minutes with me and you'd forget all about Marty-boy."

"Five minutes with you," she snapped, "I'd fall asleep from boredom."

"That's good, honey," Jason said as Corey slapped her. "Go down fighting."

"Only one going down here," Emily grunted, cheek on fire, "is you and baby-killer."

Jason laughed, turned to Covington. "All right, Mr. Governor, this is it. You've got one chance to save the damsel in distress. And yourself."

"We're ready, Lieutenant," the National Guard demolitions commander said from the top of the ladder. "There's enough C-4 on this ceiling to blow it to Pluto."

"And not collapse the entire building?"

He shrugged.

"Close enough," Annie said.

"Pardon your brother?" Covington snapped. "Like George Ryan let all those maniacs off the Row? Are you out of your mind?"

"Probably," Jason said. "But if you put it in writing and declare it was done freely and without coercion, I'll let Emily and you go."

"No way."

"Is that your final offer?"

"I said no."

Jason smiled. "I didn't think you would. Your obsession with avenging your brother precludes all common sense. On the other hand, I can relate to that." Jason looked at the clock over the viewing window. "You've got ten seconds to say yes, or Corey pushes those buttons."

"Take the deal, Wayne," Cross said. "If you don't, she's dead, and so are you."

"Corey Trent cannot go free," Covington said.

"Even if means killing an innocent like Emily?"

"Even if."

"You son of a bitch," Marty raged. "Sign the goddamn paper before I kill you myself."

"And that's ten," Jason said. "Corey, head on in."

Corey hustled to the anteroom. Ordered the frightened executioners out at gunpoint. Went inside, locked the door, laid a mop handle from the janitor closet across the three red buttons.

"All set," he hollered. "Just give the word."

Jason turned to Covington. "Last chance, Governor. Let my people go."

Covington's eyes were huge, his breathing shallow. He stared at Jason, then the anteroom, then Emily, whose eyes were equally wide. "I . . . I . . . just . . . all right, I'll—"

"Don't, Governor," Emily said quietly. "You can't give in to terrorists. It's not like they'd let us go anyway."

Jason beamed. "Well, aren't you the little Sherlock Holmes?"

Then, to Marty.

"She's right, of course. I would have let her go if you didn't love her. Unfortunately for her, you do. Which is why I set all this in motion—the twelve murders, the Riverwalk stabbing, stealing the fuel truck, blowing up her house."

"To get me," Marty said.

Jason nodded. "You had every intention of watching my brother die. So instead you'll watch your beloved woman die. Then we'll all watch your governor die."

"How? You barbecuing him? Or slitting his throat?" Marty said, stretching hard to keep Jason talking. Cross's voice tone said he needed every second he could get to launch his rescue.

"The latter," Jason said. "He's the last witness from 1966, so he has to die. Besides, he killed an innocent man in Earl Monroe. Covington's press releases say those who kill innocents must pay for it in blood. This is his chance for the justice he so freely dispenses to others."

"Like you give a damn about justice."

"Correct. I don't. I care only about my brother. We were so close growing up we were practically one person. That never changed, even when we forged our separate ways in the world. Then you arrested him."

"I'd do it again in a second," Marty said. "Your brother isn't fit to live in decent society. No wonder you disowned him."

Jason glared. "Corey understood why I did that. He knew I needed distance in order to create Leonard Hill and carry out this plan. He understood I'd be back."

"The Trent boys," Corey shouted. "Together forever."

Jason beamed. "Now we'll take care of the man who threatened all that. You. By electrocuting Emily, then dispatching Wayne through my terrible swift sword. Right, Corey?"

"Right, Bowie."

"That's the first thing my brother ever called me," Jason said with immense fondness. "Bowie. He had trouble pronouncing Jason when he first learned to talk. He saw some TV actor talk about using a Bowie knife, and that's what he started calling me. I adopted it as my middle name."

He looked through the anteroom window. "I'll count

down from ten. You push the mop handle at zero. As soon as Emily's fingernails poke through her palms, I'll slit Covington's throat. So we can watch them die together. Every execution needs its witnesses."

"Plenty of us to watch yours, freak," Marty said. "Aren't you afraid of dying?"

"Everyone dies," Jason said. "It's the grandeur of a man's accomplishment that counts. Mine is the grandest of all—saving my brother's life. Isn't that right, Governor?"

No answer.

"Very well," Jason said. "Ten . . . nine . . . eight . . ."

Annie clicked her radio twice. Guardsmen detonated the high explosives on the basement's ceiling, which was also the floor of the witness room and execution chamber. Concrete clapped like thunder in a bottle. Dust boiled. Chairs upended. Witnesses screamed. The floor cracked in six places, dropped eight inches. The door frame squealed out of shape.

Annie's demo man swept the door clear with the second ignition.

"Go, go, go," Annie barked, bounding into the chamber and putting six bullets in Jason. His eyes rolled up, and he flopped like a rag doll.

Opening Covington's neck as he went.

"Medic," she said, pointing. Two jumped on the governor as blood stained his white-blond hair.

Marty raced to the electric chair.

"I'm gonna get you out," he said, unbuckling the first leather strap. The process was too slow. He pulled Emily's combat knife from her pocket and began sawing.

"Hurry," she begged, clamping hard on her emotions to keep from freaking.

SWATs converged on the anteroom.

The second strap split open.

Corey Trent spit blood and teeth as he pulled himself to hands and knees. The earthquake knocked him to the back of the anteroom and almost unconscious. Almost.

Ram teams battered the anteroom door. The steel dented but the locks didn't yield.

"Blow it," Annie ordered.

They unwound detonation cord and slapped on shaped charges.

Fourth strap flew apart. Fifth. Sixth.

"Too late!" Corey howled, nearly back to the mop handle. "The scarred bitch dies now!"

Sweat poured off Marty's face as he sawed. SWATs joined in. Seven and eight parted, then nine and ten. Just one more, around her chest.

Corey pushed the mop handle with his fingers. Not enough leverage to trigger the kill shot. He inched forward to use his bloody palms. He tensed his abdomen and pushed.

"Fire in the hole!" the demo man shouted, twisting away.

Eight tiny, precise blasts sheared the door like a can opener. SWATs dashed inside, machine guns roaring. All three red buttons clicked as burning lead flayed Corey's chest, legs, and head.

The battery spit lightning.

The last strap parted.

"Ahhhhhgh!" Emily howled as the dragon lit her up.

She slammed the viewing window like a slapshot. Bounced sideways, hit the floor upside-down, skidded back toward the chair. Her head clanged. Her tongue tasted like burnt sirloin. Her brain became a funhouse mirror of faces, hands, feet, knives, and electric chair.

She passed out.

Jason Trent's eyelids fluttered. With the .45-caliber stitching, no one figured him alive.

But he was.

Still clutching the plastic knife, he sucked up his final particles of energy for a killing thrust.

"Come on, Emily, breathe!" Marty yelled, blowing life into his mirror image. "You're tougher than the Trents! Tougher than the chair! Kick their ass and come on home!"

Emily was drowning in dragon's blood. It was sweeter than she thought. Very thick. Not hot like its breath. Didn't hurt a bit. *Not so bad dying this way*, she thought. She relaxed, let the dragon coo in her ear, tuck her under its wing.

An air pump blasted into her lungs as a jackhammer pummeled her ribs. The dragon clawed and screeched.

It startled her enough to change her mind about dying. She spotted a hole at the top of the dragon's head. Swam toward it. Every stroke was agony.

*   *   *

"Wayne will be all right," Cross said as paramedics hustled the governor down the mountain. "Knife missed the jugular." He grabbed Emily's hand. "Come on, Detective," he whispered into her left ear. "I won't let you go out like this. You were lead detective. Remember? From the spa? The case is over now. You've got to do the paperwork." He squeezed so hard his own hand trembled. "You need to come back and finish your paperwork . . ."

Annie pushed and Marty blew cadence as paramedics readied paddles and drugs.

Dragon's blood transmogrified into Maypo. She loved that hot, chocolate cereal. Daddy and Mama made it Sundays after church, and she ate it even today. It reminded her of home.

"I got a heartbeat," Annie panted, pulling back.

Maypo became cream soda, everyone's favorite at her Sweet Sixteen. Light, bubbly, fun. Then cream became Chardonnay. Her first drink on her first date with Jack. Chardonnay became omelettes. Her first meal with Marty.

"She's breathing!" Marty said, fighting his emotions as Emily sputtered and hacked.

Emily laughed and laughed. She and Marty got silly one night, filled their bathtub with whipped cream. Jumped in with a bottle of Champagne, fooled around for hours, sang themselves to sleep. She loved whipped cream. It reminded her of home . . .

"Where are you?" Emily groaned, eyelids fluttering open. "Marty? *Marty?*"

"I'm right here, baby," Marty said, reaching for her. "Right here."

Jason Trent twisted, lifted, and plunged.

Emily caught the blur from the corner of her bloodshot eye. She smashed her boot into the murderer's jack-hammering arm. The razor-edge blade skidded off Marty's back and into the broken floor. She snatched it from Jason's hand and thrust it into his throat, picador to bull.

It pierced his jugular.

Jason croaked once, froglike. Blood gushed. The knife vibrated like a tuning fork. Jason's eyes bugged, then blanked. His mouth opened and closed without sound. His bowels released.

Then his life.

Emily melted back to the floor as Annie shot him twice in the head.

"Baby," she whispered as SWAT dragged the body away.

"Right here," Marty said.

She clutched his hands. "I made a decision. It's hard, but I have to do it because I just can't take it any more. I'm leaving."

Marty's eyes went wide. "Me?"

"No. The house. I'm selling the property and not looking back. It's time to clear away the past. We're going to use the money to pay for Troy's surgery. Then we're getting on with our lives."

"Troy? Who's Troy?" he asked.

"Your son," she said. "That's the name I came up with, Troy. What do you think?"

A slow smile broke across Marty's face.

"I think," he said, "we should talk about our son in whatever home—and life—we're going to build ourselves next."

She brushed her fingers across his lips. "Promise?"

"Hope to die," Marty said.